The Sea of Regret

The Sea

Two Turn-of-the-Century

Stones in the Sea
BY Fu Lin

TRANSLATED BY

# of Regret

CHINESE ROMANTIC NOVELS

The Sea of Regret
BY Wu Jianren

PATRICK HANAN

 University of Hawai'i Press, Honolulu

95 96 97 98 99 00   5 4 3 2 1

Library of Congress Cataloging-in-Publication Data
The sea of regret : two turn-of-the-century Chinese romantic novels /
translated by Patrick Hanan.
p. cm.
Includes: Stones in the sea / Fu Lin and The sea of regret /
Wu Jianren.
ISBN 0–8248–1666–8 (cloth).—ISBN 0–8248–1709–5 (pbk)
1. Chinese fiction—Ch'ing dynasty, 1644–1912—Translations into
English. I. Fu, Lin Ch'in hai shih. English. 1995. II. Wu,
Chien-jen, 1866–1910 Hen hai. English. 1995. III. Hanan,
Patrick.
PL2658.E8S39   1995
895.1'348—dc20   94–49173
CIP

Book design by Kenneth Miyamoto

"SEA of Regret" refers to the ancient Chinese myth that lies behind the titles of both novels in this volume. According to this myth, the daughter of the Fiery Emperor, after drowning in the Eastern Sea, returned as the bird Jingwei and spent her days carrying sticks and stones from the Western Mountains in a vain attempt to fill up the sea. At first the myth stood for futile effort or dogged perseverance, but in more modern times it came to signify the tragic consequences of romantic love. The first of the two novels, by Fu Lin, is titled *Stones in the Sea (Qin hai shi)*, literally "bird, sea, stone." The second, by Wu Jianren (also known as Wu Woyao), was evidently written in response to *Stones in the Sea* and is titled *The Sea of Regret (Hen hai)*. The two novels were published within a few months of each other in 1906.

Contents

Acknowledgments

I owe a particular debt of gratitude to Mr. Wei Shaochang of the Shanghai Branch of the Chinese Writers' Union, the doyen of scholars on turn-of-the-century fiction, who helped me obtain copies of several rare editions and also gave me the benefit of his advice on certain questions of interpretation. I am also extremely grateful to Professor Wang Jiquan of Fudan University for generously providing me with materials, and to Dr. Catherine V. Yeh for her guidance. Mr. Aixin Jiaoluo Chang Lin, Assistant Head, and the staff of the Capital Library in Beijing were kind enough to find me two rare editions of *Stones in the Sea* while the books in that section of the library were being reshelved. I am indebted also to the following for their helpful advice: William P. Alford, Chou Chihp'ing, Michael Duke, Peng Hsiu-chen, Shang Wei, Tung Yuanfang, Eugene W. Wu, and Yenna Wu. To Anneliese Hanan I am indebted in countless ways.

Introduction

THIS pair of novels, neither of which has been translated before, shows Chinese writers reacting to the influx of Western social and literary ideas at the turn of the twentieth century. It was a time when many Chinese feared that their country was about to lose its sovereignty and even its cultural identity, but it was also a time of boundless prospects for social change. I say "pair of novels," because ideally they should be read together; *The Sea of Regret* (*Hen hai,* published in October 1906), in particular, cannot be appreciated fully without knowledge of *Stones in the Sea* (*Qin hai shi,* May 1906). Although the general similarity between the two novels has long been recognized, it will be clear to anyone who reads them side by side that one must have been stimulated by the other, in which case *Stones in the Sea* would be the primary work. But if the relation were merely of this kind, it would scarcely be worth our attention. In fact *The Sea of Regret* is a response, a retort to *Stones in the Sea*—on nothing less than the place of romantic and sexual love in Chinese life.

Of the catchwords on the lips of the young and well educated in cosmopolitan cities such as Shanghai in the early years of this century—catchwords relating to a variety of freedoms, equalities, and rights—none had as direct an impact on so many people as the freedom from what was known as "family despotism," particularly in regard to marriage. Some of the leaders of the abortive Reform Movement of 1898, Tan Sitong in particular, referred to the subject in general terms, but it was first taken up as a cause by the advocates of women's rights. An article "On Freedom of Marriage" appeared in the journal *Women's Studies (Nü xue bao)* as early as the middle of 1903, after which some of the literary journals joined the debate. In the same year a novel was published, titled *Freedom of Marriage (Ziyou jiehun).*[1] It is presented in thin disguise as a translation, with the "author" appearing in the prologue chapter to address a mixed audience on the subject of free marriage. Despite its title, however, the novel is primarily concerned with political freedom rather than freedom of marriage.

Before long free marriages began to be reported. In September 1905, a much publicized free marriage took place in the Zhang Garden, a park for Chinese residents in the International Settlement of Shanghai. Rumors also circulated of scandalous free marriages in the public schools that were then being set up throughout the country.

At about the same time a series of novels were published showing the tragedies caused by "family despotism" in the arranged marriage. *Flowers in the Sea of Regret (Hen hai hua),* a short novel in classical Chinese published in March 1905, was one of the earliest. Told in the first person by the hero's confidant, it may owe something to the example of *La dame aux camélias* by Alexandre Dumas *fils,* which had caused a great stir when it appeared in Chinese translation in 1899. Like the French novel, *Flowers in the Sea of Regret* makes a conspicuous truth claim; it is represented as being written in the summer of 1904 (probably the actual date of composition) about a tragic love affair that had culminated just one year before. The first novel of the pair translated here, *Stones in the Sea,* written some time before December 1905, is narrated by the hero of a tragic love affair and makes a similar truth claim.

Public reaction against the enthusiasm for "freedom of marriage" was slow in coming but equally strong. The distinguished translator Zhou Guisheng, a close friend and collaborator of Wu Jianren (1866–1910), author of *The Sea of Regret,* wrote an article titled "Freedom of Marriage" that appeared in the March 1907 issue of *All-Story Monthly (Yueyue xiaoshuo),* the journal he and Wu edited. The article translates items from foreign newspapers to

1. See the modern edition in *Zhongguo jindai xiaoshuo daxi* (Nanchang, 1992).

show the disastrous effects of free marriage. The American divorce figures for the years from 1887 to 1907 are quoted for their shock value, and the comparative ease of elopement in America is deplored. Wu Jianren appends a commentary to Zhou's article that shows his own cultural conservatism to be even deeper than that of his friend.

If the movement toward freedom of marriage received a stimulus from abroad, it achieved its effects mainly because of conditions inside China. The marriage system, particularly the extraordinary authority it gave to fathers, was a kind of seismic strain in Chinese culture, a subterranean conflict beneath the surface of the accepted morality. It was also part of a much larger conflict, the old controversy over the role of the emotions or passions (*qing*) in moral behavior. Is moral behavior driven by the passions, or is it merely learned as a matter of duty? Can the power of the passions be harnessed for moral ends? Questions such as these held enormous consequences for parental authority, particularly in regard to love and marriage.

Marriage was normally entered into early, fourteen being a marriageable age for a girl. Arrangements were made by the parents through a go-between, usually without the bride and groom having met. Even if the pair did contrive to meet in advance of the wedding, there was no legitimate way by which they could get to know each other. The conflict between this system, however benignly applied, and the desires of many young men and women is easy to imagine.

Evidence of the conflict is perhaps best seen in literature; the most famous Chinese play—*The West Chamber*—and the most famous Chinese novel—*The Story of the Stone*—are both implicitly concerned with it. The rules of the romance, in particular the romantic comedy, call for the lovers to show extraordinary initiative, but the conflict between parents and children in these works is much more than a mere genre requirement. *The West Chamber (Xixiang ji)*, written toward the end of the thirteenth century, deals with a marriage that the girl's mother at first offers, then rejects, and finally accepts when she discovers that the young couple have been sleeping together. The play was frequently banned on the grounds of immorality and was regularly forbidden to the young. Mere knowledge of it inspires feelings of guilt in the young women of the eighteenth-century *Story of the Stone.*

The Story of the Stone (Shitou ji), also known as *The Dream of the Red Chamber (Honglou meng),* is an even better example of the conflict. Under exceptional circumstances, the hero of the novel, Baoyu, is permitted to live in a spacious garden with his girl cousins, each established in her own chalet. It should be noted that the garden was specially built for a brief visit of Baoyu's elder sister, one of the emperor's consorts. Rather than let the garden and its chalets remain idle after her visit, the consort has requested that Baoyu be allowed to live there with his cousins. Without such a request from the imperial palace, the situation he finds himself in would have been unthinkable.

The significance of the garden, which occupies the center of the novel, is that it enables a group of contemporaries, adolescent or preadolescent, to live comparatively free from the dominance of their elders. The garden is not free from discord, but no one person automatically exerts authority there by virtue of his or her age. Old age eventually asserts its dominance, of course, and the young residents of the garden find themselves married off by the well-meaning, but generally disastrous, efforts of their elders.

The conflict is never expressed in the novel. How could it be? The concept of free choice in marriage did not exist, and, given the structure of the Chinese family, a genuinely free marriage was hardly conceivable. But the conflict over marriage and parental authority lies beneath the novel, nonetheless, and contributes to its greatness.

By the turn of the twentieth century an apparent solution to the implicit conflict *was* available, a solution in terms of Western principle and practice. What had been implicit before was suddenly explicit.

Turn-of-the-century critics were quick to interpret the older fiction and drama as protesting family despotism, especially that of the father, and especially in regard to marriage. At the same time people who feared the destruction of the existing order questioned the morality of the older works. *The Sea of Regret's* prologue attacks works that claim to deal with passion while actually dealing with lechery, and a note to the first edition informs us that the author was referring to *The West Chamber* and *The Story of the Stone*. In the novel itself, Zhongai, a moral paragon, condemns his colleagues for consorting with prostitutes and claims that they have been deluded by *The Story of the Stone* into seeing themselves as so many Baoyus.

The years after 1900 were years of hectic translation. In the peak year of 1907, for example, well over two-thirds of the novels published in Chinese were translations. In terms of the romance, the most influential foreign work, after *La dame aux camélias,* was *Joan Haste,* by the popular English novelist H. Rider Haggard. The two novels tapped a gusher of moral sentimentality in the Chinese reading public. Both are about love affairs, in the first case between a gentleman and a courtesan, in the second between a gentleman and a penniless orphan. The love affair accounted for much of the attraction, but the key factor was the heroine's sacrifice of her own interests for the good of her lover's family. Her lover's parent—in the French novel the father, in the English the mother—pleads with the heroine to give up her lover for the sake of his family (his sister's marriage, the family's solvency, and so forth), and she does so, sacrificing herself for the greater good. What evidently moved the Chinese public was the combination of romantic love with the old idea of self-sacrifice in the cause of familial piety.

There was a second stage to the Chinese reception of *Joan Haste*. The novel was given a bowdlerized rendering in 1901–1902 that conveniently omitted the fact that Joan became pregnant by her lover and suffered a miscarriage, and it was this immaculate Joan that the reading public fell in love with. When the novel was translated in full in 1905 by the famous Lin Shu, many readers were appalled; Joan no longer fit their image of a virtuous young woman. (To Marguerite, the courtesan of *La dame aux camélias,* different standards applied.) It was against the background of the *Joan Haste* controversy that both *Stones in the Sea* and *The Sea of Regret* were written.

Novels like *Stones in the Sea* call for freedom of marriage within the Chinese context, even if, in most cases, it would hardly have been practicable. Significantly, they stress the hero's and heroine's rights as individuals rather than their duties as family members or citizens, and place passion (in the sense of love) above all other values.

It was this apotheosis of passion in its restricted meaning of love between the sexes that Wu Jianren objected to. The opening of his *Sea of Regret* claims that passion is the motivating force in all human conduct, whether moral or immoral. If properly applied, he argues, elaborating an older theory, passion induces the appropriate moral feelings and behavior, such as love of parents (filial piety), affection for one's children, loyalty to one's ruler, and true friendship. Wu's own romances—he uses the term *xie-qing xiaoshuo*, "stories of passion"—show passion operating in a moral, i.e., a Confucian, context. Love develops within the arranged marriage.

His attitude to love and marriage is bound up with his cultural conservatism, with his suspicion of any innovation derived from foreign practice. He often inveighs against the worship of foreign things and derides the catchwords for foreign ideas. Although a reformer himself and critical of certain aspects of the Chinese tradition, he came to regard the worship of foreign ideas and practices as destructive of China's cultural identity. In the middle of 1905 we find him nostalgically praising the oral narratives of his native Guangzhou because, although their plots are farfetched, the narratives all adhere to a basic Confucian morality. In his April 1906 preface to a collection of Chinese detective stories, he attacks the contemporary worship of the foreign. "Our country's wise men of old are reviled as fogeys," and "even fathers and teachers are scorned." "Several thousand years of the classics and histories," the entire "national essence," in fact, has been discarded, while people spend their time translating foreign works with no relevance to China's mores.

In May 1907, he remarked that *The Sea of Regret* took him only ten days to write, after which he sent the novel to the publisher without checking it. When he read it in published form, he was so affected by it that he wept, but he also claimed to be puzzled about why he had written it in the first place—an oddly disingenuous remark in view of his use of *Stones in the Sea*. His novel is full of stale ideas and holds nothing of interest, he says with evident mock modesty, but "fortunately, <u>although the whole thing is about passion, it has not transgressed the bounds of morality</u>."[2]

In his novel *Passion Transformed (Qing bian)*, serialized from June 1910, Wu tells the story of a girl who, frustrated by her parents in regard to marriage, runs away with her lover and then feels ashamed. The narrator quotes Mencius in explaining that her shame results from a guilty conscience. "If she had been someone who had lost her innate goodness, not only would she have felt no shame, I expect she would have broadcast the story of her parents' barbaric despotism in not allowing her 'freedom of marriage.' "[3]

In these attitudes to marriage he was by no means out of tune with his time. The story of the Chinese middle- and upper-class family and its changing attitudes to marriage in the first decades of this century is a fascinating one that has yet to be told. But it is instructive to consider the case of Hu Shih (1891–1962), one of the leaders of the intellectual "revolution" that took place in China from about 1917. Before Hu's departure for the United States in 1911, he was engaged to a traditionally brought up woman whom he had never met. For some years after his arrival at Cornell University, challenged by Western notions of marriage, he defended the Chinese system, even to the extent of giving speeches on the subject. His diary entry for January 27, 1914, has the gist of one such speech:

> Love in Western marriages is "self-made"; love in Chinese marriages is "duty-made." After engagement, a woman has a particular tenderness toward her betrothed. Therefore when she happens to hear people mention his name, she blushes and feels shy; when she hears people talk about his activities, she eavesdrops attentively; when she hears about his misfortunes, she feels sad for him; when she hears about his successes, she rejoices for him. It is the same with a man's attitude toward his fiancée. By the time they get married, husband and wife both

2. For Wu's comments on the writing of *Hen hai,* see *Yueyue xiaoshuo* 1907, no. 8, p. 209. For his preface to the detective stories, see Wei Shaochang, *Wu Jianren yanjiu ziliao* (Shanghai guji chubanshe, 1980), pp. 245–247. His remarks on oral narrative appear in *Xin xiaoshuo* 1905, no. 5, p. 151.

3. See the modern edition in *Zhongguo jindai xiaoshuo daxi* (Nanchang, 1991), p. 385.

know that they have a duty to love each other, and therefore they can frequently be considerate and caring to one another, in order to find love for one another. Before marriage this was based on imagination and done out of a sense of duty; afterwards because of practical needs it often can develop into genuine love.[4]

No better description exists of the way an arranged marriage was supposed to work. And this is what actually happens in *The Sea of Regret,* except that, under extraordinary circumstances, the heroine, Dihua, has met her fiancé as a child and also traveled with him in their flight from Beijing—chastely, I need hardly say. Although Hu Shih's view began to change soon after this speech, he returned to China in 1917 and to spare his mother's feelings married his fiancée. The fact that a liberated thinker of the younger generation could hold such views shows that Wu Jianren was in the mainstream of intellectual opinion in his time.

Stones in the Sea is an obscure work that does not deserve its obscurity. *The Sea of Regret,* by contrast, is one of the most famous novels of the period, certainly the most famous short novel.

Perhaps I should explain the significance of the term "short novel." Most of the well-known novels are long works that satirize a broad spectrum of official and merchant society. They were serialized, usually in fiction journals, and appeared only later in book form. Their organization is segmental rather than unitary, and they rarely drive toward a conclusion; in fact some were never finished, either because the journals in which they were appearing ceased publication or because their authors were distracted by other work. Those that were finished had the sort of structure that lends itself to the writing of sequels.

There is no necessary relation between serial publication and the comparatively loose, segmental organization of the satirical novels, but there is certainly a happy congruence of manner of composition, genre, formal structure, and mode of publication.

Short novels, by contrast, were often published in book form from the outset, as was the case with both *Stones in the Sea* and

4. From R. David Arkush and Leo O. Lee, trans. and eds., *Land without Ghosts* (Berkeley and Los Angeles: University of California Press, 1989), p. 109.

The Sea of Regret. They generally have a tight, unitary organization, and they do drive to a conclusion.

Stones in the Sea was finished before the end of 1905 but not published until May 1906. All that we know about it is derived from the first edition by a relatively small publisher, Sociology House (Qunxue she). The preface is dated December 1905, as is a rejection slip from another publisher, which the author prints at the end of the book, presumably as a blurb. The publisher concerned, Xu Nianci, had rejected the manuscript despite its merits, notably its structural perfection, because it did not fit his list, and had urged the author to publish it himself. Xu's remarks were probably something more than a polite brush-off. His publishing house, Forest of Fiction (Xiaoshuo lin), was dedicated to political and social reform, which naturally excluded the frank sensuality of *Stones in the Sea.*

The author of *Stones in the Sea* was given in the first edition as Fu Lin, which is probably a pseudonym. When the novel was republished in 1909 and 1913, the authorship was given simply as "Editorial Department, Sociology House." Perhaps Fu Lin was an editor at the publishing company.

His preface makes cosmic claims for passion as the force or principle behind all creation, animate and inanimate. Passion between the sexes, although a minor form, is nevertheless instructive because of mankind's position in the universe. Therefore the good novelist analyzes the affairs of the human heart in order to reveal the secrets of creation. The preface ends with the hope, characteristic of its time, that readers will extend their private passion to their love of country.

Stones in the Sea is in the same tradition as *Flowers in the Sea of Regret,* the novel published in March 1905 that appears to have been influenced by *La dame aux camélias. Stones in the Sea* also has a first-person narrator, but, unlike the narrator of *Flowers in the Sea of Regret,* he is the main protagonist. Wu Jianren's *Strange Phenomena Observed during the Last Twenty Years (Ershinian mudu zhi guai xianzhuang),* a long satirical work serialized between 1903 and 1905, was apparently the first Chinese novel to employ a first-person narrator, but only as a naive observer of the social scene. By contrast, the narrator in *Stones in the Sea* is a passionately engaged "I." *Stones in the Sea* may well be the first true "I-novel" in Chinese literature, a few years before the genre came into vogue in Japan.

With the first-person protagonist goes a new kind of emotional thought and rhetoric, one for which foreign literature was a catalyst and to some extent a model. At the very least one can say that the example of foreign fiction gave the Chinese novelist the freedom to explore his characters' feelings. The narrator's is a juvenile voice—he is only sixteen at the time—but he writes with a certain disingenuousness, especially on the matter of sex. Although basically a sympathetic figure, he is presented with a slight but unmistakable irony. The rhetorical flights in which he sometimes indulges can be seen as fitting the same persona.

In addition to its structural qualities, the novel is remarkable for two thematic elements. The episode in Shanghai in which the narrator meets the girl who is about to be sold into prostitution prefigures in the reader's mind the fate of Aren, whom the narrator will meet in Shanghai on her deathbed. The second element is the squirrel episode of Chapter 5. Apart from its sensuality and the narrator's disingenuousness, the episode carries a symbolic message for the reader, as the notes imply. (The notes, evidently by the author, have not been translated.) The squirrel represents a penis and the girl's sleeve a vagina, and the passage recounts a symbolic deflowering.

Along with the irony in *Stones in the Sea* goes a good deal of satire, satire of the stifling protocol of traditional upper-class China, beside which Victorian manners at their stuffiest seem positively libertine, satire of the reactionary Uncle Gu, of course, but satire also of the narrator's father who, although enlightened about the Boxers and genuinely affectionate toward his son, can be obtuse, hypocritical, and despotic. This last portrait bears comparison with the gently quizzical portraits of fathers in *The Sea of Regret* but contrasts sharply with the harsh, even contemptuous ones we find in the literature of the next generation, that of the so-called May Fourth Movement. (In a time of rapid cultural change, the father-son relationship was under particular strain.)

The main critical problem of *Stones in the Sea* has already been touched on. The narrator claims that the Chinese marriage system, especially the authority it gives to fathers, has doomed his romance with Aren. He blames the system rather than his own father or the fact of the Boxer uprising, although the novel itself belies that claim. The father has actually yielded to his son's wishes and permitted an engagement, only refusing to let the marriage take place until his son is sixteen. In the meantime the Boxer uprising has occurred and the lovers have been separated. Hardly ✓ a strong basis for condemning the system! We must allow for the youth and naiveté of the narrator, in effect, for a measure of irony, but in a more general sense the novel is indeed about freedom of ✗ marriage, or rather the lack of freedom, as it relates the lies and subterfuges to which lovers were driven under the old system.

When he wrote *The Sea of Regret,* which appeared in October 1906, five months after the appearance of *Stones in the Sea*—ample time in those days to see a novel in print—Wu Jianren, whose personal name was Woyao, was already one of the best known modern writers. Born into a Guangzhou (Canton) gentry family, he lost his father early and left home at sixteen or seventeen, ending up in Shanghai, which was by this time the cultural as well as the commercial center of China. Although he learned to speak the Shanghai dialect like a native, he never lost his Cantonese allegiance and was active in founding schools and other institutions in Shanghai for Cantonese residents. Several of his novels are set in Guangzhou, and even those that are not, like *The Sea of Regret,* have characters who come from Guangzhou.

His first novel may have been *The Strange Tale of the Four Guardian Gods, Famous Shanghai Courtesans (Haishang mingji si da jingang qishu),* published in the summer of 1898 (his authorship is uncertain). It is partly a supernatural fantasy and partly a satire of present-day courtesans on the Shanghai scene. Wu was soon to become editor of the *Caifeng bao,* a Shanghai tabloid that was dedicated to just such satirical gossip. It was the first of three tabloids that he was to edit. Occasionally his papers would take up a cause such as the campaign against opium. When the Boxers overran North China, we find his current tabloid joining other Shanghai papers in urging readers to contribute to the Relief Association formed by Lu Shufan (the Association, which is mentioned in both *The Sea of Regret* and *Stones in the Sea,* chartered ships to go north and bring back stranded southerners). In 1903 Wu Jian-ren began writing novels that were serialized in the exiled Liang Qichao's *New Fiction (Xin xiaoshuo)* journal. For a time he was editor of the American-owned *Central China Post (Chu bao)* in Hankou, but he resigned in the middle of 1905 to protest attempts in the United States to extend and strengthen the exclusion laws against the immigration of Chinese laborers. When he wrote *The Sea of Regret,* he was preparing to start his own fiction journal, *All-Story Monthly,* which was published from the end of 1906 to the beginning of 1909.

Although his career as a writer lasted only a dozen years, he published a great deal: eighteen novels (not all of them complete), stories, jokes, anecdotes, poems. He is described as a sociable man, a wit and humorist who drank heavily and thought nothing of working through the night. He was a gifted public speaker with a powerful voice, and he was also a man of strong passions. Although a staunch Confucian, he joined some of his contemporaries in blaming the Song dynasty philosophers for sanctioning an increased absolutism of imperial rule. By 1905, if not before, he had come to fear the loss of China's cultural identity in the flood of fashionable ideas from abroad.

His first so-called romance *(xie-qing xiaoshuo)* was a translation, *Strange Tales of the Electric Art (Dianshu qitan),* which was serialized in *New Fiction* from 1903 to 1905. This work has a bizarre history. The original was apparently an unidentified Victorian thriller about the art of electrohypnosis (hypnosis was a common motif in English popular fiction of the late nineteenth century). It was translated into Japanese by the novelist Kikuchi Yūhō and published in 1897. From Japanese it was turned into classical Chinese by Fang Qingzhou, who was in Japan when Kikuchi's translation appeared. It is not clear where, or indeed whether, Fang's translation was published, but Wu says that he based his own vernacular translation on it, amplifying it considerably. The novel describes a romance between the daughter of an Indian rajah and an English mining engineer. The girl follows the engineer to Southampton, and after literally incredible adventures in Europe the pair are reunited. Presumably because the novel deals with foreigners, not Chinese, Wu seems unconcerned about "freedom of marriage."

The Sea of Regret was Wu's first serious romance, but he also wrote two others: *Ashes of the Holocaust (Jieyu hui)*, serialized in *All-Story Monthly* in 1907–1908, and *Passion Transformed (Qing bian)*, serialized in another journal in 1910 and incomplete at Wu's death. In the former a couple about to be married are separately abducted on the eve of their wedding and reunited only after terrible ordeals in China and the South Seas. Although the latter novel is incomplete, one can see that a childhood love was intended to develop into a fatal obsession. Wu's sequel to *The Story of the Stone, The New Story of the Stone (Xin Shitou ji)*, the first part of which was serialized in 1905 and which was published complete in book form in 1908, is not a romance, but a combination of social satire and science fiction.

I will not go into the similarities between *The Sea of Regret* and *Stones in the Sea*, except to say that they are so many and so varied that it is hardly conceivable Wu should have been unaware of them.

One can see why *The Sea of Regret* became the most popular novel of its time—and perhaps also why *Stones in the Sea* was allowed to lapse into obscurity. The former shows in detail the process by which a girl, Dihua, betrothed in childhood, falls in love with the idea of her fiancé and then transfers that love to her actual fiancé, Bohe, who has done little to deserve it. Her actions throughout conform to the wifely ideal of Confucianism. The novel allows the reader to enjoy its hints of romance and also to be moved by the heroine's martyrdom.

There is no double standard in the novel's morality. Zhongai, Bohe's younger brother, preserves his chastity for his fiancée Juanjuan's sake, resisting the temptations of the prostitutes of Xian. However, in a cruel twist Juanjuan has herself become a high-priced courtesan in Shanghai, where Zhongai meets her in the novel's climactic scene.

Much of the novel is spent on the separate adventures of Dihua and Bohe. The novel's main achievement is its rendering of Dihua's thoughts. It describes in detail the mental, and especially the emotional, processes by which a young girl falls in love with the person chosen for her by her parents. Although Wu Jianren's rendering of the subject is not without sophistication—Dihua's love for her fiancé has to compete with her duty to her mother—it was clearly intended to exemplify love as sanctioned by the traditional system. Certain episodes, such as her erotic experience inside Bohe's bedding—in his absence, I hasten to add—are remarkable in the context of the Chinese novel.

Although Wu gives a sympathetic account of a girl falling in love under the traditional system, he also qualifies his account. One indication is the cosmic irony of his conclusion, vastly different from the outcome of the traditional moral tale. Another is the fact that Dihua is so constrained by the ideal of maidenly decorum—a full code of conduct in traditional China—that even her parents grow impatient with her. (Most readers will want to shake her, and some of the author's notes seem to encourage that reaction.) But it is a measure of the greatness of a literary work of this kind that one can appreciate the author's intention and yet read the novel in a different way, as a brilliant illustration of how a girl brought up on the Confucian texts could internalize their precepts and willingly practice them, taking the blame for things that go wrong, even when she is innocent of any responsibility. I can think of no other work that does this quite as well as *The Sea of Regret*.

Bohe, the indulged eldest son, is revealed to us by his actions rather than his thoughts. When the question is raised as to who will accompany the women south and Zhongai insists on staying by his parents' side, Bohe says not a word. Later when he finds himself in possession of eight chests abandoned in an empty shop, he reflects that he has acquired them by telling a lie, then quickly brushes the thought aside in the hope that the chests will contain something of value. On the refugee ship he is led to think of his own family, it seems, only by the lamentations of the other passengers.

The Sea of Regret is a moral work, however ambivalent, and in the Chinese context we must expect straightforward declarations of moral passion from hero and heroine. By contrast, the actual horrors of war are played down. This seems to me one of the novel's great merits. *The Sea of Regret* offers us the best picture of the Boxer uprising and its aftermath precisely because of its indirect presentation. The confusions of war—the threats, the rumors, the panic, the uncertainties, the inconveniences, the sudden, unanticipated problems—are brilliantly conveyed. Hu Shih in his 1922 essay "Chinese Literature of the Last Fifty Years" criticized *The Sea of Regret* for its lack of power and compared it unfavorably to another novel by Wu Jianren, *The Strange Case of the Nine Murders (Jiuming qiyuan),* serialized in 1904–1905.[5] But the indirectness and understatement of *The Sea of Regret* are clearly both deliberate and effective. (Actually, most of the best fiction of this period forgoes the use of dramatic power.) Stylistically, *The Sea of Regret* is bare of overt comment and represents a studied paring down of rhetoric as compared with other vernacular fiction.

Like the best novelists of his generation, Wu Jianren was mainly concerned with the condition of China. Although his subject is the traditional marriage system in the modern age, he casts his eye over the social scene. Regions, classes, generations—all are clearly differentiated. There is the relationship between parent and child, not harshly delineated as in later fiction, but still problematical. And there is the village with its popular culture, where the genteel, city-bred Dihua is as out of place as any missionary's wife from abroad. (Her reactions can easily be paralleled in the missionary memoirs of the period.) The author, in this novel as in others, is trying to define—or rather redefine—the elements of Chinese society.

The major event against which both *Stones in the Sea* and *The Sea of Regret* are set is the Boxer uprising, an amorphous movement that began among the peasantry of Shandong province and spread like wildfire throughout North China. Both novels were written within five years of the events described, an example of the almost exclusively contemporary interest of the fiction of this period. The Boxers—so named for some of their ritual exercises— had their own belief system with its motley pantheon and claimed to possess magic powers that rendered them immune to bullets and shells. Their principal motivation was xenophobia, in reaction

5. Reprinted in *Hu Shi wencun,* second series.

against the encroachment of the foreign powers and the growing presence of the Christian missions. This was a time, it should be recalled, when the dismemberment of China was an ever-present possibility, and the Boxers' rallying cry was "Support the Dynasty, Wipe Out the Foreigners."

Most officials derided the Boxers' pretensions and treated them as rebels ("bandits"), but some of the reactionary Manchu grandees about the Empress Dowager, the real source of power, claimed to believe in their magic. Eventually, in 1900, the Empress Dowager came around to their point of view and, after embracing the Boxer cause, declared war on the foreigners. An attack was made on the Beijing legations, but it was never pressed home, probably because some of the officials concerned realized its folly. In time a multinational force assembled and fought its way into Beijing, and the Empress and her court fled the city. Negotiations followed, and China was subjected to humiliating conditions and forced to pay a huge indemnity. Numerous people had been killed in the course of the uprising, mostly Christian converts and other Chinese suspected of being close to foreigners. The reprisals taken by the foreign troops were savage and indiscriminate.

Western readers are likely to know of the siege in Beijing from the spate of memoirs, novels, and even films that have poured forth ever since, notably the film *55 Days at Peking,* all of which emphasize the plight of the trapped legation personnel. Modern Chinese historians have understandably paid less attention to the siege. For the most part they have followed an ideological line in attempting to invest the uprising with exemplary value, either as an early expression of nationalism or as a foreshadowing of the Communist revolution. It is only too easy to forget, in reading them, that the great majority of Chinese commentators at the time were bitterly opposed to the Boxers.

Granted, the commentators were mostly well-educated southerners, some of whom were writing after the uprising had collapsed. But they were genuinely appalled by the Boxers' credulity, savagery, and venality—as well as by the fact that their actions, quite predictably, left China in a weaker position vis-à-vis the foreign powers than before. This eminently reasonable attitude, widespread among educated people, is the one that we find expressed in both of these novels. In this respect at least, *The Sea of Regret* is fully in accord with *Stones in the Sea*.

My translation of *Stones in the Sea* is based on a copy of the first edition in the library of the Chinese Writers' Union, Shanghai Branch, but I have also consulted the modern editions in the *Zhongguo jindai wenxue daxi* (Shanghai: Shanghai shudian, 1991) and *Zhongguo jindai xiaoshuo daxi* (Nanchang: Baihuazhou wenyi chubanshe, 1993) series. Although the modern editions purport to be based on the first edition, they are actually based on the second or third editions, which consistently refer to Aren by her formal name, Renfen. Copies of the second and third editions are preserved in the Capital Library, Beijing. My *Sea of Regret* translation is based on the edition published in 1988 in the *Zhongguo jindai xiaoshuo daxi* series, which reprints the first edition of the novel, that by the Guangzhi shuju. I have also consulted the Guangzhi shuju edition itself in the Shanghai Library.

Stones in the Sea
(Qin hai shi)

by Fu Lin

~ 1 ~

The Sea of Regret[1] proves hard to fill, as
an invalid retraces the past.

READER, let me be frank with you. I am ill, and so serious is my
illness that I have adopted a cynical view of the world and no
longer wish to live. An image flashes before my mind, and I see
her standing in front of me, my nearest, my dearest love—the perfect oval of her face, the high arch of her brows, the limpid gaze,
the rosebud mouth, the childhood dimples, her mood now cross,
now gay, now laughing, now weeping—and I am driven out of
my mind by the sight and left mesmerized, as if in a drunken
stupor. Oh, if only we had been destined to spend one night
together, a single night, my nearest, my dearest love and I, if only
I could have seen her one more time, I would never have been
reduced to such a state. Nor would I be in this state if she had
loved someone else besides me, even if I could never have seen
her again—or if I had loved someone else besides her.

Reader, who do you imagine was responsible for doing us such
grievous harm? None other, I regret to say, than the philosopher

1. The titles of both *Stones in the Sea* (literally "bird, sea, stone") and *The Sea
of Regret* are derived from the same ancient myth, that of the Fiery Emperor's
daughter who drowned in the Eastern Sea and then returned as the bird Jingwei
to spend her days carrying sticks and stones from the Western Mountains in a vain
attempt to fill up the sea. For most of Chinese history the myth has stood for
patient, Sisyphean labors, pathetic or admirable, but it also, particularly in modern
times, has signified the tragic consequences of love. As such it provides the titles
of a number of romantic works in addition to these two. In its romanticized meaning it is often combined with another myth, that of the goddess who rebuilt the

21

Mencius of the Zhou dynasty.[2] Now, Mencius lived well over two thousand years ago, so how could he possibly do us harm? Strangely enough, he once made a preposterous assertion that has been passed down to the present day. Marriage, he declared, should take place only by the parents' command and through the good offices of a go-between; otherwise the young couple would earn the contempt of their parents as well as of the general public.[3] It never occurred to him that marriage might be a matter that the young couple had a right to decide for themselves, that it was not something for parents and go-betweens to meddle in. So long as the young couple abide by the rules and wish to marry, and so long as they separately inform their parents in advance and do not engage in any illicit activity, how can those parents go making arbitrary decisions about them? I simply do not understand how a man like Mencius, who made a point of advocating equal rights and freedom, could lapse into such stupidity and say such a preposterous thing! Ever since he said it, however, perfectly decent young men and women the world over have been crushed by the weight of parental despotism in regard to marriage, with the result that ninety-nine out of a hundred married couples are at loggerheads. Those men and women who, over the course of the last two thousand and more years, have lost their lives and ended up in the City of Wrongful Death[4] far outnumber the grains of sand of the River Ganges! Some of those whose love

---

shattered vault of Heaven. The most famous use of the latter myth occurs in *The Story of the Stone,* in which Baoyu is the incarnation of a magic stone left over from the rebuilding. This myth also becomes romanticized, the "heaven of passion" being whole so long as the lovers are together, shattered when they part. Several novels include "heaven of passion" in their titles, and both *Stones in the Sea* and *The Sea of Regret* refer to this second myth in their chapter headings and also, in the latter case, in a final poem.

2. *Mencius* is one of the "Four Books" containing the essential teachings of Confucianism. Mencius lived in the fourth century B.C.

3. See D. C. Lau, trans., *Mencius* (London: Penguin Books, 1970), p. 108. The passage is "But those who bore holes in the wall to peep at one another and climb over it to meet illicitly, waiting for neither the command of parents nor the good offices of a go-between, are despised by parents and fellow-countrymen alike."

4. The limbo in Hades containing those who have died unjustly, particularly those driven to suicide.

was thwarted by their parents' overwhelming power died of frustration; others had to resort to illicit affairs and died of shame; while yet others were forced into marriage with partners who did not appeal to them—only to die afterwards of melancholia. From ancient times to the present day, how many men and women, millions upon millions, have been destroyed! Even my love and I are among those ruined by Mencius. Oh, if only we knew freedom of marriage as it is practiced in civilized countries, we would never have suffered from Mencius' stupidity and been so badly hurt. I myself by this stage in my life have tasted all the sweetness and bitterness that love between the sexes has to offer. My only regret is that in this vast world of ours there is no Heaven of Parting Sorrow, no All-Scents Kingdom,[5] where my beloved might attain nirvana. Were there such a place, my soul, now barely clinging to life, would long ago have abandoned its mortal shell and flown I know not where.

Reader, I may have been so badly harmed by Mencius as to turn into a world-weary cynic, but what business do I have to go rattling on like this to other people? I do so precisely because I was the one who harmed my nearest, my dearest love. Were I to die now without setting down in writing the whole course of our love and separation with all its ecstasies and alarms, its triumphs and tragedies, and leaving it to the world in her memory, I should have betrayed her love. That is why, even in my present enfeebled state, I must delay my death awhile and allow myself time to tell this story from start to finish so that others may learn. "By the silkworm's death all of its silk is wound / The candle is ashes before its tears dry."[6]

Well, who *am* I, to be telling you all these things? My family name is Qin, and we come from the city of Hangzhou in the province of Zhejiang. My father's name is Qin Yuan, and his courtesy name Maozhai. As a boy he accompanied his father to his official post in Hubei, and then, after his father's death, he stayed on in Hubei and made a living there by opening a silk shop on

5. The Heaven of Parting Sorrow is situated in the highest heaven. The All-Scents Kingdom is a Buddhist paradise.
6. Quoted from one of Li Shangyin's (d. 858) "Untitled" poems.

Dajia Street in Hankou with the several thousand in savings that had been left to him. However, there was a long tradition of education in our family, and Father had read widely all his life and was an accomplished writer in both verse and prose. He regularly returned to Hangzhou for the examinations and just as regularly topped the list of successful candidates. But success beyond that point came too late in life for him, and it was not until he was forty that he passed the national examinations, by which time I was thirteen.

My mother was from a Hubei gentry family whose name was Li. She had only two children, both boys. My elder brother's personal name was Ruyu and his courtesy name Placidus. When he was fourteen, Father took him away to Hangzhou and enrolled him in a school there. My own personal name is Ruhua and my courtesy name Mirus. I remember Mother telling me that at the time I was born Father was about to set off for the provincial examinations, and that in choosing my name he had in mind the quotation "examination success beneath the hibiscus mirror."[7]

As a child I was taught by Father himself, but on reaching the age of ten I was sent to a private school in the Hu family compound next door, where the teacher was said to be a noted writer of examination essays, a genuine expert. As soon as I entered his classroom, I noticed that one of the pupils there was a girl, dainty and petite. I was only a little boy at the time and knew nothing whatever of love, but although I could not have told you why, I adored that little girl with all my heart. Whenever I was punished by the teacher for something she had done, I bore her not the slightest grudge, but when she was punished for something I had done, I felt terribly upset and only wished I could have taken some of the pain in her stead. There were eight or nine of us in the class altogether, but she and I formed the closest friendship and got up to all kinds of mischief that we kept from our classmates as well as from the teacher.

I remember one occasion that winter when I pinned her against the flowering plum tree outside the classroom window and ran

---

7. A prophecy of success in the examinations. The anecdote on which it is based is found in the seventh-century *Youyang zazu*.

my hands all over her body, squeezing and fondling her at will, and she just smiled up at me and made no attempt to resist. Eventually I reached a spot where she was ticklish, and she laughed and laughed until she was out of breath. All that time my face was directly opposite hers, and she looked so enchanting that my heart overflowed with love and tenderness and, cupping her face in my hands, I planted a whole series of kisses on that rosebud mouth before letting her go. . . .

This loving relationship of ours continued for a full three years, during which "one day apart seemed like three autumns." It was solely for her sake that I never cut class unless I was actually unwell. Often she would say: "Wouldn't it be wonderful if we could go on studying together in this classroom for the rest of our lives!" And whenever I heard her say it, I found myself sharing her wish.

Unfortunately Heaven pays no heed to human desires. I was twelve that year, as was she. For some reason, at the beginning of the eighth month her father suddenly took her out of school and moved his family across the river to Wuchang. I couldn't bear to part from her, but there was nothing I could do about it. Afterwards I felt bereft and no longer had any desire to study—or even to eat. Mother assumed I had come down with an illness and twice called in a doctor to examine me. The most ridiculous aspect of all this—I was really childish in those days—was that in three years of studying beside this girl I had never once asked her about her family. I didn't know what position her father held, merely that her surname was Gu and her personal name Aren, and so after the family's departure I couldn't even find out her address—a fact that did not deter me from fantasizing about secret trips to Wuchang in search of her. Eventually, because of the tight rein Father kept me on, I had to put the fantasies aside. Oddly enough, if I had really never met her again, I am sure I could have put an end to my desire once and for all. But the intentions of the Creator, confound him, are impossible to guess. The Buddhists talk about the seed and the fruit of an action, and Aren's and my coming together on this occasion was merely the planting of the seed. If you wish to know what fruit our actions bore—well, I will come to that in due course.

Reader, you should note that Aren was the one great love of whom I have spoken.

After parting from her, I put in another year in that classroom, at the end of which I was thirteen. Unfortunately, in the summer of that year, while Father, following his success in the national examinations, was away in the capital attending the palace review, Mother came down with cholera and in less than three days had succumbed. At her death I did nothing but weep and wail, and it was left to my uncle, Li Junshi, to take care of all the funeral arrangements, even to the extent of sending Father the telegram informing him of Mother's death. Eventually, early in the seventh month, Father returned and was heartbroken at the sight that met his eyes. He took Mother's coffin to Hangzhou and buried it beside our ancestors' graves, then came back to Hubei, put his affairs in order, and turned the family business over to my uncle to run. Because my brother was about to finish school, Father let him stay on in Hangzhou while he took me with him to Shanghai. From there we changed to an ocean-going ship as far as Tianjin and then went on by train to the capital, all so that Father could offer his services. What do I mean by "offer his services"? After the palace review, he had been given the rank of assistant and assigned to the Ministry of Punishments, and he had come to the capital to report for duty. As we set off from Hankou, I can still remember passing by the Gu compound and being reminded of my old friendship with Aren. I was so overcome by the thought that I almost broke down and cried. After I got to the capital, however, her memory gradually receded from my mind.

The compound Father had rented for us was in Mutton Alley off Fruit Lane, which itself is off Horse Market High Street beyond the city wall. It faced south and consisted of two houses and three smaller buildings. On entering, you came first to the gatekeeper's lodge, to the left of which was a large reception room. Across from it was a moon gate and behind that a chief minister's screen wall. Making your way around the wall, you came to one of the houses, with its rooms set about a courtyard. On the left side was the kitchen, on the right side the servants' quarters. There was a gate in the wall on the left side, and if you went in, you found the path dividing into two. One path went north and, if followed all the way, brought you to another courtyard with a southern exposure. In front of it was a winding passageway, the south end of which led through a small gate back to the first house. The other path ran eastward, meandering over a miniature bridge and around an ornamental rock until it brought you to a good-sized study. The study faced north, with tall sophoras and willows in front and flowering plum and apple trees behind. It was well adapted to both summer and winter use and finished in exquisite taste. The previous occupant of the compound was a rich metropolitan official who had served in the provinces as commissioner of examinations. On the strength of family ties Father had borrowed the study as temporary quarters when he first arrived in the capital. Within two months, however, the official had received a new appointment in the provinces. Partly because the rent was low, partly because the houses had been newly redecorated and were set in elegant surroundings, and partly because he couldn't find anything else to suit him, Father rejected the idea of leaving and simply moved from the study into the main house. Except for the lodge, which was occupied by our steward, Wang Sheng, who served as gatekeeper, the other buildings were all vacant, and so a "For Rent" sign was posted on the gate to attract tenants.

But six months went by, and all the people who came to look at the house found fault with it in one way or another—the rent was too high, the courtyard too large, and so on and so forth. Finally, early in the third month of the new year a party of people came along who did take a fancy to it. The first to move in were the stewards, whose master, it was said, held a post in the capital comparable to Father's. Then came the family, seven or eight in all, of both sexes and a variety of ages. I was at school when they moved in and never saw who they were. Early the next morning, when a few maidservants emerged from the side gate and walked past my window, I still didn't check to find out. Not until that evening, as I returned from school and was standing in the courtyard, did I suddenly hear the sound of girlish laughter from behind the side gate. I turned to look and, sure enough, there underneath the willows behind the ornamental rock I caught a glimpse of several women talking together. But my view was obstructed by the flowers and shrubs growing out of the rock, and for the moment I couldn't make out what the women looked like, so I stepped inside the gate and, standing on the miniature bridge, peered over at them. There were two girls, both in thin bluish-gray crepe silk jackets, one with her back to the rock, the other leaning against a willow tree, while a handsome, middle-aged woman sat on the stone steps beside them. I couldn't see the face of the girl with her back to the rock, but I had a clear view of the one leaning against the willow, of the perfectly proportioned oval of her face, the high arch of her brows, the limpid gaze, the rose-bud mouth, the childhood dimples. . . . Oh, who could it be but Aren, my nearest, dearest love? At the sight of her I let out an involuntary *"Aiya!"* I was standing on the bridge at the time, and none of the three had noticed me; not until they heard my cry did they turn their heads and look, dumbfounded. The girl leaning against the tree fixed her eyes on me and looked me up and down, examining me for some time. It seemed as if she was about to ask me something but then thought better of it. At length the older woman grew a little embarrassed and stood up.

"And who are you?" she asked.

The girl and I were so preoccupied with gazing into each other's eyes that I didn't hear her. Concluding I was deaf, the older woman raised her voice and asked again: "WHO ARE YOU?"

I was so flustered that I couldn't think how to reply, except to say, in a trembling voice: "It's me." At which she burst into laughter.

Reader, when I think back on that reply of mine, I agree it was absurd. How were they to know who "me" was? What do you think of my response? Was I stupid or what?

~ 2 ~

The Heaven of Passion[8] is whole again, as
predestined lovers meet far from home.

I WAS rescued from my predicament by the girl with her back to
the rock. She broke in and asked: "Are you Master Qin, by any
chance?"

Her question brought me to my senses. "Yes—yes, I am," I
replied.

At this the older woman smiled. "Oh, so you're Master Qin."

Now that I had been brought into the conversation and had a
chance to speak, I couldn't resist pointing at the girl by the tree
and asking: "And is this young lady Aren?"

My question startled the woman. "How did you know?" she
asked.

The girl turned to face her. "Mother, he's the Master Mirus Qin
who used to go to school with me when we lived in Hankou. . . ."
Before the words were out of her mouth, I realized that she really
was Aren and felt as thrilled as if some priceless gem had dropped
down from the skies at my feet. I seized my chance to go up to
the woman and bow, addressing her as "Aunt."

"Aunt, that was very rude of me just now, I'm afraid."

"Oh, not at all," she said, returning my greeting.

I turned and bowed to Aren, at the same time asking: "And who
is this young lady?"

Aren flushed with embarrassment, fell back a step or two, and

8. See note 1 on p. 21.

29

replied: "She's my elder sister. . . ." I bowed to the sister, who
returned my greeting with a notably casual air.

When I straightened up and looked more closely at her, I saw
something about the eyes that reminded me of Aren, but she
lacked Aren's dimples and was also somewhat thinner. Now that I
had exchanged greetings with everyone, Aren's mother invited me
to join them and proceeded to ask how old I was, what I was
studying, and whether I had any brothers or sisters. As I replied to
one question after another, I kept stealing glances at Aren. Her
face was even more radiant than it had been, like a peony just in
bloom, and she also seemed more vivacious. Aware that I was
looking at her, she hung her head and appeared ill at ease. Her
mother and I went on talking until it began to grow dark—sunset
streaks in the sky, the trees hooded in mist—and suddenly I heard
Aren's sister saying: "Mother, let's go in."

"Master Qin," said her mother, turning to me, "whenever you
have nothing better to do, you're very welcome to come over and
spend some time with us." Then, taking the two girls with her, she
went off to the back, past the flowers and trees. I remained at the
foot of the rock and watched until all three had reached the gate
and disappeared into the rear court, when I slowly and dejectedly
made my way to my bedroom in our courtyard. My feelings were
in turmoil—I felt joy as well as despair—and I had no idea what
to do about it.

Still at a loss, I realized that Father had come home and that our
steward, Wang Sheng, was serving supper in the living room. I left
my bedroom and joined them.

"As I daresay you know, we've rented out the rear court," said
Father. "Our tenant's name is Gu Qingbo, and he comes from
Haining in Zhejiang. He graduated in the same class as I did,
so you should address him as uncle.[9] He has a wife and two
daughters, whom you should also address as family friends." "Yes,
yes," I replied, and quickly asked what post Uncle Gu held.
"He's a new member of the Academy," he said. "A most distinguished man."

---

9. Graduates of the same year in the national examinations were nominally
brothers.

Supper was soon over, and after returning to my room and getting Wang Sheng to light the lamp, I sat there and retraced every detail of my meeting with Aren, including the questions her mother had asked me. I wondered how happy Aren had felt on meeting me again. Had it not been for the presence of her mother and sister, which stopped us from opening our hearts, we would have told each other all the things we had been longing to tell, right there beside the ornamental rock. It also occurred to me that her mother, by asking me at our first meeting how old I was and what I was studying, must surely be thinking of marriage for Aren and me. Otherwise, why question me in such detail? Father was a ministry official, I reflected, while her father was a member of the Academy, so our two families were on an equal footing. What's more, both men came from the same part of the country and had graduated in the same year—there was *nothing* to stand in the way of a union! This thought sent my spirits soaring.

Then it occurred to me that Aren was now two years older. Moreover, she lived with her parents and sister, and eyes and ears would be everywhere. Since she wasn't able to go off to school, how was I going to get in there and court her? Even if her mother had me in mind for a son-in-law, as a woman she couldn't very well raise the matter, any more than I could with Father. Even supposing I found someone to talk Father into agreeing, I still couldn't be sure *when* he would actually send the go-between. . . . Since I couldn't see Aren regularly and couldn't wait for Father to send a go-between, I found myself in a situation so tantalizing, with Aren so near and yet so far, that it was almost guaranteed to drive me to my death from sheer frustration! This thought brought all my previous anxieties back again.

A moment later I was struck by yet another thought: if Father were to send over a go-between now, it would still be like trying to put out a fire by fetching water from a mile away, to quote the old proverb. The essential thing at this point was to find some means of bringing us together every day. Back and forth I went in my mind, trying to think of a solution, when suddenly, at the brink of despair, two ideas suggested themselves. The first was to point out to Father that the study was a quiet, elegant place and to ask his permission to install a desk so that I could work there in the evenings. Aren adored flowers and moonlight, and on moonlit evenings and crisp, clear mornings she was bound to be out in the courtyard, and I would be able to invite her in. My second thought was that in Hangzhou families the sexes were not as strictly segregated as they were elsewhere. With Aren living in our rear court, there was nothing to prevent me from going over and joining her every day. Provided I could wheedle myself into the family's good graces and remembered to dole out a few tips to their servants, I would hardly be shown the door! This thought sent my spirits soaring again. But then it occurred to me that these ideas were all very well, but what if Father refused to let me install a desk in the study? And what if Uncle Gu happened to run a strict regime and refused to let me drop in all the time? Such questions brought my anxieties back again. I was in a truly pathetic state, as these chaotic thoughts whirled through my brain, and it was not until the fourth watch that I undressed and went to bed.

The next morning I arose early and went out to ask Father about the desk, but he had left to pay a social call without waiting for breakfast. Since I had no Father to talk to, I thought of going over to the rear court to see Aren. But then it occurred to me that it was too early in the morning and she wouldn't be up yet, so my visit would be pointless. There was nothing else for it; I would just have to fall back on my old routine of breakfast followed by school. On this particular day, because I had Aren on my mind, I returned from school early, before five o'clock. On entering the courtyard I came upon Father chatting with Uncle Gu under the trees, and I went over and bowed deeply, addressing him as uncle. He was quick to return my greeting.

"This is your younger boy?" he asked Father. "What a handsome lad! You mustn't let him go gallivanting around town, or he'll be corrupted by those young hooligans out there." I couldn't help smiling to myself at this advice; with Aren installed in the house, there was no chance of my gallivanting anywhere.

I took the opportunity to put my idea about the desk to Father, but before he could respond, Uncle Gu, standing beside him, endorsed it enthusiastically: "Capital idea! If you want to move into the study and work there, why not just go and get it ready? No need to ask your father."

In the wake of Uncle Gu's endorsement, Father simply nodded. "If you want to work there, go ahead." Delighted to have permission, I gave Wang Sheng orders to clean the study and move in some furniture from the house. He was to put the desk squarely in front of the window, which was exquisitely finished and fitted with glass panes that faced directly onto the ornamental rock, so that nobody coming from the rear court could escape the gaze of anyone inside. I also sought out several really fine scrolls and hung them up. On the desk itself nothing was neglected—incense burner, tea things, and so on. Beside it I had two stands placed with pink flowering peaches. When Wang Sheng had arranged everything to my satisfaction, I sat down at the desk and began to polish my writing instruments. I was calculating that, if Aren really did pay me a visit, she might be persuaded to sit for a while amid such spotless surroundings.

Polishing away, I caught a glimpse of someone passing by and assumed it was Aren out for a walk. I looked again and saw it was a woman all right, but not one that I had seen before. She appeared to be about thirty, with a round face, a prominent nose with pockmarks on either side of it, and a stocky figure, and she was dressed all in white. She certainly didn't belong to Uncle Gu's family, and yet she didn't appear to be a servant either. From her position beside the ornamental rock she was craning her neck and peeping at something or other beyond the side gate, but when I saw she wasn't Aren, I lost any interest in what she was doing. After watching for some time, she turned and went back to the rear court.

That evening, reciting texts in the study, I saw to it that my voice was loud enough to reach Aren's ears and let her know I was there.

Reader, I went to endless lengths for Aren's sake. I doubt that anyone in the world has ever gone so far to impress a girl.

Next day I attended school as usual, but a little after four o'clock, on the strength of a fib told to the teacher, I came racing home again. In my bedroom I changed into a new suit of clothes and headed straight for the rear court. Then, as I entered the living room, I came upon the woman I had seen the day before, chatting with Aren's mother. When they saw me, they broke into

smiles, got to their feet, and asked me to join them. This time
I used a new form of address with Aren's mother, calling her
Aunt.[10] "Do sit down, Aunt," I said. "You've been living in our
compound for several days now, and I haven't been over to pay
my respects, which is really very remiss of me. Is Uncle at home,
by any chance?"

"The master hasn't come back yet," said Aren's mother. "But
you're welcome to stay and amuse yourself."

I asked who her companion was. "This is my younger sister,"
said Aren's mother. It came to my mind, once I realized she was
Aren's aunt, that it was the custom in Hangzhou to address a
woman of the older generation as "foster mother," so I presented
myself before her, bowed, and addressed her in that fashion. She
laughed as she returned my greeting. I then joined them, but
although I kept a close watch all around, I saw no sign of Aren.

Soon a maidservant brought in some tea. After I had had a long
chat with Aren's mother and there was still no sign of Aren, I lost
patience. "My two cousins—why haven't *they* appeared?" I asked.

"They're in their room doing their needlework," said Aren's
mother. I didn't care to pursue the matter and, after sitting a while
longer, took my leave.

On my way back to my room I kept thinking: I may not have
managed to see Aren today, but the good news is that I now have
a regular means of access and will always be able to visit her. That
evening I again recited my texts in a voice loud enough for her to
hear.

On the afternoon of the following day I made another surprise
visit to the rear court in hopes of seeing Aren but instead found
only her sister, with whom I exchanged a few pleasantries. I was
put off by the sister's coolness toward me and ended up making
small talk with her mother. We chatted until evening and then,
when Aren had still not appeared, I took a rather awkward departure. I was surprised at missing Aren two days in a row. Was she
sick, perhaps? Or was Uncle Gu's regime so strict that, except
under extraordinary circumstances, she was not allowed to see

10. I.e., as his examination "brother's" wife. In calling her "Aunt" before, he
was using a less specific term.

any visitors? Otherwise, well, our relationship was exceptionally close—as close as if, in Lady Guan's words, "you smashed up two clay figures, mixed the clay together, and then molded it into two new figures"[11]—and she knew perfectly well that I was there in the living room chatting with her mother, so why on earth didn't she come out and see me? I racked my brains for a long time without coming up with an answer. Then the thought struck me that my evening performances were a kind of incantation designed to lure her forth and that I ought to keep them up, even if she had failed to appear so far. That evening I again recited my texts in a loud voice, and I also went on longer than before.

On the third day I returned to the rear court, but this time I was really out of luck, for Uncle Gu happened to be in, and I was forced to observe a nephew's protocol and respectfully exchange a few highly reactionary sentiments with him before I could decently take my leave.

The fourth day I went over even earlier. I greeted Aren's mother, her sister, and her aunt, and chatted with them for some time, but Aren still did not appear. Back to my study I went in a blind fury. I felt sure she had jilted me, that she was no longer the Aren I had known. We had been apart almost two years now, and so clever and beautiful a girl must surely have had other young men pursuing her. If one of them had managed to seduce her and she had fallen in love with him, or if she was engaged to be married, of *course* she'd be ashamed to meet me! That would explain why she flushed with embarrassment the first time we met and why she had been hiding in her room ever since. *Yes, that was it!* The facts clearly showed that there was no longer any bond between us and that it was no use cherishing any foolish hopes about her.

And yet, I thought, addressing her in my mind, although I can't blame you for falling in love with someone else, or for being engaged for that matter, you really ought to meet me and tell me

11. The artist Zhao Mengfu (1254–1322) is said to have written a song to his wife, Lady Guan, informing her of his desire to take a concubine. Her reply, from which these lines are quoted, is one of the most passionate avowals of love in Chinese literature. Unfortunately, the story is almost certainly apocryphal; it first appears in a much later work.

so to my face, not shilly-shally and keep me in suspense. At this
thought I began grinding my teeth in fury. I felt as if my heart had
been deluged with icy water and my limbs had begun to freeze.

It was the tenth of the third month. The moonlight projected
the shadows of the flowering branches onto my whitened wall.
Wang Sheng came in to call me for supper, but I excused myself
on the grounds that I wasn't feeling very well and just sat there on
my own in the gathering darkness. The longer I thought, the more
likely my fears seemed and the more furious I became. After
Wang Sheng had called in to light my lamp, I no longer recited my
texts, or rather my incantations, but lay brooding on the couch
instead. Before long the moonlight outside my window was flood-
ing half the garden. Suddenly my ears picked up a sound—it
seemed like a girl's faint cough—from the stone path beside the
ornamental rock. I assumed it was Aren's maidservant going by
and thought nothing of it, but then after a pause I heard a faint
tapping on my study door. I got up from the couch, walked over
to the door, and slowly opened it. On looking up I received such
a shock that I let out a cry: *"Aiya!"*

～ 3 ～

Birds of passage meet beneath the
dragon-flower tree.[12]

READER, who do you suppose it was? None other than the bodhi-
sattva Guanyin,[13] savior of those in distress—my nearest, dearest
Aren! The moment I saw her all the suspicion and fury I had felt
were banished to the ends of the earth. I grasped one of her
hands in mine and, putting my other arm around her shoulders,
pulled her toward me and hugged her tightly, intending to kiss
her, but she became agitated and pushed me away with all her
might: "You're fourteen and *still* behaving so badly! No wonder
everyone in my family calls you an idiot!"

At once I let her go and invited her into the study, where I
showed her to a seat on the couch and sat beside her. I felt as if
there were a million things I wanted to say and didn't know
where to begin, but Aren couldn't wait to tell me what was on her
mind. "I imagine that after missing me several days in a row you
must be blaming me for not coming over before," she whispered,
"but you don't understand how things are in our family. My aunt
was recently widowed and now makes her home with us. She
loves nothing better than gossip, and my mother believes every
word she says. If you cross my aunt in any way, she'll make life
extremely unpleasant for you. My sister Asou serves as a personal
secretary to my father. She received an education at home and
writes beautifully; all my father's letters to his friends are written

12. Buddha met disciples under this tree to preach his doctrine.
13. The goddess of mercy.

by her. He thinks the world of her, and she sets very high standards for everybody she comes in contact with. At that first meeting, when she saw how tongue-tied you were, she formed a low opinion of you and told us you were an idiot and we should have nothing more to do with you. I've been longing to tell you what has happened to me since we parted, but because of these two menaces in the household I've had to keep my distance. Now that I'm living in your compound, I don't doubt that we shall meet, but I'm afraid it will not be very often."

I became terribly upset. "Are you trying to tell me it will be almost impossible for us to meet?" I demanded.

"No, I don't mean that at all. Let me tell you something. My sister never gets up before eleven, and my aunt is a rather grasping woman with a passion for wine. If you can win those two over to your side, we should have no trouble in meeting regularly." She stood up to go, but I held fast to her hand and begged her to stay.

"Look, I came here today behind my mother's back," she protested. "If you're going to be so pushy, I won't dare come again."

There was nothing I could do but show her out of the study. Peering into her face, I found that in the moonlight her beauty was more dazzling than ever. As I walked along, I plucked a rose from her hairpin and slipped it into my pocket. She didn't object, but after I had escorted her over the miniature bridge, she broke away from me. "Don't forget what I said," she added. "Think it over." Then she dashed back to the rear court. After she had gone, I stood by myself beneath the blossom. Moonlight flooded the courtyard, and the scent from the blossom was overpowering. I lingered a while, in the spirit of the lines

> The song has ended, the singer gone;
> Above the river the peaks stand green.[14]

Still musing, I heard Father calling from the other side of the gate. Because I hadn't eaten any supper, he had given Wang Sheng special instructions to make me a bowl of Shandong noodles and had brought them along to my room. I raced frantically back.

---

14. From a poem by Qian Qi (722–c. 780), "Examination Poem: Drum and Zither of the Xiang River Spirits."

"What's the matter with you?" Father asked.

"I feel all right now," I said. After gulping down the noodles, I undressed and went to bed.

The West Chamber puts it well: "Sleep denied / Cheek in palm / Pursuing languid thoughts."[15] Although I did get some sleep, I kept thinking of Aren and carefully analyzed what she had said, which made a great deal of sense to me. Her aunt's acquisitiveness and fondness for wine, like her sister's arrogance and inability to get up in the morning—these were two themes, and now that they had been set, I could begin to write my essays. But what approach should I adopt in my writing? I pondered the question for a long time, and then, eureka! The first essay would be simplicity itself to organize. I would start the next day by snapping up my chances wherever I found them, and eventually I'd get that essay done.

After school the following day I told Father I needed some more winter clothes and asked him for a few taels to buy them with. Then I went off to an imported goods store on Dashalar, where I bought fourteen yards of dark green foreign silk in a fashionable design and had a tailor whom I had dealt with before cut it in two and make one part into a padded gown for my own use. The other half I brought home and stowed away in my book chest. With the few coins I had left over, I sent Wang Sheng to the Guangyi dried fruit store on the west side of Horse Market High Street to get two bottles of premium Wujiapi, which I also put away in the study. Mindful of what Aren had told me, I did not venture into the rear court that day.

Two days later, in the morning, I sent Wang Sheng back to the tailor's, and rather to my surprise the gown was ready. I was thrilled with it, and slipping it on went gaily off to the rear court in hopes of finding Aren's aunt. Instead I found only Aren and her mother in the living room. Aren hadn't done her hair, and when she saw me come in, she got up, gave me a broad wink, and went back to her room. I had to exchange a little chit-chat with Aren's mother before I could escape. It was generally in the afternoons

---

15. *The West Chamber (Xixiang ji)*, written toward the end of the thirteenth century, is the most famous Chinese play. These lines come from a song by the hero at the end of part 1, act 2.

that I ran into the aunt, I reflected, so I decided to drop by after school that day.

I had guessed right. This time I had no sooner reached the passageway than I came upon her, playing with a baby in her arms. She had been widowed not long before, and the baby was her late husband's posthumous son. The moment she saw me, she proceeded to scrutinize my new clothes.

"Oh, Master Qin!" she exclaimed. "That gown of yours—it's a brand new design and in the *loveliest* shade! Where did you get it?"

I told her I had had it made up from some material of my own.

"Baby would look so *cute* in a little outfit made out of that! But where did you buy the material?"

Confident that I had her in my trap, I gave a calculated answer: "I doubt that you can get this in the capital. I had a friend pick it up for me in Shanghai. But I do have another seven yards left over, and I'll gladly make you a present of it."

At this offer her face broke into a broad smile. Although she protested that she couldn't possibly accept the silk as a gift, needless to say she was really only too eager to do so. Smiling to myself, I returned to the study, took the rest of the material from the chest, and brought it back and presented it to her with both hands. As she took it, she beamed with delight and couldn't thank me enough. Privately I was just as elated as she was—the first essay Aren had assigned me was already half written.

From that time on, whenever I got up early in the morning I would go over to the rear court and look for Aren. Sometimes I saw her, sometimes I didn't, but even when I did see her we couldn't really talk, and I was far from satisfied. When I was free in the afternoon I would stroll over there, and if I had any candy or fruit, I would give some to the aunt's baby. Within a matter of ten days or so, I had the aunt securely locked in my Eight Trigrams Furnace[16] and could do whatever I liked with her.

One morning I happened upon Aren, who remarked with a grin: "The lad is showing promise."[17] I reflected that on my daily

16. The Furnace was used by Lao Zi to trap Monkey in *Journey to the West;* See chapter 7.

17. Quoted from Sima Qian's (c. 145–c. 85 B.C.) *Historical Records* ("Hereditary Household of Marquis Liu").

visits to the rear court I could never get farther than the living room; I didn't dare venture into her room. The sage Confucius spoke of "ascending the hall" and "entering the inner room."[18] Well, I could ascend the hall, all right, but I could not enter the inner room, so that even if I did manage to see Aren it was to very little purpose. The trouble was that Aren's sister was one of those superior creatures who could be neither bullied nor bribed into compliance, and if I wanted to get into that inner room, I'd have to curry favor with her. Reader, I ask you, how do you imagine I was going to curry favor with someone as high and mighty as the sister? How should I set about writing my second essay?

Where there's a will, there's a way, of course, but in this second essay I had help straight from Heaven and did not need to lift a finger. Now, women in the capital like nothing better than visiting temples to burn incense and pray to Buddha, and when it came to that kind of superstition, Aren's sister was no exception. It was the sixth of the fourth month, just two days before what is known as the Buddha Bathing Festival. The steward of Aren's family, Li Gui, who shared the lodge with Wang Sheng, happened to have some business in the city that day and had entrusted his duties to Wang Sheng. I had just run home from school and was feeling rather hungry, so I asked Wang to go out and get me a snack.

"The men on the gate are all off," he said. "Would you mind staying here a moment yourself, sir? Don't go away, now."

I nodded and stood outside the gate as Wang Sheng went off.

Before long an eleven- or twelve-year-old boy approached the gate with a letter. "Is this Mr. Gu's residence?" he asked.

"Yes."

"Please take delivery of this," he said, and walked off.

I picked up the letter. On the outside it read "For Young Master Guo from Sick Butterfly." I called after the boy: "The name here is Gu, not Guo. You've brought this to the wrong house." To my surprise he continued to stride away as if he hadn't heard a word I said. Then I looked at the letter again and became a little suspicious. I felt the envelope between thumb and forefinger; there was something stiff inside, like a piece of cardboard. My suspi-

18. See D. C. Lau, trans., *The Analects* (London: Penguin Books, 1979), p. 108.

cions grew until finally I picked it up and slipped it into my breast pocket.

Before long Wang Sheng returned with my snack, which I took with me to the study. Munching as I walked along, I brought out the letter and slowly and carefully opened it. How odd! There was nothing inside but two snapshots, one of a young man, the other of a group of buildings, and I was utterly baffled. Then I looked at the back of the first photograph and found what appeared to be a few penciled characters. I tried to decipher them; they *seemed* to read "noon on the eighth." But I had no idea who the person in the first photograph was or where the buildings in the second were located. Even if such a person and place existed, why send the photographs here? I pondered this question for some time before suddenly spotting the answer. The letter *had* to be intended for either Aren or her sister, and the handsome young man *had* to be the lover of one or other of them! But since the letter was addressed to "Young Master," Asou was the more likely recipient.[19] As for the buildings, they must be the site of the rendezvous, while "noon on the eighth" would be the date and the time. I had better keep this information to myself for the time being, I thought, and simply seal the letter up again and have it delivered to Asou, then wait and see what transpired. With this idea in mind I sealed up the letter and told Wang Sheng to take it over to the rear court. Unfortunately he handed it to a maid, who disappeared inside with it, and I never did learn which of the sisters took delivery. Still, from the fact that someone had accepted it, I felt that my suspicions had been more or less confirmed.

On the morning of the eighth I got up early and went over to the rear court to find out what the sisters were doing. I had hardly reached the passageway when I ran into Asou and asked her why she was up so early. "Aren't I *allowed* to get up early?" she asked with a smile. I smiled, too, and left it at that.

However at noon, as I came by the lodge on my way home from school, I heard one of the maids from the Gu household telling Li Gui to order a rickshaw for the elder young lady, who

---

19. The word translated as "young master" actually specifies an eldest son. Note that Asou is an elder daughter.

wanted to give thanks at Lotus Flower Temple. My ears buzzing with this piece of news, I skipped lunch and went straight out again to lie in wait for the lovers at the temple in Westbrick Alley.

No sooner had I entered the gate than among the crowd I came upon a handsome young man who on closer inspection proved to be identical with the one in the photograph! It dawned on me then that the buildings in the other photograph must be those of this Lotus Flower Temple. I kept an eye on him as he emerged from the temple gate, took out his pocketbook and removed a note from it that he gave to a rickshaw man, then turned and went inside again. I waited until he was some way off before approaching the rickshaw man. "Excuse me, but who was that gentleman you brought here just now?" I asked.

"He's the son of Mr. Lu in the Ministry of Punishments. Why do you want to know?"

"You mean Mr. Lu of Nanheng Street?"

"That's right."

The handsome young man was the son of Lu Xiaocang from Haining, who was an acquaintance of Father's and had actually visited our house. Just as I was about to ask more questions, I saw Asou and a maidservant arriving in another rickshaw. I caught a glimpse of them in the distance, then spotted an opening in the crowd and slipped through it into the temple, where I waited for them on the steps of the Hall of the Great Hero. I was not disappointed. In a matter of moments I saw Asou emerging from the hall with the handsome young man in tow. (I have no idea what became of the maid.) As I watched, they walked a dozen yards along the west side of the passageway, taking care to keep their heads down, then looked up, noticed a certain room, and ducked inside. Lest Asou recognize me, I had to watch from a distance, not follow them in. After I had waited a considerable time and they still had not come out, I slowly approached the room, peered inside—and found that it had a back door! Asou and the young man had left, and I didn't even know when. Cursing myself for a fool, I made a thorough search of the temple before returning home, where I took Wang Sheng aside and asked him: "The elder Miss Gu, is she back yet?"

"Yes," he replied.

A sigh escaped me. Those two had arranged to meet for a tête-à-tête at the temple, I thought, where they could unburden themselves to each other far more freely than Aren and I ever could, even though we met practically every day. She and I might just as well have been living at opposite ends of the earth for all the good our meetings did us! But then I was struck by another thought, one that lifted my spirits again. All the evidence I needed against Asou was now in my hands, and no matter how arrogant she was, from now on she'd have to knuckle under. The period of *my* own freedom was about to begin. Oh, Master Lu, Master Lu, what a savior you have been! But for the help you gave me today, instead of finishing my essay, I might have had to hand in a blank sheet of paper.

~ 4 ~

Soulmates affirm their vows of love.

I BOLTED down some lunch and then, on the pretext of leaving for school, went off to see a Hangzhou friend of mine to check up on Lu Xiaocang's background and find out the name of his eldest son. Xiaocang proved to be an assistant director at the Ministry of Punishments, and his son's name was Boyin. When they first arrived in the capital, they had taken up temporary quarters at the All-Zhejiang Guild. At about the same time, Uncle Gu had brought *his* family to the capital and stayed at the same place. Early in the third month both families had moved out.

Now that I understood how the relationship between Asou and Lu Boyin had come about, I bought a few apricots and carried them home, hoping to find Aren's aunt and curry favor with her—and at the same time set Asou a tricky theme to write *her* essay on. At this point it should be noted that Father was far from being a puritan. After Mother's death he had found the celibate life little to his taste—in fact he was bored to death at home—and every day after lunch would either go to a friend's house to play mahjong or else accompany his cronies on visits to the singsong girls or the nancy boys.[20] As a result I was left alone in the house and could come and go as I wished without anyone to restrain me. On this occasion, with the apricots in my pocket, I dashed around to the rear court, where I found Aren on a couch in the passageway trying to coax a smile from the baby. Her aunt was sitting beside

---

20. Officials in the capital, unable to supplement their meager salaries by influence peddling, were relatively poor, as in *The Sea of Regret*. Their duties, however, were often light, as in Mr. Qin's case.

her. I went up to them and stretched out my hand near Aren's breast to attract the baby's attention, then pulled two apricots out of my sleeve. The baby tried to grab them, but he did so with too much force and succeeded only in knocking them into Aren's lap, from which they rolled onto the ground. Laughing, I bent down to pick them up from beneath Aren's seat. But at the same time she jumped up, and her knee happened to catch my temple a glancing blow and send me sprawling. Her aunt roared with laughter at the sight, and even Aren joined in. Hearing the laughter from her room, Asou came out to see what was going on.

"Who's having all the fun?" she asked.

I scrambled to my feet, meaning to have a talk with her, but she took one look at me, clapped a stern expression on her face, and without another word turned on her heel and went inside again. I realized then that she held me in too much contempt even to speak to me, and I was seized by such an ungovernable rage that I nearly told Aren and her aunt right then and there about the unsavory goings-on I had witnessed in the temple. But a moment's reflection was enough to convince me that in the long run it would be wiser not to tell them, and so with a great effort I suppressed my anger and merely confided to Aren's aunt: "I picked these up along the passageway in Lotus Flower Temple and popped them in my pocket to bring home for Junior. Otherwise they'd have been eaten long ago."

"I find that hard to believe," she said, smiling. "There aren't any apricots lying about in Lotus Flower Temple!"

"You don't believe me? Well, I was visiting the temple today when I happened to notice a young friend of mine walking behind a strikingly beautiful girl. They were dashing into a room on the west side of the passageway, and the apricots fell out of his pocket without his being aware of it. I found the whole scene highly amusing, so I went over and picked them up."

"Who was this young friend of yours?"

"Oh, a fellow named Lu. Someone I've known for ages."

Our little exchange was proceeding merrily when it was overheard by Asou. "Aunt, you'd better come quick and see what's happened!" she called out. "That dish you left out to cool has been knocked over by the cat."

Her aunt sprang to her feet and rushed inside. I knew perfectly well what Asou's call meant—that eventually she would have to lay down her arms and surrender. With a smile to Aren I left the house. Nothing else of interest happened that day.

On the evening of the following day I was in my study looking through my books when I saw Asou come out along the path beside the ornamental rock and start picking flowers. She very rarely appears, I thought to myself; no doubt the flowers are just an excuse to come and have a talk with me. I pretended not to notice her, in order to see what she would do. There was a pause, then I saw her pick a flower and make her way purposefully around to my door.

"What are you looking for, Master Qin?" she called out.

I saw my chance. "Oh, I had two photographs that a friend sent me. I only *wish* I knew what Wang Sheng has done with them. But won't you come in and sit down?"

Flushing, she stepped reluctantly into the study. I pulled up a chair for her, but even so it was only after a good deal of bashful hesitation that she finally began to speak: "What I did yesterday at Lotus Flower Temple—I wonder if you could find it in your heart to overlook it? I know it was wrong."

Ah, those few words of hers could not have been purchased for a whole mint of money! Looking into her face as she spoke, I felt as if I had been granted an imperial pardon—I was literally speechless with delight. The gods and bodhisattvas in Heaven are rewarding me for all the trouble I have gone to, I thought to myself; they've delivered her into my hands. Without their help, I could never have done it!

"My dear 'Sou," I said, "of course I shall respect your wishes. Let's have a tacit understanding between us."

Slowly her color returned to normal, and before long she stood up to take her leave.

"I think I hear Mother calling. I have to go."

"Just one moment," I said, pouring her a cup of Dragonwell tea and holding it to her lips. "You have to drink a cup of my tea before I'll let you go." She had no choice but to take the cup and drain it, after which, with a hurried "Thanks," she dashed out of the study and back to the rear court.

After reaching my understanding with Asou, I was constantly visiting the rear court. It was as if I had been released into "a sea where fish could leap at will, a heaven where birds were free to soar."

Reader, you should understand that Uncle Gu, although strict in terms of family discipline, spent most of his time away from home dancing attendance on powerful figures and so had no inkling of the fact that both of his daughters were engaged in love affairs. Even if I did on occasion let slip a hint or two in his presence, Asou was always there to cover up for me. In the case of her mother, I had nothing to worry about, for the aunt was constantly singing my praises. It was chiefly the maids I had to be on my guard against. Although I kept doling out tips, still, since maids and servants are the hardest people of all to handle,[21] I was careful never to give them any evidence that they could have used against me.

The next day was the tenth of the fourth month. I returned from school in the evening and headed as usual for the rear court. This time, however, I found the living room deserted. The right side of the courtyard was occupied by Uncle and Aunt's bedroom, with the maids' quarters next door, while the left wing was the girls' bedroom and adjacent to it a room that Asou had converted into a study. The aunt's room was behind a partition in the living room; to the right of it was Uncle Gu's parlor and to the left a kitchen. Since no one else was about, I went up to the girls' bedroom window, beside which a giant elm tree grew and, standing beneath the tree, poked a tiny hole in the paper and peeped inside.

On a platform bed facing south a beautiful girl lay on her side. Her eyes were closed, and she was fast asleep. She had on a lined gown of rose-pink foreign silk with a ripple effect and lined trousers of lotus-green silk. The front of the gown had been blown half open by the wind, exposing a snowy white midriff. I looked more closely—it was Aren, my love! I listened—a slight sound came from the adjoining study as if someone were grinding up ink. Assuming it must be Asou, I gave a faint cough, but no one

21. Quoted from *The Analects* 17.25; see p. 148.

heard me, so I went up to the study window and tapped lightly on the sill. This time I did hear sounds, and someone came to the window and called out: "Who is it?"

"It's me," I whispered.

There was a creaking sound as the little door near the window swung open. Asou pulled aside the door curtain, saw who it was, and broke into a broad smile. "Come on in and sit down!" At these words I felt as if I were melting with joy. I had never set foot in this room since Aren moved into the house, I reflected; Asou's gracious invitation marked an entirely new development for me. Reader, you should bear in mind that following this visit I went back and forth countless times without any need for prior negotiation.

I followed Asou into the study, where she showed me to a painted rattan chair and personally served me tea. The warmth with which she treated me, when compared with her previous disdain, made her seem like an entirely different person. Looking about me, I saw that the walls were papered in a glossy silver, which gave them a shiny snow-white glow. Beneath the window on the north wall stood a very long desk, which I assumed was where she did her work. Outside the window were a few banana plants, newly placed there. On the west wall hung a pair of scrolls three feet long in seal script:

> Passionate the fragrant flowers, wordless the setting sun;
> After the crabapple blooms, soon the swallows call.

I glanced at the inscription—the calligraphy was by Deng Shiru.[22] To one side of it was a horizontal scroll of corn poppies from the hand of Yun Shouping.[23] In addition, artistically placed about the room were bronzes and rare editions, all far superior to anything I had in my study.

"So this is your study?" I asked, after drinking my tea.

"Yes."

"Does Aren have one, too?"

"That little desk along the south wall is hers."

---

22. An eighteenth-century calligrapher who specialized in the seal script.

23. A seventeenth-century artist who specialized in painting flowers and insects.

"Where is she?" I asked, a trifle disingenuously.

"Asleep in the other room. Go in and see for yourself, if you don't believe me."

"But I couldn't possibly go into your *bedroom!*" I exclaimed as disingenuously as before.

Asou gave a snort of laughter. "You can come in here, but you can't go in there, is that what you mean?"

I couldn't help laughing at her retort, as I got up and went into the outer room. Ah, reader! You should mark this down as another new development for me—the first time I had ventured into that room since Aren moved into our compound.

She was just awakening when she saw me come bursting in, and she gave a start: "Are you *crazy?*" she demanded. "This is my *bedroom!* Who said you could come in here?"

"What if it *is* your bedroom?" I replied with a grin. "Anyway, your sister said I could."

Aren looked blank. "Why would she *say* such a thing?" she eventually asked.

"I have no idea. Why don't you ask her?"

In the midst of this exchange her aunt parted the curtain and came into the room, the baby in her arms. More than a little embarrassed, I turned and was on the point of leaving, when with a faint smile she urged me to stay: "There's no harm in joining us for a while, Master Qin. You're not trying to *avoid* me, are you?" I saw my chance and quickly took a seat by the window. But as soon as Aren saw me sit down, she turned and retreated to the other room. I assumed she had gone to get the truth out of Asou and took no notice, merely played with the baby in its mother's arms. I stayed there for some time without a sign of Aren, and since it was getting late I felt I had to go back. When Aren's aunt saw me leaving, she stood up. "Do come by a little earlier tomorrow!" she said.

Asou, who had been watching us from the other room, bustled out to say good-bye. "Yes, do come and see us again!" I accepted both invitations and left, smiling to myself as I walked along. How ridiculous they were, Aren's sister and her aunt, both of them successfully coopted and powerless to do me harm! And yet, how extraordinary it was that Aren, who had fled at the first sight of me, was now acting more coolly than before!

I had intended to wait until evening before visiting her and trying to clear matters up. But unfortunately it began to rain before then, and a steady, soaking rain persisted for the next three or four days. "Never used to be this wet in the capital during the rainy season," Father said. "It all comes from the southern climate moving up north, you know. Only been like this the last twenty years."

Finally, on the evening of the fifteenth the skies began to clear. I had eaten my supper and was sitting alone in the study at the time. In my anxiety over Aren, whom I hadn't seen in three or four days, I stepped outside and began pacing back and forth. A full moon like a jade disk or golden mirror was rising over the corner of the eastern wall, and in the fresh, clear light that followed the rain, it looked incandescent. After one glance at the moonlight, I forgot all about the soggy ground underfoot and stole noiselessly over to the rear court to see Aren. As I brushed past the trees on each side, the raindrops gathered on the tips of their branches came pattering down behind me. At the passageway in the rear court I found Aren standing by herself under the elm and gazing up at the moon. I tiptoed up to her, but in her sharp-eyed way she had already seen me. "What are you doing at our place in the middle of the night?" she demanded.

"I'm bent on robbery or rape," I said with a grin. "You really ought to be a bit more careful, you know."

"Oh, pish! You're talking nonsense again. Tell me, what scandal to do with my sister has come to your ears, that you can manipulate her like this?"

I assumed from her question that she had not been told the story of Asou's adventure in Lotus Flower Temple, so I took her by the hand and led her along the passageway and out the side gate to the ornamental rock, where I told her all about the photographs I had found in the letter and the events I had witnessed at the temple. When I came to the part about Lu Boyin following Asou into the room at the temple, I stopped.

"Why have you stopped?" she asked impatiently. "What did they do then?"

I compressed my lips into a faint smile. "My dear 'Ren," I said, "for such an intelligent girl you can sometimes be awfully dim. What they did then must have been that singularly fascinating thing that you and I have never done. . . ."

Before I could finish the sentence, she blushed furiously, slipped her hand out of mine, and dashed back to the rear court.

~ 5 ~

Perfect bliss! Wine with a lover at midnight.

I LAUGHED and followed her into the rear court, where I found her leaning against the trunk of the elm tree, one finger in her mouth and her head bent low over her breast, deep in thought. Silently I approached. "You didn't let me finish!" I said, taking her hand and leading her back to the ornamental rock.

She looked up and saw there was no one else about. "My sister is far too proud to do any such thing! I simply don't believe you," she said.

"My dear 'Ren," I explained, "you can't judge people by their appearances. The more pride they *seem* to have, the more likely they are to be doing just such things as that. Take the people in power in the capital these days. To all appearances they're incorruptible—never pull any strings or take any bribes—but they all have their back doors open. So long as the money ends up in their pockets, they'll stoop to any sort of shady business. The public are the only ones who are taken in. . . ."

At this point there came a sudden knocking at the main gate; either Uncle Gu or Father must have returned. Aren tore her hand out of mine and dashed back to the rear court.

It was Father who had come home. I returned to my room and lay on my bed pondering the situation. I had overcome the threat posed by Asou, and there was nothing to stop me from slipping into the sisters' room at midnight. However, so long as I continued to sleep in this room, my every move would be subject to Father's scrutiny. How could I ever get away at midnight? I wrestled with this problem for a long time, and then . . . eureka! The back window of my bedroom used to open onto the passageway in the rear court, but it had been blocked off with a bookcase. Tomorrow I would complain that it was too dark in the room to write properly and get Wang Sheng to come in and move the bookcase aside. Then I'd go to an imported goods store and get a couple of rubber bands to put around the ends of the top bars of the window sashes so as to prevent any creaking sound when the window was opened. At midnight I'd be able to come and go as I pleased. No one would be any the wiser, even if I slipped out of the window and sneaked over to Aren's room.

The next day I put my plan into operation, moving the bookcase aside and fitting rubber bands around the ends of the window bars. That evening I returned to the rear court and, seeing no one in the yard, went up to the window of the nearest room on the lefthand side and again tapped three times on the sill. Asou soon appeared, but when she saw who it was, her tongue popped out in surprise. "My, what a *chance* you're taking!" she exclaimed. "It's a good thing Mother left a moment ago. If she'd been in here and heard you tapping on the window-sill, we'd be in terrible trouble!"

She had barely finished speaking when Aren came running up. "What a *chance* you took!" she said, shaking her head. "From now on, if you want to come into our room, you'll have to call out our names a couple of times first, then walk casually in. Whatever you do, you *mustn't* go tapping on the window!"

The scolding I received sent shivers down my spine, as it dawned on me that I really had done something rather foolish. "What if from now on I don't come over after supper, but wait until midnight?" I whispered.

"How are you going to get out of your bedroom at midnight?" asked Asou.

"I'll climb out of the window at the back," I said. "I've thought of a way of stopping it from creaking."

"Your window may not creak, but our door certainly will," said Asou. "If you want to visit us, you'll have to think up a secret signal, so that I can leave the door ajar and you can come and go as you please." Asou's suggestion filled me with admiration for her intelligence, and I felt even more grateful that she was willing to put it to work for me.

"Let's handle it this way from now on," I said, stepping into the study and standing in front of the two girls. "When you see the light in my bedroom go out early, that will be a signal that I want to come over, so please leave the door ajar!"

"That's fine," said Asou.

"But what if there's someone else in here at the time?" said Aren. "What shall we do then?"

"At midnight there won't be anyone else in here but the two of us," said Asou. "You can rest assured on that point."

"You mean *you* don't have a friend like me?" I asked Asou with a smile.

She gave me a wry look. "If I had a friend like you," she said, "I wouldn't worry about getting my new shoes soaking wet. I'd take him by the hand and lead him over to the rock for a little chat."

I leapt to my feet in astonishment. "You must have seen me yesterday beside the rock!"

"She never saw a thing," Aren explained. "She only said that because she noticed my shoes were wet through."

At this point Asou gave me a couple of meaningful glances, as if to say there was something else she wanted to tell me. But suddenly we were interrupted by Aunt Gu's voice calling the girls, and they ran off to the living room while I raced home.

Every midnight after that I slipped over and hung about in the sisters' room. Sometimes we'd talk poetry; sometimes we'd play chess; sometimes, on moonlit nights, we'd drink wine beneath the moon (and on occasion I'd drink too much and end up taking a nap on Aren's soft and scented couch); and sometimes I'd pick out some romantic stories of heroes and heroines from ancient and modern fiction and discuss them in detail with the girls by the light of the lamp.

As time went by and Asou got to know me better, she was even willing to reveal something of her affair with Lu Boyin. Occasionally, though, she would touch on some secret concern, and the tears would well up in her eyes, and she would lapse into silence.

Aren, however, was abnormally sensitive. Embarrassed anyway in her sister's presence, she was also a virgin and, whenever she came to some delicate matter, would turn shy and refuse to go on. I remember one night when Asou was feeling unwell and had gone to bed in the other room. I took Aren's hand in mine and, sitting beside her at the desk, had the nerve to demand a kiss: "Come on, 'Ren, we haven't kissed in ages. Let's have a kiss."

Turning her head away, she looked outside and smiled. "I'm afraid you'll end up just like Tedmore. One day you'll have to go to court and pay me three thousand dollars in compensation for my kisses!" That year a Shanghai magazine had carried a news item about an American woman named Ford who had been abandoned by her husband, Tedmore, after fourteen years of marriage. Taking him to court, she had pleaded: "In fourteen years of marriage he demanded one thousand, two hundred and thirty kisses from me. If he's not forced to pay compensation, I'll never be able to hold my head up again!" In his verdict the American judge had awarded her two dollars forty-two cents for each kiss and made Tedmore pay a total of three thousand dollars. Aren had seen the item in the magazine.[24]

"My dear 'Ren," I replied, "how many kisses have *I* ever asked you for? If you took *me* to court, I'd give you *twice* as much as Tedmore had to pay!"

"Now you're being silly. Think what *they* were to each other, and then think what *we* are. It's too soon to be asking for kisses."

I had no answer for that and had to let her go, not daring to offend her. Thinking back on the incident now, I feel confident she would not have refused me had I taken a somewhat stronger line. But Aren and I were both able to control our feelings, often taking stern measures to do so, and although over the course of a year or more our intimacy, to quote Zhang Chang, "went far

24. A note in the first edition of *Stones in the Sea* says that this incident appeared in the *Continent (Dalu bao),* a Shanghai journal published from 1902 to 1906, first at monthly, then at fortnightly intervals. I have been unable to find the item, and Tedmore and Ford are just guesses on my part as to the original names. (The Chinese has Tie-di-mo and Fo-di.) If the case occurred in Shanghai, it would have been heard by an officer of the U.S. Consulate. The word "kiss" is no doubt a euphemism.

beyond the painting of eyebrows,"[25] we never did sample the delights of the flesh.

After I had opened up my back window and could visit Aren in secret, time flew by until suddenly the season of pomegranate blossom was upon us. So far neither Father nor Uncle and Aunt Gu had any inkling of our midnight trysts. Our one fear was that Aunt Gu's sister, whose bedroom adjoined Aren's, would give us away. To stay in her favor, my only recourse was to cold, hard cash, and I must say she always did manage to keep our secret.

It was the third of the fifth month. I had been to a cosmetics shop on Dashalar to buy two sandalwood rosaries and a pair of incense sachets and then dropped by Wallet Lane and was strolling about the market there when I noticed someone holding up two or three squirrels for sale.[26] I was so taken with the little creatures that I paid three hundred cash for one and then another two hundred for a brass chain that I found at a street stall. Back home I kept the squirrel in my study tethered to the chain and gave Wang Sheng instructions to keep it supplied with fruit and nuts. The rosaries and sachets were intended as presents for Aren's aunt.

That night I told Aren about the presents and asked her advice on tipping the servants. At the Dragon Boat Festival, only two days away, how much should I give their two maidservants when they came to offer me their compliments of the season?

"One rosary and one sachet are enough for Aunt's baby; the others you can keep for yourself," she replied. "With the maidservants, though, you ought to be more generous. To buy their loyalty, you'll need to give them anywhere from eight hundred to a thousand cash each." I nodded.

"Well, haven't you bought anything for *me* to amuse myself with?" she added.

"My dear 'Ren, I'll buy you anything your heart desires. Today I got a squirrel and brought it home. The moment it sees an open sleeve or spots a hole somewhere, it wriggles inside. It's great fun!"

25. A first century B.C. official who won lasting fame from his habit of painting his wife's eyebrows.
26. Presumably small ground squirrels or chipmunks.

"A real, live squirrel?"

"That's right."

"Where is it now?"

"I keep it in the study."

At this point Asou came in from the other room. "What are you two talking about?" she asked.

I told her what I had just told Aren, then noticed that she had a pomegranate flower of a charming crimson pinned to her hair. I looked back at Aren and found that she had one exactly the same, which gave me an idea.

"In the six months you've been up here, have you ever seen those artificial flowers they have on sale in the Flower Market?"[27] I asked.

"Yes, someone gave us a few at the end of last year. Fascinating things!" said Asou.

"Were any of them pomegranates?"

"No."

"Then tomorrow I'll get you each one."

"Don't you have to go to school tomorrow?" asked Aren.

"School's closed. I won't be going tomorrow."

Aren did not pursue the matter, but turned and took several unfinished sachets out of the cupboard, after which she and Asou began sewing under the lamplight, their heads bent low over their work. Casually I picked up one of the sachets. It was a little Buddha's hand of yellow silk, exquisitely made.

"What fun these are!" I exclaimed. "May I have one?"

"They're for us girls to amuse ourselves with," said Aren. "We can't let you have any."

When I realized that they were not going to oblige me, I went to snatch one.

"Oh, don't be such a bully!" said Asou. "Tomorrow, when we're finished, you'll get your share. Look, it's late. You'd better go home."

It was just after the "Grain in Ear" season,[28] and the nights were

27. Situated outside Front Gate, the market sold paper flowers for women to pin in their hair.

28. Falling in the fifth month, it was one of the twenty-four designated periods of the year.

short. I glanced at the clock on the wall—nearly twelve. Taking leave of the girls, I went back to my room.

Early the next morning I visited the market and bought some artificial pomegranate flowers for Aren and Asou. Then, lest their aunt feel envious, I thought I had better buy a couple of lotus flowers for her, too. I brought the flowers home packed in a jewel case and distributed them in the rear court to general appreciation.

After supper that evening, it occurred to me that I hadn't put any money aside for the maidservants' presents the next day. I couldn't very well ask Father for it, so what was I to do? The problem weighed heavily on my mind as I walked over to the study, but I thought I had better wait until Father came home before deciding. I had been in the study only a little while when Aren slipped inside my door, unaccompanied. I wasn't expecting a visit from her and was filled with apprehension. But before I could ask her what the matter was, she caught sight of the squirrel and went over to it, smiling with delight. Unfastening the chain, she took it in her hand.

"Watch out!" I cried frantically. "They *bite!*" But before the words were out of my mouth, the squirrel had darted up her right sleeve. She gave a start, let out an *"Aiya!"* and clutched desperately at the little animal through her clothes, but it crouched down beside her right breast and could not be dislodged. "What shall I do? What shall I do?" she cried in panic.

"Quick! Take your clothes off and let me catch it for you!" I said, standing beside her and trying to be helpful.

By this time she had lost all concern for modesty and began hastily stripping off her clothes. Reaching out, I helped her with the buttons.

The weather was warm, and under a well-worn gown of grey-green silk all she had on was a white muslin shift. In her panic she undid both garments, revealing the pink breast-band underneath. There below her nipple crouched the squirrel. I shot out a hand to grab it, but it scurried away under her armpit and ended up at her back, beneath the lower part of the shift. She was so shaken that she stripped off both garments and flung them to the ground, at which point the squirrel finally scampered away and took refuge under a chair. All this while, Aren had had eyes only for the squirrel. There she stood in front of me, naked from the waist up, her swelling breasts, like flowers in bud, faintly visible through the breast-band. Her upper arms and shoulders were a soft, lustrous white—simply adorable! I gathered up her clothes from the floor and draped them around her, then felt her left breast. "Did it scratch you here?" I asked.

She flushed scarlet and pushed my hand away. "I'm all right," she said. She was so obviously embarrassed that I hadn't the heart to trifle with her. I waited until she was fully dressed, then invited her to sit on the couch.

～ 6 ～

Endless frustration! The search for
Yellow Robe.[29]

FOR A long time she sat on the couch in a state of shock; then she
broke into a giggle. "You almost scared me to death with that
wriggling squirrel of yours," she said.

"If you'd left it alone, it would never have gone up your
sleeve."

"Of course it's all *my* fault."

" 'Ren, why did you come over?"

She put her lips to my ear and whispered: "You said yesterday
you were going to give presents to our maids. I guessed you
wouldn't have any money of your own and that, even if Uncle
Qin gave you some, it wouldn't be enough. But those presents
must on no account be skimped on, so without letting on to my
sister I've brought you some of my savings."

I was overwhelmed by her offer. "Look, I appreciate your concern, but I couldn't possibly take your money," I protested.

"Oh, don't be so *conventional!*" she said. "At this stage what do
you and I have to do with convention?"

She stood up, took a bank note from her pocket, and thrust it
into my hand. "Here, take this!" Then she slipped out the door.

I saw that the note was for five taels and raced after her. " 'Ren,
I don't *need* all this!" I called out.

29. In the ninth-century tale "Huo Xiaoyu," Yellow Robe is the name of a
mysterious knight-errant who arranges a meeting between the heroine and her
former lover.

"If you have any left over, keep it for something else," she said, continuing to walk away. Then suddenly she stopped, turned her head, and beckoned to me. I caught up with her and asked what she wanted.

"Don't tell my sister what happened with the squirrel," she whispered.

"I understand," I said, and she continued on her way.

The next morning I waited until Father had left the house before telling Wang Sheng to cash the note for me. Then, after grooming myself carefully, I went over to the rear court to present my compliments to Uncle and Aunt Gu. He had already gone to the office, but she invited me to stay for refreshments. The two maidservants presented themselves, kowtowing before me, and I gave them one tael each. When Aunt Gu saw the amount, she tried to stop me: "Oh, that's *far* too much!"

"No, no, it's nothing," I replied. The maidservants, in high spirits, thanked me and left.

Next the aunt came out with the baby in her arms, and I greeted her and offered her my compliments. She politely protested. Then I produced the rosary and sachet and hung them around the child's neck. "These are for Junior to amuse himself with," I said. She protested again before accepting them. Asou and Aren did not come out, perhaps because they were too embarrassed; later that evening we would be meeting as usual in the study next door.

From this time on I joined the girls at midnight every night.

After a few more days the weather became even hotter and the nights shorter. Before I had spent very long in the rear court, it would be time to return to my bedroom. Worse still, beginning early in the sixth month Uncle Gu, who was distinctly overweight, took to bringing out a rattan couch on returning home every day and lying down beneath the elm tree to enjoy the cool air. Sometimes he stayed there until twelve o'clock before going in to bed, completely disrupting my system of communications with Aren. I would see her occasionally during my morning and afternoon visits, but in the evenings I felt as wretched as a child deprived of its mother's breast. Back and forth I would pace, stopping from time to time to peer through a crack in the window at the sisters' bedroom, which, like some sanctum of the blessed immortals, could only be gazed at from afar.

Two months passed, months in which Aren and I enjoyed not a single rendezvous. On the eve of the Double Seventh, celebrating the annual tryst of Herd Boy and Weaving Maid,[30] and during the Mid-Autumn Festival in the eighth month, when the moon is full and the flowers are at their best, I sat alone beneath the blossoms outside my study and raised a cup of wine to the moon, then lingered awhile amid the sharply etched shadows, my mood reflecting the lines

> Now that Beauty has gone away,
> None is left to share my joy!

How hard it was to endure my loneliness until that time of chilling frosts and northerly winds that follows the Mid-Autumn Festival, when Uncle Gu no longer came out to take the air and I could sneak back into the study at night and resume my meetings with Aren!

Within a couple of days, however, Aren's mother came down with a dangerous fever that continued without remission and left her delirious and prone to hallucinations. The doctors took one look at her and knitted their brows, pronouncing her complaint next to incurable. Her daughters were fearfully concerned and kept vigil at her bedside night and day. Sometimes, after listening to the doctors, they would weep together in private until their eyes were so red and swollen that they looked like peaches. Since Aren was now inaccessible to me at night, I often went over to Aunt Gu's room in the daytime on the pretext of visiting the invalid and then, if there was no one else present, offered my words of comfort to Aren. After a few days Uncle Gu found a noted doctor and invited him to call. He actually prescribed a laxative, after which she purged twice in quick succession and her illness abated. Unfortunately the doctor was equipped only to deal with the disease, not to restore the patient to health. Although her fever subsided, he never did find the right treatment for her,

---

30. The romantic myth of Herd Boy and Weaving Maid, who represent the stars Altair and Vega, situated on opposite sides of the Milky Way. The lovers meet only once a year, on the seventh day of the seventh month.

and she developed symptoms of a general physical decline such
as sore joints and muscles, shortness of breath, and a hacking
cough.

Asou and Aren saw that her illness had not entirely left her and
felt obliged to resume their round-the-clock vigil. When the
invalid, who had no son of her own, saw how assiduous I was in
visiting her bedside, she remarked on what a nice boy I was and
told Uncle Gu to ask Father if she could consider me her adopted
son. Of course Father had to agree; he could hardly do otherwise.
And so from this point on she regarded me as her own flesh and
blood and told Aren to address me as a brother. No longer did I
need to worry about appearances; even in Uncle Gu's presence I
could talk openly to both girls. From the time of Aunt Gu's illness
my relationship with Aren reached a new level of intimacy.

Another odd thing happened to me. In the ninth month, on the
Double Ninth, Father took me to Taoran Pavilion for the custom-
ary climb,[31] and we ran into Lu Boyin, there for the same purpose.
On seeing Father, he approached and addressed him most
respectfully as uncle, then bowed in my direction. We introduced
ourselves, and he behaved toward me in an extremely friendly
way. The next day he sought me out at home, and the two of us
hit it off splendidly.

"Is there anyone else in your household, apart from Uncle?" he
asked.

"No, just the two of us."

He was two years older than I and on the basis of seniority
addressed me as "younger brother." "Younger brother," he said on
this occasion, "do you happen to have a newly appointed Hanlin
official from Haining named Gu Qiquan staying with you?"

"Yes, we do."

"Well, he has two daughters, Souyu and Renfen,[32] whom I daresay you've met. To be honest with you, Miss 'Sou used to be a
very good friend of mine, and we still keep in touch by letter. The

31. On the ninth day of the ninth month people took wine with them and
climbed up to a high place. Taoran Pavilion was a favorite destination in Beijing.
32. These are their actual names, of which "Aren" and "Asou," used uniformly
elsewhere in the first edition, are familiar versions. "Qiquan" is Gu's courtesy
name.

trouble is that the rules are so strict in her household that she can hardly ever get out, and although *she* can write quite freely to me, I wouldn't dare reply in the same fashion, lest my letter go astray and fall into someone else's hands—particularly her father's, which would be fatal. For that reason I often have to use a secret code, which would allow her to deny any involvement. Now, however, by this marvelous stroke of luck I have met up with you, and in future I would like to entrust you with all my private letters. My only hope is that from now on I'll be able to say exactly what I want to. You'll have to buy off the maids and servants, of course, but whenever you need to give them anything, just send the bill to me."

I agreed and took on personal responsibility for the letters. Later, when I told Asou and she realized that I had struck up a friendship with Lu Boyin, her feelings for me also reached a new level of warmth.

One evening I had a chat with her in private. "For several months now," I complained, "I've not had a single chance to talk freely to Aren. Although we often see each other in your mother's room, we can never say all the things we want to say. You've got to find a solution for us."

"What do you have in mind?"

"Aunt still isn't completely better, and she definitely needs someone with her at night, but that doesn't mean both of you have to be there at the same time. My suggestion is that you take turns, each one staying with her a night. That would lessen the burden on you two and allow me a tête-à-tête with Aren when she's back in her own bedroom."

Because I was constantly doing favors for her lover, Asou did as I asked. That same night she spoke to her mother and put my plan into operation. From then on I often met Aren in Asou's study at midnight, just as I had done in the past. Whereas before the Dragon Boat Festival I had been with her every night, during the hot season I never met her at night and only occasionally did so during the daytime. Then, after the Mid-Autumn Festival, although we were together all the time, she was so depressed and tearful that I found the situation even worse than during the period of separation, when I was spared the sight of her suffering. This new arrangement was far superior; I could count on meeting her every second night and, when we did meet, no one else was there to inhibit us, and so we could say whatever we wished. From dusk to dawn, this was the most delightful time of the year for both of us. Eventually Asou began to suspect that we were sleeping together, and whenever she came into the room and found us huddled in an intimate conversation, she would turn on her heel and leave. Ah, the truth was that our relationship was one of passion, not of lust; our love was based on a natural affinity rather than on carnal desire. But not only was this hard for Asou to accept, even my readers may be reluctant to believe it.

After the ninth month the weather in the capital turned unseasonably cold. On the tenth of the tenth we had a light snowfall, and although the skies cleared the following day, it grew even colder, and stoves were lit in both our houses. That evening I was huddled around the stove in Aren's room chatting with her until about one o'clock, when we both began to feel a little hungry. To make matters worse, Aren's fur coat was still in her mother's room, from which she could hardly retrieve it at that hour, and in the meantime she was so cold that her teeth chattered.

"What we need is a drop of wine to warm us up," she said.

Her remark reminded me of the two bottles of Wujiapi that I had bought in the fourth month to give to her aunt. They were still sitting in my study. Why not bring them over and have a drink?

"You'd like some wine to warm yourself up with? I still have two bottles in my study. Let me go and get them."

"Great!"

I got up and went out, thinking to go through the side gate, but I was barely out of the door when I glimpsed a human figure darting away from the window. A fierce north wind was gusting at the time, and in the hazy moonlight I couldn't see at all clearly. Without bothering my head as to whether it was man or ghost, I dashed frantically over to the study, grabbed a bottle of wine, and raced back to Aren's room.

When she saw me come in with the wine, she fetched a warming flask and heated a cup of wine with water boiling on the stove. Then from an earthenware jar on the bookcase she filled a bowl with marinated peanuts and placed it on the table.

"I have only this one cup. Let's share."

"Great!"

We sat around the stove and sipped the wine in turn, drinking to our hearts' content. Because she felt so cold, she sat close to the stove, and in the glow of the fire her face was absolutely lovely. As soon as the wine touched her lips, she drank it down without a second thought, and before long, between the two of us, we had finished half the bottle. The spiritual and physical bliss I felt on that occasion is impossible to convey, but I am convinced that Commander Dang,[33] making merry inside his silk curtains, was no happier than I.

Soon Aren became a little tipsy, and a faint rosy hue appeared in her cheeks. Smiling happily, her beautiful eyes gazing directly into mine, she made one think of Yang Guifei in Aloeswood Pavilion.[34]

I saw that the cup was empty and was about to pour another when I heard a thud outside the window as if someone had slipped and fallen down. It brought to mind the figure I had glimpsed before, and a chill ran down my spine.

"Would you like another cup?" I asked hastily.

"No, I've had enough."

"I, too." With a quick goodnight, I rushed back to my room and went to bed.

The next day I recalled the sounds outside her window and was completely mystified. After supper I sat in the study trying to puzzle out whether the figure I had glimpsed and the sounds I had heard were evidence of mortals or ghosts, fox spirits or burglars. I wondered, too, whether Aren had heard anything. I was still just as mystified, when all of a sudden the door curtains began to move and someone entered the room. My heart pounding with fear, I looked more closely—and saw that the intruder was none other than Aren's aunt. I watched as she stepped into the room and blew out the lamp on the desk, then rushed over to me and flung her arms about me in a tight embrace.

33. A tenth-century general, he was a voluptuary of fabulous wealth.
34. Aloeswood was the pavilion in which Yang Guifei dallied with the Tang emperor.

"Foster mother!" I exclaimed, aghast. "What are *you* doing here?"

"Don't be alarmed, Master Qin," she whispered, her arms still around me. "I've admired you for the longest time, and I've come over specially for a little tête-à-tête with you. I remember my sister's mentioning you when we moved in and saying what a handsome young fellow you were, and I made a point of coming over once or twice just to see for myself. But later on I noticed how thick you were with Aren and wouldn't have dreamt of interfering. In fact I took your side with my sister, to give you a chance to succeed with Aren. These last two nights I've even watched you two making love together. Oh, do take pity on me! I'm . . ."

At this point she choked on her words, then after a pause hugged me again and continued: "I've done such a lot for you, is it asking too much of you to do for me, just this once, some of the nice things you do for her?" She stood up and without so much as a by-your-leave pulled me over to the couch and began unbuttoning my clothes. I flared up at that and was on the point of crying out, when suddenly there came a thunderous knocking at the main gate—Uncle Gu was home! At once she let go of me, heaved a sigh, and raced frantically back to the rear court.

~ 7 ~

A loving father permits his son to marry.

IT WAS not until some time after her departure that I managed to catch my breath and pull myself together. Slowly I made my way over to the desk, groped for the matches and lit the lamp, then sat down and began going over in my mind what had just taken place. It was a terribly dangerous situation I was in, there was no doubt about that. Had it not been for Uncle Gu's knocking at the gate, a fearful disaster might have ensued. Then I thought what a monstrous injustice it was for her to talk as if Aren and I had already made love. Finally it occurred to me that, although she had let me go this time, sooner or later she would surely come back and make further trouble for me. I couldn't avoid her, but I couldn't very well reject her either. What was I to do in such an impossible situation? I agonized over the question half the night without coming to any conclusion. There was nothing else for it but to return to my room and go to bed, leaving the whole matter for discussion with Aren the following night.

The next evening I waited anxiously until eleven o'clock before sneaking over to her room. Once I saw she was alone, I gave her a detailed account of all that had happened the night before and asked her advice. She was so alarmed that her tongue popped out, and it was some time before she replied. *"It's all your fault!* I promised to marry you ages ago, and if your family had only sent over a go-between to arrange it, Aunt wouldn't have dared to interfere! But now she's in a position to blackmail us, and if you disappoint her, she'll destroy our relationship and leave us helpless to do anything about it."

"My dear 'Ren," I said, "when did you ever promise to marry me?" The words were hardly out of my mouth before she flushed crimson around the eyes and gritted her teeth.

"If I hadn't promised to marry you, do you imagine for one moment that I would have let you kiss me, hold my hand, and touch me all over my body? Is there *anything* we haven't done together, you and I, here in this room in the middle of the night? Except . . ." Here she stopped in mid-sentence and went blue in the face.

I rushed forward and bowed several times in apology. "Dear 'Ren, don't be angry. It was wrong of me to say that." I had never seen her in such a state, but fortunately, after I had pleaded with her for some time, she began to calm down.

" 'Ren, you've got to think of a solution!" I said.

"What solution can *I* come up with? Since you didn't reject her outright, from now on you'll just have to try and keep in with her—while getting on as fast as you can with what you have to do."

I had nothing better to suggest and was forced to agree: "Yes, yes, of course. I'll do as you say."

Reader, consider my situation for a moment. Keeping in with her aunt, that was something I could force myself to do, but when it came to proposing marriage, that could only be done, as I have said before, "by the parents' command and through the good offices of a go-between." Otherwise, even if I were dying of love-sickness, I would get nowhere. But I wasn't old enough to approach my father's friends, and even if I were, I could hardly broach the matter myself and get one of them to serve as my go-between!

I thought long and hard without coming up with any solution, so I waited until the next day and went over to the Lu compound on Nanheng Street to see Boyin. I told him that I was in love with Aren and wanted his father to act as an intermediary with my father.

"Father's certainly in a position to help you," said Lu Boyin. "The only problem is that I can't very well speak to him about it myself. However, he does have a friend who joins him on visits to the pleasure quarter, a man called Guan Geru, with the nickname

Horn-in.[35] So long as you provide Guan with a few taels in brothel expenses, he'll tell Father anything you like, and Father has only to hear a suggestion from him to act on it, no matter what it is. Since you're so eager to marry Aren, as long as you're willing to put up a few taels, I'll ask Guan to take the job on, and I guarantee you'll be successful."

I cheered up at once and offered to give Boyin ten taels to use in persuading Guan Geru. He readily agreed, and after chatting a little longer I went home.

That evening I told Aren about the idea I had discussed with Boyin.

"Ten taels is a small price to pay for making our wishes come true," she said. "But how are you going to get your hands on so much money at short notice? I know, let *me* put up the go-between's fee!" She promptly unlocked her trunk and took out a four-tael note as well as some loose silver and handed it to me. "Here are four taels," she said, "and here are another six taels thirteen. Put the money together and offer it to him."

Embarrassed but also touched by her offer, I accepted the money.

In the midst of our discussion we heard a cough outside the window. Aren gave me a wink, and I rushed out of her bedroom and back to my own.

The next day was the fifteenth of the tenth month. After returning from school in the afternoon, I tucked the money in my sleeve and went back to Nanheng Street to see Lu Boyin, whom I found chatting with a friend in the living room. He got up as he saw me come in. "Ah, you've come just at the right time!" he said. Pointing to his friend, he added: "This is Uncle Guan."

I looked at the friend, a man with pinched cheeks and a sprinkling of pockmarks on either side of his nose. He was in his thirties and spoke with what sounded like a southern accent. I bowed to him, and he at once responded.

"So you are Cousin Qin?" he asked. "What an honor!"

Boyin motioned to me and then turned and went into a side room, where I followed him.

35. A dialect term for a man who cuts in on a courtesan patronized by someone else.

"I told Guan about that matter you mentioned yesterday," he murmured in my ear, "and he accepted at once. Were you able to raise the money, by any chance?"

"I've brought it with me. Here you are."

"No hurry. Just so long as you're able to keep your side of the bargain."

"Since I have the money on me, let me leave it with you. You be the judge of how much to give him and when to give it." I took the money from my sleeve and handed it to Boyin.

"Wait here a moment," he said, and left the room to hold a lengthy, whispered discussion with Guan. Not until I heard Guan leaving did Boyin return.

"Guan says he'll take it on and you can set your mind at rest."

"I shall owe it all to you," I said. We went on to talk of Asou's situation, and only after an hour or more had passed did I say good-bye and make my way slowly home.

When six or seven days had gone by and nothing had happened, I began to suspect that I had been swindled by Guan and dashed off a note to Boyin to that effect. Back came a reply saying that I would have to wait another four or five days before I could expect any news. Sure enough, after another five days Boyin's father, Lu Xiaocang, arrived to see my father, who invited him into the parlor and held a long discussion with him. I was so concerned about the decision that I stood beneath the window and eavesdropped.

"If they weren't living in the same compound," I heard Father say, "this whole problem of appearances wouldn't arise." I sensed an unfavorable drift to the conversation, but although I listened intently, I couldn't make out anything more. After a while Lu Xiaocang left. Anxious though I was, I couldn't very well go up to Father and ask him about the decision. Nervous as an ant on a hot stove, I paced back and forth in my study, thinking that if Father were going to play the hypocritical puritan and refuse us permission to marry, he would be sending us to our graves.

By evening I could stand the strain no longer, so I dashed off a secret note to Boyin and had Wang Sheng deliver it to Nanheng Street and wait there for a reply. After what seemed like ages, he returned empty-handed. "Master Lu has gone out to a dinner party," he said. "The steward took the note and told me to call back tomorrow for an answer." That meant one more night on tenterhooks for me.

The next day was the twenty-ninth. As soon as Wang Sheng had had his breakfast, I sent him around again, and before long he was back with a note from Boyin, which I snatched from his hand. "With regard to yesterday's meeting," the note ran, "your father proved to be exceedingly stubborn and insisted that people living in the same house had to hold themselves above suspicion and in such cases marriage was not appropriate. Father tried hard to persuade him otherwise, but to no avail. See that you take your time deciding on a course of action. Don't do anything rash. . . ."

At this point I felt as if I had been struck in the face with a bucket of icy water, my hands and feet began to tremble, and I could read no further. I had always been an unemotional person, but now for some reason the tears began spilling from my eyes like pearls from a broken string, spattering onto the floor. Stuffing the note into my breast pocket, I rushed into the bedroom and flung myself down on the bed. My cheeks were streaming with tears, and I would have let myself go and bawled aloud, had I not been afraid that Aren would have heard me, realized that marriage was out of the question, and taken her own life, involving us all in a case of homicide. Imagine my state of mind as I thought back on her behavior toward me and the hopes she had expressed that we would spend eternity together—and surrendered myself to utter despair! Then I began to worry about how I should act toward her right now. If I told her the truth, she would certainly stick to her code of loyalty and either take her own life or go into a nunnery. But if I told her nothing, how would I respond when she questioned me? Even if she didn't question me, I would inevitably look and sound so wretched that she would quickly deduce what had happened. All that day I lay on my bed, crying and agonizing over this decision, and by noontime when Wang Sheng came to call me for lunch, I couldn't bear the thought of food.

That afternoon I dropped into a deep sleep from which I awoke toward evening with a slight fever. In my half-demented state, without the slightest desire to go on living, I was not about to worry over a mere fever. In the evening Father came to see me

and urged me to eat something, and I realized that, insensitive as
he was to my feelings, he had always cared deeply for me, a
notion that left me even more confused. I felt I had to do as he
told me and force down half a bowl of rice. Afterwards it occurred
to me that Aren's suspicions would surely be aroused if I failed to
visit her that night, and at this thought I felt another stab of grief
and began sobbing again. Unfortunately my grief affected my
spleen, which promptly ceased to function, and by midnight gas-
tritis had set in from the rice I had eaten. My temperature rose to a
dangerous level, the saliva in my mouth dried up, and the lamplight became a yellowish blur before my eyes. Because it was so
late, I didn't go and arouse Father. By dawn all my joints were
aching, and I began to feel dizzy and lacked the strength even to
get out of bed. Before long Father came in to check on me, and
when he saw my scarlet face, parched lips, and raging fever, he
was alarmed.

"How did you get so sick all of a sudden?"

"I think it must be from eating a bit too much rice last night."

He felt my forehead and then rushed from the room, to return
soon afterwards with a doctor, who felt my pulse and wrote out
a prescription. I was actually suffering from a gastric disorder
brought on by a depressed level of vital spirits, but he diagnosed
my complaint as winter-warm syndrome and prescribed the wrong
treatment. After a single dose of his medicine, my illness took a
turn for the worse, my eyesight becoming so dim that I couldn't
recognize anyone and kept mistaking Father for Wang Sheng.
From time to time in my comatose state I would babble Aren's
name. Father had always had a soft spot for his younger son, and
now, seeing that I really was quite ill, he came into my bedroom
and sat with me, at the same time asking a friend to call in a certain well-known doctor to treat me. Then he heard me babbling
"Aren" and "Asou" in my delirium and guessed the cause of my
illness. When my fever was at its height, he called Wang Sheng
into the room. "Has the young master heard the news?" he asked
him in my hearing. "I accepted a match for him today. I understand his fiancée is the younger daughter of the family in the rear
court."

At this news my spirits revived, and I took the first opportunity to ask Wang Sheng: "Is this true?"

"Of course it's true."

I broke into a broad smile. Suddenly I was supremely happy. After I began taking the new doctor's medicine, my health steadily improved. When Father realized that my illness really was due to Aren, he had no choice but to call on Lu Xiaocang and beg him to obtain Uncle Gu's agreement to the marriage. Because of Father's chopping and changing, he had to endure a good deal of ribbing—as well as pay up for a dinner party complete with singsong girls—before Lu Xiaocang would consent to approach Uncle Gu.

Uncle Gu's first reaction was exactly the same as Father's— adamant opposition. But then Aren's mother came to hear of the proposal, and she insisted on my fine character, good looks, and agreeable personality, and confidently predicted high examination honors and an Academy appointment for me. So hard did she press Uncle Gu that he agreed.

I was already half over my illness by this time, and when I heard the joyous news I felt able to get out of bed. By the fifteenth of the twelfth month, the day our engagement was celebrated, I could even walk to the parlor and join Father in greeting the guests.

I was wonderfully happy, and I assumed Aren felt the same way. But we had been apart so long that I simply *had* to see her and tell her about my ordeal during the period of separation, about the misery of my illness (as well as the reason for it), and about all the trouble I had had in getting our two families to agree. Then another thought struck me; I couldn't very well go over to their house any more, because if I met Uncle and Aunt Gu, I'd have to call them "Father-in-law" and "Mother-in-law" or some such thing. Even with the aunt and Asou I'd have to use new forms of address, and I simply hadn't the nerve to start calling them something different all of a sudden. Moreover, Aren was bound to be even more bashful than before and to refuse to see me. I became depressed, fearing that she and I would not be able to see each other again until our wedding night.

Two days later, however, Father brought along some special news: "Your Uncle Gu has been over to say that you don't need to change the way you address the members of his family. That can be left until after the wedding."

I was immensely relieved and, unable to restrain myself any longer, slipped over to the rear court that very day. I did feel a little awkward on first meeting the family, but they welcomed me with smiles and behaved toward me more warmly than before, asking me if I was completely better and ordering the maid to pour me a cup of tea. After that I paid several visits, until it seemed quite natural to do so and I gradually lost my sense of awkwardness. There was just one thing that continued to bother me; I had met the whole family—with the solitary exception of Aren.

~ 8 ~

A farsighted man leaves the capital in haste.

I MAY not have been able to see Aren, but I did have one consolation: now that we were engaged, the time would eventually come when we would be together night and day, a far cry from that moment of despair when Lu Xiaocang failed in his attempt to persuade Father. There was just one problem: You can't put out a fire by fetching water from a mile away, to quote the old proverb. I might have taken a pill to calm my nerves, but the pangs of hunger were still far more than I could bear. So great was my longing for Aren that I felt compelled to ask Lu Xiaocang to intercede with Father again, in the hope that the wedding could be held as soon as possible. With this thought in mind, I went over to Nanheng Street, told Boyin of my problem, and pleaded with him to ask his father for me. A few days later Boyin came by to say that with the approach of the New Year the pressure of official business was greater than usual and his father had no time now but would see to it as soon as the Lantern Festival was over. This seemed reasonable enough. I would have to get through the festivities as best I could, while still trying to find some way of meeting Aren. On New Year's Eve and New Year's Day, I asked Father for a few taels and kept up my practice of giving gratuities to the staff of the Gu household.

Once the New Year festivities were over, it was soon time for the Lantern Festival. On the evening of the fifteenth I was returning from a visit to the Bridge of Heaven to see the lantern display. It was late, but the moon was particularly lovely that night, and I couldn't bear to go straight to sleep, but strolled over to the study instead. Suddenly at the foot of the rock I glimpsed what appeared to be a human shape darting away from me. Suspicious, I walked over and was surprised to find Asou there, enjoying the moonlight on her own. I went up to her and called out: " 'Sou, is Aren in bed?"

"What if she isn't?" she responded with a wry smile.

That sounded promising, so I told her how I was longing to see Aren and begged her to think of a way for us to meet.

"I know you've been apart for ages, but I'm wondering just what *my* reward will be for doing you such a favor?"

"My dear 'Sou, you name it, it's yours!" With a laugh she turned and went to the rear court.

Soon she was back to say: "Your lover is inside, longing to see you. Why don't you go in and see her?"

Stealthily I followed Asou through the side gate and along the passageway into the study, where I found Aren sitting by herself with her back to the lamp, cracking melon seeds. At my entrance she stood up and motioned me to a chair, looking distinctly ill at ease.

"This isn't the first time you two have met," said Asou. "Sit down and talk, why don't you?"

I took a seat by the window and told them the whole wretched story of Lu Xiaocang's mediation and Father's refusal, which had brought on my sudden illness.

"You didn't need to tell us all that," said Asou. "We know about Lu Xiaocang's attempt to persuade your father. And if *you* got sick because it didn't work out, what makes you think Aren didn't?" This was my first inkling that she had been ill.

"But how did you hear?" I asked.

Aren laughed and gestured in Asou's direction. "Oh, her lover wrote her a letter with all the news." I now understood why she had fallen ill. That night Aren and I, together again after a long separation, went on talking until dawn, and still it seemed that many things were left unsaid.

As we were saying good-bye, she set out the rules for our future meetings. I was to be allowed only one a month; the rest of the time her door would be kept locked. Her rules were designed to keep our meetings secret and also to prevent her aunt from blackmailing us. We would have to wait for the blessed day itself before we could really bare our souls to each other. I had no choice but to accept her conditions, but from then on I lived in the hope that Lu Xiaocang would succeed in persuading Father about the wedding.

A few days later Lu did call on Father to discuss the issue, but curiously enough, this time Father objected on the grounds that I was too young—early marriage would only deplete my primal essence, preventing me from living to a ripe old age—and insisted that the wedding wait until I was sixteen. Lu continued to press my case, and eventually Father agreed to reconsider during the first half of my sixteenth year. Meanwhile there was nothing I could do but curb my impatience and wait.

That was the year with the intercalary eighth month.[36] Shortly after the New Year celebrations, the capital began buzzing with rumors. Somewhere or other spirits were supposed to have been summoned to earth who prophesied that this year the Jade Emperor[37] would visit war upon the north, wiping out all the foreign devils and Christian converts, and as a result of the rumors no one on the streets of the capital dared buy any more imported goods or foreign publications. By the end of the fourth month self-styled "Brothers" began to make their appearance in the Bridge of Heaven neighborhood, spouting nonsense. They claimed to be disciples of someone called Holy Mother Yellow Lotus[38] and boasted that they could cast spells and summon the Six Yin and Six Yang Spirits to wipe out foreign devils and Christian converts. Provided you learned their spells, you could dodge bullets and make houses burst into flame. The Brothers told people to learn their fist and quarterstaff exercises and prophesied that the day of

36. An indirect reference to 1900, the year the Boxer rebellion broke out. An intercalary month in a *geng* year (1900 was a *gengzi* year in the Chinese cycle) signified bad luck.
37. The Taoist emperor of Heaven.
38. A female magician and the best-known Boxer leader. The word I have translated as "Brothers" actually means "brother-disciples," i.e., disciples of the same master.

the so-called Red Lanterns³⁹ would be the foreigners' last day on earth.

At first it was only a handful of the simple-minded who believed in this nonsense, but within a few days their numbers had begun to swell, and they took to wearing their red turbans in public and rampaging through the city streets, until even the nobles and high officials came to believe in them. Now, Father was an enlightened man who could see the writing on the wall, so he held a private discussion with Uncle Gu and suggested that they take their families south. Uncle Gu, however, proved to be a die-hard conservative.

"These folk with their fist exercises and their spells happen to be loyal, upright citizens who have recently taken on the title of 'Militias of Righteous Harmony.'⁴⁰ What this means is that the fortunes of our great dynasty are due for a revival, and these supernatural warriors have been sent from the other world to possess the bodies of the common people in order to save the dynasty and wipe out the foreigners. The court has decided to appoint Prince Duan⁴¹ commander-in-chief of the militias. Provided we throw in our lot with the Brothers and follow their orders, it goes without saying that we'll enjoy their protection. What's the point of leaving for the south?"

When Father realized that Uncle Gu had been taken in by the Boxers' claims, he pleaded with him not to trust them but to come south with us, citing the case of the Song dynasty magician Guo Jing,⁴² whose attempt to drive off the Jurchen army with the

39. The Red Lanterns were a corps of young female magicians among the Boxer forces whose magic was said to be even more potent than that of their male counterparts. Their leader was Holy Mother Yellow Lotus.

40. The name universally translated as Boxers was actually Yihequan (Fists of Righteous Harmony), which was later changed to Yihetuan (Militias of Righteous Harmony).

41. Zaiyi, Prince Duan, was a court adviser of reactionary, even obscurantist, views. He helped the Empress Dowager crush the Reform Movement of 1898 and also influenced her decision to support the Boxers and declare war on the foreigners.

42. A twelfth-century Taoist magician, who was allowed to try out his magic in a vain attempt to repel the Jurchen invaders. He chose his soldiers according to their horoscopes rather than their fighting abilities.

magic of the Six Yang Spirits had ended in disaster. Uncle Gu, however, turned a deaf ear to all such warnings, and Father had to give up. Well into the night he and I packed our bags, sending Wang Sheng off to order two long-distance mule traps for the journey. By this time the railroad track between Tianjin and the capital had been torn up by the Boxers, and we would have to travel by trap over the Marco Polo Bridge and down the eastern highway.

I was heartbroken. I hated Uncle Gu with a vengeance for rejecting Father's pleas and forcing Aren and me to part. If by some chance the Boxers did provoke a catastrophe in which the innocent perished along with the guilty, our parting in life might well turn into a parting by death. I was overcome with anguish at the thought, and my tears streamed down. Waiting until Father was asleep, I slipped over to the rear court and approached the study. Just as I was about to knock, I noticed that the door was slightly ajar and on stepping inside found an array of delicacies on the lute table. Beside the table sat Asou, as if expecting a visitor. She stood up and welcomed me in with a smile.

"Why isn't Aren here?" I asked.

"I'll call her. She hasn't had her supper yet."

What with the delicacies and now this remark of Asou's, I was thoroughly mystified. Soon she was back from the other room with her sister on her arm. Glancing at Aren, I was surprised to find her the picture of misery.

"My dear 'Ren," I asked, "why so sad?"

She began to sob, and the words she was about to say caught in her throat.

"She knew you were leaving and has spent the whole evening in her room crying her eyes out," said Asou, answering for her.

"Who's responsible for the delicacies?" I asked.

"I felt sure you'd be over to say good-bye, so I put this together as a farewell party," said Asou, drawing me to a chair beside the table and seating Aren on my right. She herself sat opposite us and poured the wine.

"Drink this," she said, handing me a cup of wine. "Here's to a safe return south! This is only a temporary separation for you two.

You'll certainly be reunited one day and then spend the rest of your lives together. There's no need to be too upset about it."

After I had thanked her, she turned to Aren. "If there's anything you want to say to him, now is your chance! The nights are short, and it will soon be dawn."

Aren's tears spilled down. "The city is in such chaos I'm afraid we may never meet again," she sobbed. "Li Shangyin has a line, 'This life is over, the next not yet divined,'[43] that fits our situation perfectly. Here's hoping that you'll take good care of yourself on your journey and arrive home safe and sound. You have a great future to look forward to, and you mustn't worry about an ill-fated wretch like me. That's all I wanted to tell you. I have nothing more to say." Her eyes brimming with tears, she handed me her cup of wine.

I felt as if a knife were twisting inside my heart, and before I knew it my own tears were streaming down. I had to force myself to offer her any words of comfort.

"My dear 'Ren, life and death are in the hands of fate, as the saying goes. In a city as large as this, even if some catastrophe does occur, the chances are that you yourself won't be affected. What's more, Uncle has decided to throw in his lot with the Boxers, so you'll certainly be in no danger from them. I beg you to take special care of yourself and not to ruin your health by too much grieving." I took the cup from her hand and passed her the one in front of me. Her eyes welled up with tears.

"It's getting light outside," said Asou. "Drink up, you two!" Aren brushed the cup against her lips, then set it down. I saw that the window panes really were getting brighter, and I stood and drained my cup.

"Whatever you do, 'Ren, don't take this too much to heart," I said. "I'll write to you as soon as we get there. I have to go now. I'm afraid Father will be up."

She stood, too, and grasping my hand managed to say "Take care" before she broke off, choking with sobs. Affected by the tone of our farewell, Asou also began to cry. The two girls saw me

---

43. From Li Shangyin's poem "Mawei," which is about the death of Yang Guifei.

out of the study and all the way to my bedroom. I climbed in through the window, then turned and looked back at them as they stood in the courtyard, the tears still glistening in their eyes.

By now there was a hazy light outside, and the neighborhood roosters were in full cry. I felt the weight of a thousand sorrows that I could not begin to express, and the tears ran down my cheeks like water from a spring. Before long I heard a cough outside my room—Father really was up. Sleepless though I was, I joined him for a little breakfast. Then Wang Sheng came in to say that the traps were harnessed up and ready to leave. The fare to Dezhou would be fifty taels for each trap, exclusive of tips. He had scarcely finished telling us this when Uncle Gu came out to see Father off.

"When you get to the south, if you hear that the foreigners in the capital have all been wiped out," he said, "you must come straight back again without delay." Father felt this was hardly the time to argue the point and merely asked him if he would look after our belongings for us while we were gone. Uncle Gu nodded. Then we bowed our farewells, scrambled aboard the traps, and set off in a westerly direction along Horse Market High Street to Zhangyi Gate.

At the gate several Boxers with strips of red cloth wound about their heads came over and began questioning us. Luckily our drivers knew them and following a brief discussion with them persuaded Father to contribute a couple of taels to the upkeep of their spirit altars, after which no further objections were raised. Once out of the city, we made straight for Marco Polo Bridge. The road was lined with tall willows and the ground covered by a thick frost. In the trap that I shared with Wang Sheng, I kept murmuring the lyric "Willows along the shore, a dawn wind, a waning moon."[44] My heart was full of concern for Aren. I wondered if she had cried herself into a state of delirium, and I felt a sudden stab of grief and began crying myself.

We traveled for many days on our wretched, lonely journey, and Aren was never absent from my thoughts; no sooner had my head touched the pillow than I would start dreaming of her.

44. Liu Yong's (987–1053) lyric to the tune "Yu lin ling."

Sometimes I dreamt that we were holding hands beneath the blossoming trees and gazing up at the moon. Sometimes the house was hung with lanterns and festooned with streamers, and there was music playing; I was the bridegroom awaiting the arrival of her bridal chair, after which she and I would make our wedding bows. And there were times, too, when I dreamt of hordes of red-turbaned Boxers with flashing swords and spears who burst in and dragged her off weeping and sobbing, and I would cry out in the middle of my dream.

In this fashion we eventually reached Dezhou, where we took a boat south to Qingjiangpu by way of Linqing and Jining, then changed at Huaicheng to a small steamer for the journey to Zhenjiang. I spent the whole time longing for Aren. Father's original intention had been to return to Hubei, but our travels proved so exhausting that he decided to stop for a few days' rest at the Liujiyuan Inn on Ocean Street.

It was the twenty-third of the sixth month, and Father and I had gone out that morning to a teahouse, where there was a man hawking an assortment of Shanghai newspapers. Father fumbled out a dozen cash and bought a copy of the *News,* in which a cable at the top of the front page ran: "On the nineteenth of the sixth month the combined forces of the allied powers took the capital. Their Imperial Majesties have departed on a visit to the west and are reported today to be residing in Guanshi."

Father went pale with shock. "Just as I feared! Just as I feared!" he exclaimed. Snatching the newspaper from him, I asked what he meant. "What do you think?" he replied. "They had this crazy notion of killing all the foreigners, and now that Beijing has fallen to the foreign troops, I can't *imagine* how that city is going to suffer!"

I was so alarmed as I listened to Father that my limbs turned to ice. I felt sure that Aren must have met with disaster and that we would never see each other again. Although I hated to cry in front of Father, the tears were already trickling down my cheeks.

He noticed and smiled. "You're being foolish, my boy. What does it matter to you if the allied army attacks the capital? Why are you crying?" He paid for the tea, and we went back to our inn.

All that day and the following night I hid in my room and sobbed my heart out. Father guessed the reason but was too embarrassed to come and console me.

On the afternoon of the following day he moved us out of the inn. We boarded a large China Merchants ship and, with Father, Wang Sheng, and me sharing a cabin, set off for Hubei.

~ 9 ~

As she flees the carnage, her past life
becomes a distant dream.

IT was the twenty-ninth when the ship docked in Hankou. Our
house was leased to tenants, so Father found us other accommo-
dations above a silk shop by the name of Gonghe Tai with which
he used to have dealings. The owner, Yang Jintang, was a close
friend of his, and he let us have our board and lodging free of
charge. Noticing that a Shanghai paper was delivered at the shop
every day, I read it without fail. It carried such headlines as "Imperial Majesties Reach Taiyuan," "Gov. Li Northbound for Peace
Parley,"[45] and "Court Officials Flock South Via Dezhou," as well as
the news that the Shanghai philanthropists had formed something
called a Relief Association[46] and sent a ship north to rescue the
officials and others who were trapped there. The one thing the
paper never mentioned was the whereabouts of Aren and her
family. I kept hoping against hope that she had been able to
escape and we would be reunited. My days were spent worrying
and my nights weeping, and in less than a month I showed all the
symptoms of a breakdown; I was reduced to skin and bones and
had completely lost my appetite.

Father was greatly perturbed. At first he appealed to me on
grounds of general principle, but then he tried to raise my spirits

45. I.e., the veteran statesman Li Hongzhang (1823–1901) was called in to
negotiate the peace.
46. Lu Shufan organized the rescue of many of the tens of thousands of officials and merchants from the south who were trapped in the north by the Boxer
rebellion.

by feeding me the false news that Uncle Gu had gone west as part of the imperial retinue. Since I had seen no reliable evidence, I didn't believe a word of it. Father also told Wang Sheng to take me out to a variety of places. I saw mountains and rivers galore, but they all looked the same to me, and I ended up feeling even more depressed. By the time the Mid-Autumn and Double Ninth festivals were past, my longing for Aren had grown more intense than ever.

Then from someone or other Father picked up the rumor that Uncle Gu and his whole family had lost their lives when the allied army entered the capital.

One day a boyhood friend of his named Jin Lizhi visited us with a proposal of marriage for me. The girl, whose father was one Bi Boxie, was fifteen years old, the same age as I. According to Jin, her beauty, when considered along with her exquisite calligraphy and poetry, made her the most desirable match in all of Hankou. Bi Boxie himself, who was worth twenty or thirty thousand and had bought himself an intendant's rank, was a prominent member of the local gentry. But heavens above, even if Miss Bi had been more beautiful than Aren, even if she had had more talent, she still would not have aroused my interest. In fact, of course, her beauty and talent depended solely on Jin Lizhi's highly partisan appraisal; no one else had seen her, to tell us what she was really like. Aren and I, however, enjoyed a perfect spiritual and emotional communion. Why, even if some legendary paragon[47] had been reborn on earth, I would not have paid court to her. And so when Jin Lizhi came to Father with his proposal, I wasn't in the least perturbed. My own engagement was already arranged, and Father would never do anything so rash as to betroth me to someone else. But the world seldom behaves as we expect it to. Father assumed that once I was engaged to Miss Bi I would be more inclined to forget Aren, and the proposal had barely been put before him when he accepted it and chose the first of the tenth month as the date of our engagement celebration. He even consulted Jin Lizhi about the possibility of holding the wedding itself before the end of the year.

---

47. The text actually refers to Wang Zhaojun and Xie Daoyun, paragons of beauty and talent, respectively.

When I found out what Father had done, I leapt to the conclusion that Aren and her whole family must have perished in the
capital—otherwise he would never have betrothed me to anyone
else—and I was in agony at the thought. I was convinced that
Aren and I really had parted forever, confirming the truth of the
line she quoted as we said good-bye—"This life is over, the next
not yet divined." From that day on my illness grew steadily worse.
Father became dreadfully anxious and announced that he wanted
to take me to Hangzhou to visit the family graves, when all he
really wanted was to get me to Shanghai, which he hoped would
shake me out of my depression. Perhaps that city's "three-mile foreign mall"[48] would possess some miraculous cure for whatever
ailed me. Actually I was just as eager as he to get to Shanghai, but
only to visit the Relief Association and find out if Aren was among
the people brought back from Beijing and Tianjin, or if there were
any refugees who had news of her. And so on the ninth of the
tenth month we set off on a China Merchants ship with Wang
Sheng again in attendance. Docking in Shanghai after a three-day
journey, we took rooms at the nearby Tai'an Inn at Sanyangjing
Bridge.[49]

Next morning Father ordered a horse and trap and took me out
on a sightseeing tour from which we did not return until late in
the evening. But neither the Zhang nor the Yu Gardens, nor such
diversions as a French restaurant or the theater, were sufficient to
dispel my gloom. On the following day he wanted to visit his
friends and had no time to take me out, so Wang Sheng was
detailed to accompany me downtown. I was so drained by my
experiences that I could barely walk, and after going along a few
streets, we returned to the inn, where I lay on my bed and rested.
Wang Sheng brought me in a cup of tea and then went about his
own business.

I was lying there quietly when I heard footsteps on the stairs.
Someone was opening the door of the vacant room next to mine
and moving in what sounded like a lot of luggage. Soon several

48. The phrase refers to downtown Shanghai, the area of the foreign conces-
sions.
49. One of the bridges linking the International Settlement with the French
Concession.

people with Jiangxi accents arrived in the room, one of them seemingly a woman. After much argument, the men apparently went out, leaving behind the woman, who moaned and sighed as if suffering some unbearable grief or pain. Suspicious, I forced myself to leave my own room and peer into the one next door. I found a girl of fourteen or fifteen sitting there, the picture of misery. Although her hair was uncombed and she wore no make-up, she was by no means completely unattractive. I had been silently observing her for some time when all of a sudden she came to the door and asked me a question.

"Excuse me, sir, but can you tell me what this place is?"

"It's a Cantonese inn."

She sighed. "I'll *never* get out of their clutches!"

I followed up this extraordinary remark with some questions of my own: "Where are you from? What brings you here?"

She gave another sigh. "It's no use telling you. It's better if I say nothing."

This only increased my suspicions, and I pressed her to tell me why she had come to Shanghai.

Her eyes reddened. "I suffered first at the hands of the Boxer bandits in the capital and then was tricked into coming here by some people who want to sell me into prostitution. I'm from a gentry family, too, and engaged to be married. My young man is a cultivated gentleman much like yourself, sir. My parents had set the wedding for next spring, but all of a sudden the rebellion broke out, and they were killed by the bandits. I myself fell into the hands of the Boxers, and they sold me off to Shitiao Lane, where I was forced to do all those shameful things. Several times I tried to kill myself before I was rescued by the allied soldiers and locked in an empty room, where I suffered further weeks of misery. And now some scoundrels from back home who pass themselves off as relatives of mine have bailed me out of the foreigners' custody and brought me here on a Relief Association ship."

"But in that case you've escaped from the fiery pit,"[50] I said. "Why did you say just now that you'd never get out of their clutches?"

50. I.e., prostitution.

"What do you mean 'escaped from the fiery pit'! They know
perfectly well that I have no home to go to, and last night they
had their heads together plotting to sell me to some 'house' or
other."

My thoughts turned suddenly to Aren. "Where was it you used
to live in the capital?" I asked.

"At Hufang Bridge."

"Did you happen to know the Gu family in Mutton Alley? From
Haining."

"You mean Academician Gu?"

"That's right."

She was about to go on, when two shifty-looking characters
appeared on the stairs, and she broke off and withdrew. Furious
as I was at the interruption, I, too, had to shrink back into my
room, where I lay on my bed waiting for the men to leave so that
I could resume my talk. But after coming upstairs, they began a
commotion that lasted until dawn, when they suddenly ordered
two or three traps and carried their luggage and the girl away with
them. I was lying on my bed at the time, and when they took their
rowdy departure I felt I could scarcely step forward and plead
with the girl to stay, just in order to question her about Aren. I
was left in utter despair.

Two days later Father told Wang Sheng to get us tickets on a
small steamer bound for Hangzhou. We embarked at the Guan-
yinge Dock and spent a day and a night on board a Daisheng-
chang steamer before arriving at Gongchen Bridge in Hangzhou
on the fifteenth of the tenth month. We then took a lighter into the
city and put up at a relative's house on Mill Lane. The following
day my brother, hearing of our arrival, got leave from his school
and came to see Father, who took us out through the Qiantang
Gate to the West Lake to visit the family graves and, incidentally,
to enjoy the lake's beauties. In all we spent three days on the lake.
I admired the frosty green of the wintry hills and the still waters
of the distant sea. How true it is that the lake is equally pictur-
esque whether richly adorned or not![51] My one regret was that

---

51. Su Shi (1037–1101), in the second of his "Drinking on the West Lake"
poems, compares the lake to the legendary beauty Xi Shi and claims that it is
equally beautiful whether lavishly or sparingly adorned.

Aren wasn't there to enjoy it with me, but that regret was enough to make the clouds and trees forlorn and to strip the hills and streams of their color—a dreadful shame! After spending seven or eight days in Hangzhou, Father brought us back by steamer to Shanghai, where we put up at the Dingsheng Inn on Fourth Avenue.

This being my second visit to Shanghai, I did not need Wang Sheng's company on outings downtown. It was the first of the eleventh month, and I had strolled as far as Second Avenue when, in the midst of all that dense traffic, more than the eye could take in, I happened to notice someone in the crowd with ragged clothes and a dark complexion making his way slowly along the street. There was something about him that looked familiar. I thought for a moment—it was Li Gui, Uncle Gu's steward! "Mr. Li! Mr. Li!" I shouted.

He turned his head, looked hard at me, then broke into a broad grin. "Master Qin! When did *you* get here?"

"Yesterday. Is your master with you?"

He frowned. "Don't talk about the master!" he exclaimed. "He died back in the capital."

I asked when he had died.

"It's a long story." He pulled me into the doorway of a paint shop and began slowly to explain. "To be frank with you, sir, after you and your father left, the master took charge of official business for Grand Secretary Gang.[52] The Boxers were going from strength to strength at the time. One day they attacked the embassies, the next day they set fire to the cathedrals. Early in the sixth month you heard people saying that the foreign countries had sent warships against us, but the master wasn't unduly worried. Then on the nineteenth of the sixth month the foreigners launched a sudden attack on the capital. Those pathetic Boxers with their big talk were mowed down by the foreigners' guns, and in no time at all the city was in chaos. At that point the master panicked and rushed to do what everyone else had already done; he stuck a flag on his gate with the words 'Peaceful Citizens' on it. It worked, because the foreign soldiers made one search of the

---

52. Gangyi, another reactionary court politician.

house and then didn't bother us again. However, three days after that they got word that the master had been a high court official, and they arrested him and set him to work with all the other people who were burying the dead and clearing away the rubble. As you know yourself, sir, the master was a cultivated gentleman who couldn't possibly stand up to that kind of treatment. Within a few days he came down with an acute case of the colic and retched and purged for a day and a night before he died. It was the height of summer, and there were bodies all over the place. Coffins weren't to be had at any price, but fortunately Master Lu of the Lu compound on Nanheng Street managed to get us one made out of pine. Without any ceremony the master was laid in it and given a hasty burial near Taoran Pavilion.

"The mistress felt so indebted to Master Lu for doing us this favor that she accepted him as a son-in-law and let him take her elder daughter off with him. Following the tragedy she and the younger daughter spent their days commiserating with one another, at a complete loss as to what to do. Twice the daughter had to be recued from attempts at suicide. Then a friend of Master Lu's named Guan Geru offered the mistress a solution. He said he was a confidant of one of the foreign generals and claimed he could wangle us a safe-conduct pass as far as Tianjin, from where we ought to be able to find a way of getting to the south. The mistress trusted him and, packing up all her valuables, accompanied him to Tianjin along with her younger daughter and also that widow, Mrs. Zhao. Before we had been in Tianjin two months, however, the valuables were all in the pawnshop, and we were still not able to leave. Later, I don't quite know how, Guan took up with that Mrs. Zhao, and the pair of them actually slept in the same room, unconcerned about all the taunts that came their way, just as if they had been husband and wife. Early in the ninth month, on the grounds that I was doing nothing to justify my keep, I was driven out. Later I had the good luck to fall in with a former colleague of the master's, and he brought me south with him. As to what happened to the family after I left, I'm none too clear about it."

"But what became of the daughter and your mistress?" I interjected. "Do you really know *nothing* more about them?"

"A couple of weeks after I got here," he went on, "I ran into a friend from Tianjin and happened to mention Guan Geru's name to him. Eventually Guan did find some way of bringing the mistress and her daughter to Shanghai, where they took rooms at a small inn. But because there wasn't enough money to pay for their board and lodging, he sought out a procuress by the name of Sister Trey and arranged to make a living sacrifice out of the girl by selling her to a deadbeat named Lin. On the surface she was being sold as Lin's concubine for a hundred and fifty silver dollars, but in fact she was being sold to a house as a prostitute. When the girl found out, she got someone to smuggle in three drams of opium and swallowed it. It was midnight, and nobody knew what she was doing. . . ."

At this point my heart began to pound, and everything went black before me; there was a sudden roar in my ears, and tears started from my eyes. If only I could have battered myself to death against the doorway of that paint shop, the sooner to seek her out at the gates of Hell!

Li Gui was astonished at my reaction. "Master Qin!" he exclaimed. "Don't take it like that! She didn't *die!*"

At these words I revived and, clutching at him, demanded that he tell me at once what happened next. For my own sanity, he *had* to say: Was Aren alive or dead?

~ 10 ~

Splendor vanishes, but regret will last
a thousand years.

"THIS is no place to talk," said Li Gui. "Let's go on a bit and find a teahouse where I can take my time telling you." His reply drove me nearly frantic, and I could scarcely contain my impatience to get to the teahouse, where I insisted that he give me a full account of everything that had happened.

"Fortunately the mistress, who was asleep at the time, heard the death rattle in her daughter's throat and jumped up in alarm to find the girl blue in the face and unable to speak," he explained. "At first the mistress froze up with shock, but then she began screaming for Guan Geru to get out of bed—she was going to have it out with him once and for all.

" 'It's a case of opium poisoning,' Guan barked. 'Don't panic, either of you. I've seen whores in Beijing who swallowed raw opium and were saved with a dose of bombax.' He charged out of the inn and somewhere managed to find a quantity of bombax flower, which he burned to ashes and steeped in boiling water, then dribbled down the girl's throat. Sure enough, by morning she had brought up little by little all the opium she had swallowed. Our poor young mistress, such a beauty she used to be! But after this ordeal, so I'm told, she turned all sallow and haggard, like a consumptive. Guan was hoping to get a few dozen taels for her, but when he saw what a temper she had, he realized he'd never be able to deceive anyone, so he picked a quarrel with the mistress and moved out with Mrs. Zhao, I don't know where to. The mistress had no idea how to cope. She was reduced to begging the cashier to write to her relatives in Hubei asking for their help. I gather she and her daughter are still at that inn."

"Where is it?" I asked at once. "Have you been there?"

"I was driven out by the mistress at Guan Geru's urging. Why would I go back? As for the inn, it's not far from here. You just go up to the top of Fifth Avenue, and there you are."

When I heard that Aren was still alive and staying at that inn, my spirits soared, and I allowed myself to hope that one day she and I might still be able to marry. I seized Li Gui's hand and demanded that he take me there.

"Don't keep on at me!" he protested. "I haven't had a bite to eat all day!"

I fished some change out of my pocket and told him to get himself a meal in the little restaurant across the street, then take me immediately to Fifth Avenue. But with the money in his hand he decided against a meal and bought himself a couple of wheatcakes instead, munching them as he walked along. I stuck close behind him, a multitude of thoughts swarming through my mind. When we left the capital, no one could have imagined that Aren would ever be brought so low. It was the fault of that swine Guan Geru, of course, but her ordeal must also have resulted from her own destiny. Now that I was going to see her again, I must do my level best to persuade Father to help them find somewhere to live and to see that she received proper care. She might look pale and haggard now, I thought, but with the right medical treatment she should be able in time to regain her health and beauty.

As these fancies raced through my mind, I noticed a small inn ahead of us, just where Li Gui said it would be.

He stopped. "Master Qin, this is where the mistress is staying. Please go in and see for yourself. I won't be going with you."

Again and again I pressed him to come, but he refused, and in the end I had to pluck up my courage and go in alone. "Excuse me, but do you happen to have a Mrs. and a Miss Gu here, refugees from the north?" I asked at the desk.

A man behind the desk pointed inside. "Number 8," he said.

I went in the direction indicated, found No. 8, then pulled aside the door curtain and stepped into the room. At the far end of it stood a bed with the screen half down. A woman in ragged clothes sat on the edge of the bed wiping away her tears. Her face was so sallow and haggard that I had trouble recognizing her, but on a closer look I realized that she was Aren's mother. I approached and called to her: "Aunt."

She looked up, saw who it was, then leapt to her feet and grasped my hand. "Oh, Master Qin, if *only* you'd come a little earlier, my Aren would have died in peace and been spared the extra agony of these last few days. The poor child has been starving herself for five or six days now and has come close to death on several occasions. Every time she revives she asks me, 'Is Master Qin here yet?' and I say, 'Master Qin's your predestined lover. What makes you think he'll come *here*? If you want to die and be reborn, go ahead, but there's no need to be so concerned about your predestined lover!'" At this point she opened the bed screen and let me see Aren.

She was propped against the pillow, her cheeks shrunken and drained of color, looking for all the world like a paper funeral figure. At the sight of her, with her mother's words still ringing in my ears, I was filled with a range of emotions—alarm, fear, sadness, anxiety. My tongue thickened and my throat contracted, and I stood there a long time before finally letting out a cry: "Oh, 'Ren, 'Ren, how ever did you come to such a state? And it's all my fault!"

Hearing my voice, she suddenly opened her eyes wide—Aren, so close to death for so long!—and sat bolt upright and wanted to tell me something. But before she could speak, she began gasping for breath, and it was some time before she recovered. "Come here," she said, in the feeblest of voices.

When I looked at the state she was in, I felt as if I had been stabbed to the heart. I sat on the edge of the bed, gripping her hand in mine. "I'm here now," I said, fighting back my tears. "If there's anything you want to say, please say it."

She shook her head twice, then said with a visible effort: "You've shown me your love in a hundred different ways, but I never had the good fortune to become your wife. I'm still a virgin. . . ." At this point she began gasping for breath again, but then after a while with another great effort continued: "After I am dead, you mustn't grieve too much. So long as my soul remains intact, there's a chance we may meet in the next life." As she said this, I felt her hand growing cold and couldn't help bursting into tears.

" 'Ren," I said through my tears. "You were always so clever— how could you *do* such a thing to yourself? If anything happens, I'll never be able to face you." Her mother, watching us, wept too, her tears streaming down.

Then I heard Aren continuing: "Now that I have seen you again, my last wish has been fulfilled. Let go of my hand and allow me . . ." Before she could finish the sentence, the phlegm began rattling in her throat, and although her eyes continued gazing into mine, the expression on her face had changed utterly. Dropping her hand, I beckoned to her mother to come and help me lay her out on the bed.

By this time the staff had heard the wailing from our room and come rushing up in twos and threes. Aren's mother and I faced the bed and stamped our feet and beat our breasts in grief. The staff waited a considerable time, then grew impatient and broke in: "Now that your relative has unfortunately passed away, you ought to be making arrangements for the funeral. You can't just go on grieving like this."

Their advice sent Aren's mother into paroxysms of sobbing, and it dawned on me that she didn't have the money to pay for a funeral. I stopped my wailing and asked her to wait for me, then took a rickshaw back to the inn, where I found Father and, after sobbing out the story of Aren's death, pleaded with him to pay for the funeral. He was genuinely moved and at once accompanied me back to the inn. After paying his respects to Aren's mother and glancing at Aren's body, he gave the cashier some money for the purchase of new silk burial garments and a coffin, and also for hiring several funeral assistants. Then with Father and myself as witnesses Aren's body was laid in the coffin. By that time I had cried myself into a state of virtual oblivion and wanted nothing more than to leap into the coffin with her and accompany her to the other world. Father waited until the laying in had been completed, then asked the cashier to hire musicians and buy quantities of incense candles and paper money. He had the assistants carry the coffin to the guild house, which would serve as its temporary resting place. Aren's mother and I escorted it there, weep-

ing every step of the way. At the guild house I grieved once more
and gave the staff a little money to take good care of it, after
which Father and I took a rickshaw back to the inn.

Noticing how emotionally drained I was, he told me to get some
rest. He himself went straight out again to take Aren's mother
some travel money and urge her not to grieve too much. He also
devised a scheme to get her safely home, writing to all his colleagues and friends along the way and asking them for their help.
Because of Father's love for me, he extended his love to Aren and
his kindness to Aren's mother, a prime example of the old saying
"A parent's love knows no bounds." The debt of gratitude that I
owe him can never be repaid.

Unfortunately, the day I returned to the inn I fell seriously ill,
and ever since then my illness has grown worse. When I consider
my present state, I doubt that it will be very long now before I
follow Aren to the grave. Oh, how fondly I had always hoped,
ever since I first met her in that Hubei compound at the age of
ten, that she and I would form a loving couple forever! But our
meeting was followed by a surprise separation. If we had really
never met again, I could have borne it, but to my surprise we
chanced to meet in the capital, where our love for each other
deepened and the incubus of sexual desire grew stronger. However, even at this time if her family had maintained a really strict
regime in which boys and girls found it difficult to meet, or if our
parents had been adamantly against the match when Lu Xiaocang
proposed it, our love would gradually have cooled. But to my surprise she was able to meet me morning and night, and eventually
we were pledged to marry. At that point I was certain beyond the
shadow of a doubt that we would become husband and wife, but
to my further surprise Father delayed the wedding and then—
another surprise—the Boxer rebellion broke out in the capital,
and suddenly she and I had to go our separate ways. After that we
might have been expected to remain at opposite ends of the earth
and never see each other again, but to my great surprise we were
brought together under tragic circumstances. And there was an
even greater surprise in store—the day we met was also the day
of our final parting! So tortuous, so bizarre was the fantastic
course of our love for each other! I simply cannot understand why

the Creator, confound him, assigned us these roles as phantom lovers and made us act out all these joys and sorrows, partings and reunions, only to bring us to such a conclusion![53]

However, I blame neither Father nor the Boxer bandits for my ruin. Instead I hold Mencius responsible. But for his stale formula "by the parents' command and through the good offices of a go-between," I would long since have joined Aren in a free marriage. No matter how much turmoil the Boxers caused, she and I would still have been able to travel south together. At this very moment I could be by her side again, sitting around the fire drinking wine or taking moonlit walks beneath the blossoming trees. In addition we could be showing our love for each other by night and embracing by day, enjoying all the delights of the flesh without plumbing the depths of anxiety, hardship, frustration, and misery. Instead of that I am left with mounting loneliness, desolation, sorrow, and pain. My life hangs in the balance, my hopes lie in ashes. Not only have I brought grief to Father, I have burdened Miss Bi with a dubious reputation. I hope above all else that one day this China of ours will change its marriage system and grant people their freedom, before the City of Wrongful Death claims countless more millions of aggrieved and anguished souls. That would be an achievement of unimaginable, incalculable proportions!

And now an image flashes before my mind, and I see my Aren standing in front of me—the perfect oval of her face, the high arch of her brows, the limpid gaze, the rosebud mouth, the childhood dimples, her mood now cross, now gay, now laughing, now weeping—and I am driven out of my mind by the sight and left mesmerized, as if in a drunken stupor.

Those lovestruck young men and women that we read of in verse novels old and new are described as plucking orchids or peonies, peaches or plums—or choosing golden jewel boxes or hairpins, jade ornaments or pendants—and presenting them to each other as clandestine gifts to serve as pledges of love and tokens of commitment. Or else we see them exchanging poems

---

53. Note that the word translated as "conclusion" conceals a reference to the "fruits" of action mentioned in Chapter 1.

and love lyrics, which are then passed down to posterity and turned into immortal tales of high romance. Or else their spirits are transformed into such miraculous things as trees that intertwine or fish that cannot live apart—the Queen of Qi turning into a mourning cicada, Han Ping into a butterfly[54]—and these things, too, are apt to make us recall the past and shed a tear.

But the only thing Aren and I ever gave each other was this one word "passion." For us there were no keepsakes or love letters to preserve our memory into the future. Yet the passion she felt for me was truly as deep as the waters of Peach Blossom Pool.[55] If I were to die now, would I not have betrayed that passion? That is why, ill as I am, I must let my tears run together with the ink and force myself to pick up my brush and set down the course of her boundless passion from beginning to end, so that in ages to come lovestruck young men and women will read my novel, reflect on the past and pause awhile, sigh and shed a tear, and perhaps, if the spirit moves them, write a pair of sad lyrics in our memory or dedicate to us a rhapsody of regret.[56] When that time comes, from her abode in the Nine Springs Aren will manage the faint trace of a smile, and the deep love she bore me will not have been in vain. Reader, reader, you should know that Aren died on the first day of the eleventh month and that this novel was written after her death. From first to last it is concerned with just one word, *passion,* and no man or woman of passion anywhere in the world should hesitate to read it. Only those people who spend their time talking of nothing but *lust,* who fail to understand even the meaning of the word *passion,* are forbidden to read this book.

54. The queen died lamenting the king's treatment of her and then turned into a cicada and continued her lament. Han Ping and his wife killed themselves when oppressed by the king (a different king). She left a request to be buried in the same grave as her husband, but the king spitefully placed their graves opposite each other. However, a tree grew between the graves and united them with its roots. In one version of the story the couple turn into butterflies.

55. This bottomless pool is referred to in Li Bai's (Li Po, 701–762) poem "For Wang Lun."

56. The actual "Rhapsody of Regret" by Jiang Yan (444–505) describes the fates of various historical figures.

The Sea of Regret
(Hen hai)

By Wu Jianren

~ 1 ~

Matchmakers are called in to convey
marriage proposals,

And refugees are held up by illness
in a remote village.

I TAKE up my brush to write a novel and then, before setting
brush to paper, run through my mind all the events I am going to
relate. When complete, my novel will qualify as a story of passion.
Now, I have long maintained that passion is something that we
possess from birth, well before we know the meaning of sexual-
ity. In the most general sense of the term, a baby's crying and
laughter are both passion, although certainly not the kind the
world is referring to when it speaks of passion's "awakening."[1] In
the eyes of the world, you must understand, passion is confined
to sex, whereas the passion I am speaking of, the kind we possess
from birth, is an innate quality that, as we grow up, can be applied to any sphere of life, the only difference being in the *manner* of its application. When applied to a ruler, it is loyalty; when
applied to parents, it is filial piety; when applied to children, it is
parental love; and when applied to friends, it is true fellowship.
Clearly the cardinal virtues all derive from passion.

As for sexual passion, the only word for that is infatuation.

There are even people who have no need to employ such passion, indeed who ought not to employ it, but who *abuse* it—and
such people can only be described as lechers.

According to one interpretation, the chaste widows lauded by
our forefathers had hearts like dead trees or dry wells; they were
utterly unmoved by passion. I categorically disagree. The occa-

1. I.e., puberty.

sions on which the widows remained unmoved were precisely those on which their passion was at its height. In its conviction that passion is confined to sexual love, the world inevitably takes the term too lightly. What is more, there is many a "story of passion" that in reality describes not passion, but lechery, which it then tries to portray as passion. A true crime of the writer's brush!

It would be rather awkward for me, in relating this story of mine, to tell you in advance just what kind of passion I am going to describe, but I assure you that I shall not commit the crime of describing lechery. If you wish to know more, you must read the story proper.

In the year *gengzi* of the Guangxu reign period [1900], the whole northern part of the country was thrown into turmoil by the rise of the Boxer bandits. Eventually the turmoil brought the allied army into the capital—and led to Their Imperial Majesties' departure on a tour of the west. Untold numbers of officials at all levels were humiliated, among them a certain Chen Qi, courtesy name Gelin, who came from Nanhai in Guangdong province. After succeeding at both levels of the civil service examinations, he had been given the rank of secretary and assigned as trainee to the Ministry of Works, after which he returned to Guangdong and fetched his family to live with him in the capital.

He and his wife, Miss Li, had two boys, the elder named Xiang (courtesy name Bohe) and the younger Rui (courtesy name Zhongai). Once back in the capital, Gelin installed his family in a house that he had rented on Nanheng Street.

At about the same time a first cousin of Gelin's had brought *his* family to the capital from his home in Suzhou and was having trouble finding a house to rent. Gelin, whose house was too large for his own needs anyway, sublet part of it to his cousin, and so the two families came to share the same courtyard.

The cousin was named Wang Dao, courtesy name Letian. His wife was a Miss Jiang and their only child a daughter whose childhood name was Juanjuan. Wang Letian held the rank of secretary at the Grand Secretariat; like Gelin he had not yet been given a regular post. Now, metropolitan officials are always hard pressed for money, life in the capital being far from easy. Apart from the five rooms to the north of the courtyard occupied by Gelin and the three to the west occupied by Wang Letian, there were three other rooms to the east that stood empty, costing Gelin money that he could ill afford, and so he posted a notice advertising them for rent.

Before long someone came to inquire, and after showing his visitor through the rooms, Gelin asked him his name. "I'm Zhang Gao, courtesy name Heting," he said, "and I come from Xiangshan in Guangdong." Gelin was delighted to find that his visitor came from the same part of the country as he did. A rent was quickly agreed on, and Heting chose a date to move in. Like Letian, he had a wife and a daughter, the wife being a Miss Bai and the daughter Dihua.

These events all took place in the years *xinmao* [1891] and *renchen* [1892]. As I have related them, they conform exactly to the old saying "Without coincidences, there'd be no stories." In this one compound lived three families with four children among them, all five or six years old at the time. The Wangs were relatives of the Chens, while the Zhangs were fellow-Cantonese. Sharing a courtyard as they did, the womenfolk saw a great deal of each other and became fast friends, while their children played together every day. When Gelin engaged a tutor to teach his boys at home, the Wangs and the Zhangs sent their daughters along to attend class, and the children drew closer still. In fact they became quite fond of one other and got along remarkably well.

Every so often Zhang Heting was obliged to make a trip to Shanghai. He was a businessman who had started a shop in Shanghai selling imported goods and, after doing well in that line, had opened a branch on Qianmen Avenue in Beijing. Each year he had to go back and forth checking on his shops, and when he went to Shanghai, he would entrust his family to Gelin's care, an arrangement that brought the two men closer together.

In this manner five or six years went by. Meanwhile Gelin received a regular post in the Building Department, where he so impressed the senior officials, both Manchu and Chinese, with his abilities that he was appointed superintendent of sawmills, after which his financial position was somewhat improved.

One day Miss Li remarked to her husband: "Xiang [Bohe] will

be twelve this year and Rui [Zhongai] eleven. They've been working hard recently, and I fully expect them to follow in their
father's footsteps."

"What an odd thing to say!" said Gelin with a laugh. "Out of the
blue you suddenly start praising our boys!"

"But it's *not* out of the blue. When you see your sons doing
well, it's natural to feel pleased and try to plan ahead for them in
every way you can."

"Plan for what?"

"For their engagements."

"But what's the hurry? They're still *very* young."

"There's something I've been meaning to talk to you about. I'm
convinced that the two girls who share our compound would
make ideal wives for Xiang and Rui, and I'm hoping we can
arrange it."

"There's no danger of the girls' running away, you know—they
do live in the same compound, after all. There'll be time enough
to arrange things a couple of years from now."

"I'm not worried about their running away. But I've seen
what splendid girls they are, and I'm afraid we'll be beaten out
by someone else. We'll have missed out on a golden opportunity!"

Gelin thought for a moment. "That Juanjuan really is a very
bright little thing. Not long ago I saw her practicing poetic
couplets, and even if she didn't get them quite right, it was a very
creditable effort that she made. She's extremely smart, in speech
as well as behavior. Dihua, the Zhang girl, strikes me as a little on
the dull side by comparison—never smiles or says anything.
Moreover Heting's a businessman who doesn't ever unbend, but
manages to keep up that stiff Cantonese manner of his all the
time. He may not even be interested in allying himself with a civil
service family like ours."

"Let's get a matchmaker to take our proposal over and see. So
far we've not even raised the question with him, so how can we
know what he will say?"

And so it was decided.

The next day Gelin asked two matchmakers to take separate
proposals to the Wangs and the Zhangs. Wang Letian accepted at

once, betrothing Juanjuan to Zhongai. Zhang Heting, however, preferred to talk the matter over with his wife first.

"This is the most important event in a child's life," she said. "*You* make the decision. What do you want a woman's advice for?"

"That's not the point. I'm out every day—in fact I'm rarely at home—while you see the children all the time. What's young Xiang's character like? People always say you never know with children, but surely you can tell *something* from their behavior and temperament. They study side by side—do they get along together? That's another important thing."

"Xiang is much livelier than his brother. And I'm always hearing it said that he's brighter in class. But as to how they get on together, there's really no point in asking that. They're children, and naive in the way children are. What do *they* know about such things?"

"But that's not the case at all. If they'd never known each other, that would be one thing, but they've been thrown into each other's company day after day. Suppose they felt a certain antipathy for each other and we forced them to marry. Can you just imagine what their lives would be like?"

"They play together as brothers and sisters every day of the week. What antipathy could they feel?"

Rather than continue the argument, Heting went to the classroom to observe the children, whom he found bent over their desks practicing their writing. After exchanging a few words with the tutor, he stepped out again. For the life of him he couldn't think how to decide the issue. But there *was* one consideration: Gelin came from a long line of officials, and his children had been well brought up, which was why Xiang and Rui, although only eleven and twelve, had such grownup manners. Heting had noted this fact long ago and filed it away in his memory. One reason for consulting his wife was to get her reaction; the other was that, having just the one child, he was extremely cautious where the great event of her life was concerned. The truth was that he had been more than half inclined to accept the proposal all along.

He returned to the east wing, discussed it once more with his wife, and decided to accept. But he also declared that it would be far easier for all concerned if they moved out of the compound.

Otherwise, the situation might get rather unseemly, with the children growing up. . . .

The next day they gave their instructions to the matchmaker, who conveyed their acceptance to a gratified Gelin. Heting found another house on West Riverbank and moved in with his family, after which Gelin renovated the vacant east wing and turned it into a study. Wang Letian did not move out, partly because he was a relative, and partly because Miss Li begged him to stay. An auspicious date was set for the engagement ceremonies, and horoscope cards were exchanged. Meanwhile Juanjuan continued to attend class with the boys. She was a pretty girl, and when school was out she would often go over to Miss Li's rooms to play, smiling and laughing all the while. Miss Li took a great fancy to her and lavished endearments upon her as if she had been her own daughter.

After Dihua moved away, she gave up her lessons and confined herself to studying needlework with her mother. Gradually she came to neglect her *Maxims for Women* and *Classic of Filial Piety for Girls,* forgetting the words and retaining nothing but the general meaning.

In this manner several more years passed until by the year *gengzi* [1900] the children had grown up. Dihua and Bohe, who had been born in the same year, were now seventeen, Dihua being the elder by a month; Zhongai was sixteen; and Juanjuan, the youngest, was fourteen.

That year Chen Gelin was promoted to be assistant director of his department.

That was also the year when the Boxer bandits started their havoc. Rumors had been circulating from the year before, rumors that in the first and second months of the new year grew daily in intensity. Now, people from Suzhou are notoriously timid and, in addition to his nervousness, Wang Letian also suffered from a weak constitution. In the third month, with rumors arising on all sides, he obtained leave from his department and, taking his wife and daughter with him, left for his home in Suzhou. Before his departure he arranged with Gelin that if no trouble had broken out within two or three months, he would bring his family back again. However, if trouble did break out and the capital became unsafe, they would all meet up in Shanghai. Gelin agreed to both suggestions and, after accompanying Letian some distance out of the city, said good-bye and returned home.

By this time both Zhongai and Juanjuan understood something of the world and were extremely reluctant to part.

Not long before these events occurred, Heting had traveled to Shanghai, leaving his family behind in the capital.

Following Letian's departure, an endless stream of officials also applied for leave, a development that so infuriated the government that it issued an order prohibiting any further applications. At that point the entire corps of capital officials, at least all those with an ounce of worldly wisdom, realized that they were being asked to die at their posts. A panic-stricken Miss Bai paid several visits to Gelin to get his advice on leaving for the south. Unfortunately it was now too late for Gelin himself to apply for leave, and since Miss Bai and her daughter could scarcely undertake such a long journey on their own, there was nothing he could suggest.

This situation dragged on until the end of the fourth month, when Gelin received a telegram from Heting: "DISTURBING NEWS STOP IF TROUBLE SEEMS LIKELY STOP URGE COME SOUTH STOP REQUEST BRING MY FAMILY. . . ."

Gelin did not know what to do. New rumors were springing up every day. Suddenly it was reported that the ambassadors had wired for troops to enter Beijing ready for action. Another rumor had Grand Secretary Ronglu ordering Dong Fuxiang into the capital on garrison duty; some people claimed that all of Dong's troops were Boxer bandits, while others held that Prince Duan had declared war on the legations and was going to launch an attack the very next day.[2] By this time the entire population of Beijing was on tenterhooks.

By the beginning of the fifth month they were in an even worse state, with the Boxer bandits rampaging through the city streets.

---

2. Ronglu (1836–1903) was a Manchu statesman with some influence over the Empress Dowager. He realized the futility of the reactionaries' policy and did not press home the attack on the legations. Dong Fuxiang (1839–1908) was the commander of an unruly army of soldiers from Gansu province who were stationed near Beijing. His troops' murder of a secretary from the Japanese legation set off the conflict in the city. On Prince Duan, see *Stones in the Sea,* note 41.

Gelin himself became nervous and, calling Miss Bai over to the house, told her to pack up her valuables and bring her daughter with her; he would detail one of his servants and both of his sons to escort them south. She complied at once, packing up her luggage and bringing Dihua over the same day. When families were being torn apart, it was no time to worry about such niceties as the rule that engaged couples should avoid each other's company.

When Gelin told his sons to escort the women, Zhongai objected: "But you and Mother will be staying behind! When families are forced to part, it's not right for both sons to leave. Let Bohe escort Aunt Zhang, while I stay and look after you. If fighting should break out, we'll all flee together."

"As an official, I have to follow orders and cannot ask for leave, but there's no need for the rest of you to go putting yourselves in harm's way. Far better if I stay here, while you and your brother look after your mother and aunt on their journey."

"With you still here," put in Miss Li, "how can we all leave? Let the boys go on their own."

"You go with Xiang, Mother! I'll stay and look after Father."

"What do *you* know about such things, my boy? Come on, off you go with your brother!" said Gelin.

"In any other matter I wouldn't dare offend you, Father, but in this case you may punish me as much as you like, I still won't go."

There was nothing Gelin could do but tell Bohe to take their servant Li Fu and escort Miss Bai and her daughter out of the capital. Hiring two traps, they set off for the railway station to catch the train for Tanggu.

However, when they reached the station, they found it deserted. No trains would be running that day, they were told; the tracks had been torn up to prevent any foreign troops from entering the city. Bohe talked the matter over with Miss Bai, and they decided to go on by trap; with any luck they might find a train waiting for them at Fengtai. Negotiations followed with the drivers, and after the fare had been raised, they set off. The drivers didn't dare follow the railroad tracks in case they met an oncoming train and there was no time to get out of its path, so they took a roundabout route. The travelers drove on until dusk and that night had to make do with a country inn, which had just one guest room containing a single platform bed. Thoroughly embarrassed, Dihua was reduced to sitting on one side of the room and hanging her head. The inn did not provide any meals either, and Bohe had to send Li Fu out to pick up some wheatcakes. Fortunately no other guests wanted to stay the night, and Bohe, the servant, and the drivers all slept in the entrance hall.

The next morning the drivers refused to go on, and the fare had to be raised again. Bohe promised them seven taels a day for each trap regardless of how many miles they covered, and on that understanding they harnessed their mules and set off. At Fengtai, however, the travelers found the station a smoldering ruin, and once more the drivers refused to go on, relenting only after much heated argument. Failing to reach Huangcun station that day, they spent a second night at a village inn.

Because Bohe was not yet married to Dihua, he was careful to avoid her company and slept a second night in the entrance hall. Now, in North China the entrance halls of village houses have no doors, and he caught a chill and began to run a fever. That day he could not travel, but had to stay behind at the inn and rest.

Greatly concerned, Miss Bai told him to come and lie down on the platform bed in the guest room. Dihua retreated to a rickety chair beside the bed, where she sat with her back to him. Fortunately they had brought with them a quantity of Canton medicinal tea. Miss Bai herself heated some up for Bohe, and by the afternoon he felt a little better.

Then the drivers began agitating again: "Even if we don't travel, we'll still need our seven taels a day." Li Fu started to argue with them, but Bohe intervened. "Don't argue!" he said. "Let them have their way!"

That night Bohe slept in the guest room. Fortunately platform beds in the north are very wide, taking up fully half the room, no matter how large it is, and can always sleep at least ten people. Miss Bai placed a low table in the middle of the bed and let Bohe sleep on one side of it, while she and her daughter slept on the other, an arrangement that to a northerner's mind qualifies as segregation of the sexes. But Dihua had never experienced such a situation in her whole life, let alone in her fiancé's presence, and she refused to lie down. Turning her back to the lamp, she hung her head and sat there in silence.

Bohe had taken some medicine during the day to bring on a sweat and as a result had slept so soundly that now he couldn't get back to sleep. He lay in bed watching the flickering of the lamp, while Dihua sat by herself and Miss Bai slept on the other side of the bed. Moved by the little scene, he whispered to Dihua: "Cousin, go to sleep!" (Reader, you should understand that Dihua was two months older than Bohe and as children together in the same classroom they had addressed each other as cousin.[3] That was why he reverted to the old form of address on this occasion. You should not conclude that husbands and wives in Guangdong regularly address each other in this manner.)

To return to our story. When Dihua heard Bohe's whisper, she hung her head and said nothing. "There's a table in the bed between us," said Bohe, "and you have Aunt on your side, too. Just look at the tear in that paper window. It may be summer, but we're sure to feel a draft later on. You mustn't catch cold!"

Dihua still did not look up. After a long pause she whispered her reply, hesitating over every word: "Do get some rest, cousin! You've only just recovered, you know!"

At these words, Bohe sat bolt upright. But if you wish to know why, you will have to turn to the next chapter.

---

3. Chinese does not distinguish between "brother" or "sister" and "cousin" in this case.

～ 2 ～

One is deeply in love, yet filled with unease;
The other is caught in the turmoil and driven away.

WHEN Bohe sat bolt upright in bed, Dihua was startled. *Why is he getting up?* she wondered. *It was kindness on his part to tell me to lie down, but he can't go foisting himself on me just because I don't do as he says—that would be too absurd!* But all she heard him say was: "Lie down, cousin! Don't wear yourself out fretting over things. We shall have to go on again in the morning, you know."

"Lie down yourself, cousin!" she whispered back. "Don't catch another chill when you've only just recovered from the last one. I'm tired. Of course I'll lie down."

Bohe said nothing, just pushed the bedclothes aside, bent over to slip into his shoes, and stood up.

"I'm going outside again to take a nap. Sleep well, cousin!" He left the room.

We used to play together as children, mused Dihua. *Isn't it amazing that he's still so considerate of me after five or six years apart? While still not completely over his own illness, he says he's afraid I'll wear myself out with worrying and goes off to avoid me. But that last illness of his was caused by sleeping outside for that very purpose. How can I put him through the same ordeal again?* Too shy to call out and yet too tenderhearted to leave him outside, she stood up and gently shook her mother. "Mother, wake up!" she called.

Her mother awoke with a start and asked what the matter was. Dihua hung her head and said nothing.

Miss Bai laughed. "What's going on? First you wake me up, and then you have nothing to say." She sat up and repeated her question, but Dihua still hung her head and said nothing, which only added to Miss Bai's suspicions. She turned and, noticing that Bohe was no longer in bed, asked where he was. As she pointed outside, Dihua flushed a deep red.

Miss Bai was about to get up when Bohe walked in. "She wouldn't go to sleep with me in the room," he said, "so I went out again to avoid her company."

Miss Bai broke in. "That's *so* unnecessary! At a time like this when we're fleeing for our lives, we can't be concerned about all these niceties. Nephew, go to sleep this minute! And you, child, come over here and lie down on this side of me! If anyone gets ill, we'll all suffer!"

Bohe looked over at Dihua, but she still hung her head. "Lie down, nephew!" said Miss Bai. "I know how to get her to sleep." Bohe lay down, and Miss Bai reached out an arm and drew Dihua to the edge of the bed. "Now, you lie down! Don't go upsetting everybody!"

Dihua continued to hang her head, but then finally, after repeated urging from her mother, she crossed her legs and lay back fully clothed. If I don't lie down, she thought, I'll be preventing Mother from getting any sleep. But this is such an unseemly situation, it makes me feel highly uncomfortable. If we'd married before we left, that would be one thing, but we're still bound by the rules of behavior, and I can't even ask him how he's feeling without encouraging him to show concern for me. If I don't lie down, what a poor return *that* would be for all his kindness! Then she began to wonder how an unmarried couple could possibly sleep in the same bed, and at the very thought she felt a sharp, prickling sensation down her spine. Several times she was on the point of sitting up, but for fear of disturbing Bohe she forced herself to stay down. That whole night she kept thinking of one thing after another and never did get to sleep.

At first light she sat up, half opened her eyes, and glanced over at Bohe, who was lying on his side with the bedclothes partly off. It's just at this hour, shortly before dawn, she reflected, that people are most susceptible to the early morning chill. Moreover, he's lying right opposite that torn window pane. He'll *never* survive another illness. I'd be far too embarrassed to cover him up myself, but I'm afraid that if I awaken Mother she won't get back to sleep. I expect she'll want to set off again today, and if she doesn't get more sleep than this, she won't be able to stand the strain of the journey. Dihua tried to call out and awaken Bohe, but the words stuck in her throat. She thought and thought, but there was no other course open to her. Stepping silently out of her bed, she tiptoed over, gently stretched out her hand, and pulled the quilt up to cover him.

It so happened that Miss Bai was already awake, lying in bed with her eyes closed, quietly relaxing her mind. As Dihua covered Bohe with the quilt, Miss Bai chanced to open her eyes. "See you tuck him in properly!" she volunteered.

A trifling remark, perhaps, but one that made Dihua blush all the way to her earlobes. Falling back a step or two, she collapsed into a chair. If we were husband and wife, she thought, it wouldn't matter what I did, but I'm in this terrible bind in which there are *so* many things I have to guard against, more than I can stand. We should have gone our separate ways as refugees. We'd have missed each other, of course, but that's all. As things are, we are together all the time. I long to take care of him, but I can't, and I'm at my wits' end! At this thought she felt a pang of grief and began to cry.

Miss Bai sat up in bed and noticed her tears. "Why are you crying?"

Dihua wiped away her tears and forced herself to reply: "I wasn't."

Miss Bai sighed. "Look, I know how hard this is on you. But it's a special situation you and he are in. You were together as children and got used to treating each other as cousins. It's not your fault that you're both refugees cut off from your families. In any case, you have me here with you. The fact is, the rules of behavior can be set aside for the time being. I've noticed Juanjuan and young Rui talking and laughing together all day long. They may be relatives, but they're also engaged to be married, yet she *never* behaves the way you do! It's a good thing we moved away from that house. You couldn't have stood it there!"

Her remark set Dihua wondering about that very possibility; if they had never moved away, what would her life have been like? She was only a child then, and naturally she wouldn't have known anything about the rules of behavior. If that situation had continued to the present, they'd have simply grown used to being together, like a child wife and her child husband. It was just this situation that was so difficult.

As these fancies crowded her mind, Bohe rolled over, sat up, and began rubbing his eyes. "How come you're both up so early?"

"Are you completely better now?" asked Miss Bai.

"I am indeed. Today we can get started. I wonder what things are like outside."

"Can we find out from the people here?"

"They're terribly stupid. Yesterday I asked them something, and their answers made no sense at all. All they know is that the Brothers are killing the hairies.[4] Plus a load of nonsense about heavenly soldiers and heavenly generals—not a single thing worth listening to. Let's set off as early as we can and ask someone along the way."

He went out and told Li Fu to heat up some water, and Miss Bai and Dihua washed and dressed themselves. But when Bohe ordered the drivers to harness up, one of them declared: "I'm not going on! I'm through with this job! Last night I heard people saying the hairies' soldiers have arrived in Tianjin and are fighting the Brothers. The hairies have rifles and cannon, while the Brothers have heavenly weapons and fire on their side. *They* may not be afraid of rifles and cannon, but we certainly are. I'm not getting myself blown to bits with you people just for the sake of a few extra taels."

The other driver tried to talk him out of it. "Look, we're all subjects of the Great Qing Dynasty, and since the Brothers are trying to 'support the dynasty and wipe out the foreigners,' of *course* they'll protect us. Come on, there's nothing to be afraid of."

"We may not even go to Tianjin," put in Li Fu. "We could well stop at Huangcun, Anding, or Langfang—wherever we find a

4. The Boxers' pejorative word for foreigners was *maozi* (hairy ones). A separate term, *ermaozi* (secondary hairy ones), was applied to Christian converts and others closely associated with foreigners. I translate the latter "hangers-on."

train. What makes you think we're so set on going to Tianjin ourselves and getting blown to bits?"

"Nonsense!" said the driver. "Trains, you say? You can forget
about trains! The railroad tracks have all been melted down by
heavenly fire."

Bohe overheard the argument and came out. "What's the
trouble?" he asked.

"You needn't bother to ask," said the driver. "The long and the
short of it is that I'm through with this job. As soon as I get my
pay, I'm off."

Bohe turned to the other driver. "And what about you?"

"If he doesn't want the job, that's his affair," he said. "The only
trouble is that if all of you ride in my trap, it will be too much for
my mule. If we'd known we were coming on such a long journey,
we should have brought a two-mule trap."

"I wonder if there's a trap around here that we could hire?"

"In a little village like this they wouldn't have any traps," said
the driver, "but I suppose you might find a mule or two."

"Then go and hire us a couple," said Bohe.

The other driver began clamoring for his pay. As soon as he
received it from Bohe, he drove off in his empty trap.

Before long the driver who had been sent out to look for mules
returned. "There isn't even a mule for hire," he said. "All people have are their private ones, which they're not prepared to
rent out."

"There's nothing else for it, then. We'll just have to share the
one trap."

"It's not that *I'm* unwilling," protested the driver, "but it's simply
too much for my mule."

"Drive a little slower, then. Anyway, those of us who've been
riding on top can always get down and walk."

"In that case you'll have to raise my pay."

"I'll give you two taels more a day," said Bohe.

The driver laughed. "You're just too shrewd, sir!" he said. "The
traps were costing you seven taels a day each. Now that the other
fellow has quit, if you pay me only two taels more, you'll be saving yourself five a day."

"How much are you asking for, then?"

"Isn't it only fair to give me the money that he turned down?"

"Rubbish!" exclaimed Li Fu. "We'd be paying out an extra seven taels a day just for riding on top!"

"Never mind," said Bohe. "Give him what he wants. In an emergency like this there's no point in haggling!" The driver then took himself off, and when they needed him to load the luggage, he was nowhere to be found.

Bohe went back to the room and whispered something to Miss Bai. "Just now as I was standing in the courtyard talking to the driver, I noticed far more refugee vehicles on the road than there were yesterday or the day before. The situation is getting more and more chaotic. Without letting anyone see what we're doing, let's divide up our valuables and tuck them away in our money belts."

The suggestion alarmed Miss Bai. "Why, what's going on outside?" she asked.

"Mother, don't ask," said Dihua. "It's a good idea. It's much safer to carry things in our belts than in our cases."

Miss Bai quickly produced a key, opened her small suitcase, and took out her jewel box. She shared the two pairs of pearl hairclips and some pieces of gold jewelry with her daughter, and they both tucked them away. Dihua noticed another ten ounces of gold leaf left in the jewel box.

"What shall we do with these?" she asked, taking them out.

"Oh, give them to my nephew," said Miss Bai.

Meanwhile Bohe, on opening his own suitcase to remove the silver, found himself in a quandary. If he carried too much on his own person, it would slow him down, but if he took too little and some of the cases got lost, they might well run short. On hearing Miss Bai's remark, he turned to look, and Dihua handed him the gold leaf, which he tucked away in his money belt along with twenty or thirty taels of loose silver. Then he took something from his own money belt and handed it to Miss Bai. "This little trinket is a family heirloom that my mother gave me. I have so many bulky things on me already that I can't take this one too. Please put it away for me, Aunt."

Miss Bai took it in her hand, and Dihua saw it was a "double happiness" disk of white jade. As her mother was putting it away in her case, she intervened: "It won't be safe there. Let me take it!"

Miss Bai gave it to her. Dihua once more removed the things at her waist, added the disk, and tied her belt up again. Bohe took out several dozen taels and gave them to Li Fu to put in his belt. Before relocking the case, he also brought out enough money to cover the last few days' fare. After dividing the gold leaf in two, he undid his leggings and bound half of it up in each.

He then called the driver, who still had not returned. Eventually he reappeared, and Li Fu helped him load the luggage, after which Miss Bai and Dihua emerged from the inn arm in arm and climbed aboard. Bohe paid for the room, then called in the driver and handed him the fare. "This includes your fourteen taels for today," he explained. "See you keep it on you. I'm afraid our luggage may get lost along the way, and without it I won't be able to pay you. You'll have put in several days' work for nothing."

This pleased the driver. "Just as I thought, there are even more refugees on the road today," he said, accepting the money. "Some of them told me they left the capital two days ago, while others said they left only yesterday. It just goes to show how serious the situation must be, that they've come this far." He put down his whip and tucked the money away in his belt, then left the inn. Bohe and Li Fu took their places on top of the trap, one on each side.

"Great!" said the driver with a touch of bravado. "We're off to chance our luck. Bad luck—and we get blown to bits. Good luck —and I make a little extra." He cracked his whip, made a series of clicking sounds with his tongue, and the mules started up.

From his perch on top of the trap Bohe noticed the second mule and asked: "Where did you get that one from?"

"Oh, I managed to hire it. Costing me half a tael a day, it is, too! A single mule would have been done in by this load."

"How is it that when you were sent off to hire some mules for us, you told us there weren't any?" asked Bohe.

"In the case of draft mules, I'll be back this way again and can return them. But with riding mules, it's a different matter. Since there's no one to receive them at the other end, and since you won't be returning yourselves, how would the owners ever get them back?"

"But even if we hired some mules, we'd still be with you," said

Li Fu. "Surely you could have taken them back with you after we arrived in Tianjin?"

"I didn't think of that."

Li Fu gave a cynical laugh. "What do you mean, you didn't think of it? The point is that you wouldn't have been able to charge us double if we'd had our own mules."

The driver ignored the remark and concentrated on his driving.

From the top of the trap Bohe observed the dense traffic in both directions. Of course those leaving the capital are fleeing from danger, he thought. But surely the people coming in this direction aren't deliberately heading into danger! Where could he find someone to explain the situation? But although he scrutinized the passing traps for a long time, he found nobody he recognized and ended up asking the driver.

"The people coming in this direction—what are they trying to do?"

"Who knows?" said the driver. "Rumors are flying about all over the place. The people in the capital are fleeing to Tianjin, the people in Tianjin are fleeing to the capital. The truth is there's no peace to be had anywhere, in the capital or outside. One day when the Brothers take on the hairies in earnest, you and I won't care who wins or loses, just so long as they don't trample on us bystanders."

At noon they stopped at a village inn for a quick lunch. The inn was packed with people, every seat taken. Miss Bai and her daughter did not leave the trap, but Bohe went in and got himself something to eat. He also bought two wheatcakes, a dish of scrambled eggs, and a pot of tea, and had Li Fu deliver them to Miss Bai and Dihua in the trap. The driver unharnessed the mules and took them away to be fed. For himself he demanded a jug of wine, then rolled some scrambled eggs up in his wheatcakes and ate them along with the wine.

Bohe, who was the first to finish, stood waiting for the driver in the entranceway. By now even more traps had stopped at the inn. Although the road was a main thoroughfare and extremely wide, it was jammed with vehicles.

As Bohe watched, a trap stopped at the gate, and three older men got out and came in for lunch. No seats were available in the dining room, so they sat down at a dilapidated table outside. Taking them for merchants, Bohe approached and asked: "Excuse me, gentlemen, but have you just come from Tianjin? You're on your way to the capital, I take it?"

"We've come from Tianjin, but we're not heading for the capital. We're off to Bao'an to get out of harm's way," said one.

"Things still quiet in Tianjin, are they?"

"Don't talk to me about that! The place is a *shambles!* Yesterday the foreigners sent several hundred troops to the capital to protect the legations. The trains had stopped running, and they wanted to commandeer them to get the troops there, but Intendant Tang, assistant director of railways, was unwilling to give them up, and an argument developed. One of the foreigners picked up a rifle and threatened to shoot him, so Tang *had* to hand them over. I've heard that much of the track has been destroyed. I wonder if the troops have arrived yet?"

"We left days ago," said Bohe, "and weren't able to follow the railroad. We're anxious to get to Tianjin as soon as possible."

"I daresay you want to go south," said the old man. "As soon as you get to Tianjin, you should leave the city at once. In my opinion heavy fighting is going to break out in the next couple of days. The good thing is that the railroad track between Tianjin and Tanggu hasn't been cut. Once you get to Tanggu, you'll be able to breathe a little easier."

"What are those Brothers hoping to achieve?"

The old man shook his head. "They're just a bunch of children acting up, but I've no doubt they'll cause major bloodshed. Poor old Tianjin—it hasn't been sacked in all the centuries from the Ming dynasty down to the present, but I'm afraid it won't escape this time. . . ."

As they spoke, the driver finished his wine, harnessed up the mules, and wanted to get started. Bohe said good-bye to the men and climbed on top.

That day they made good progress and got beyond Langfang. Bohe felt bloated from the food he had eaten. He also found the trap's lurching uncomfortable while he was riding on top, so he got down and walked beside Li Fu. But before they had gone another mile, a crowd of people suddenly came surging toward them. There was no knowing how many there were, but they were all running for their lives and screaming at the top of their lungs: "Help! The hairies are coming!" Not only was Bohe unable to push his way through the crowd, he was forced to turn back the way he had come and run with them. He was utterly confused, and had no idea what was happening to him and no control over where he was taken. The surge of people from the rear was simply too strong; no matter how hard he tried to resist, he could never stand his ground, but was swept along for a distance of several miles, and not down the road he had come, either. He lost sight of both the trap and Li Fu. But if you are wondering what happened to him after he was separated from the others, you must turn to the next chapter.

~ 3 ~

Their journey halted in Eight Hundred Village,
The travelers fail to arrive in Bamboo Grove.

DRIVEN away from his companions by the mass of people sweeping down upon them, Bohe had lost sight of both the trap and Li Fu. What was behind the panic? he wondered, and tried asking some of the people who were fleeing with him, only to find them as much in the dark as he was; they had simply seen other people fleeing and fled themselves. After running pell-mell for some time, the crowd gradually dispersed.

Bohe retraced the way he had come, looking for the trap, but by the time he found his way to the place where they had been driven apart, it was dark and there was no sign of any traps on the road. By this hour they've probably stopped somewhere for the night, he thought. His only hope was to inquire at the nearby village inns, which he did, without success. By now he was extremely worried, but it was nighttime and there was nothing more he could do, so he put up at an inn himself and passed a restless night.

At first light he rose and went about asking for news of his companions. He called at several inns, at all of which the people disclaimed any knowledge. Perhaps they've gone on, he thought, and began slowly walking in a southerly direction, full of apprehension and uncertainty, indeed without an idea in his head. Even Li Fu had vanished without a trace. The few dozen taels that Bohe had strapped to his legs now felt heavier and bulkier than ever and made walking difficult. He plodded mechanically along, and whenever he came to a village he would go in and ask, invariably without success. On and on he went until he came to a place from which a tall building stood out in the distance. Approaching cautiously, he found a train halted beside the building, its locomotive belching smoke. Bohe's heart leapt with joy; perhaps they're already on board, he thought. He rushed ahead, cutting through a field to get to the train faster. But as he hurried along, his head down, he heard a shout from directly in front of him. Some way off stood a foreign soldier holding a rifle, while many other foreigners were at work on the tracks. In fact this was Luofa station, and the foreigners had commandeered the train to transport their troops to the capital. Arriving at this point, they had found a section of the railroad track destroyed by the Boxer bandits and were busy repairing it. Not knowing any of this, Bohe had come to see what was going on and also to ask for news of Dihua and her mother—only to be ordered to halt by the sentry on duty.

Bewildered, he stopped, and seeing him stop the sentry took aim and was about to fire. In a panic Bohe turned and fled. The sentry gave chase, but Bohe ran for his life and managed to get away. By this time he was even more alarmed, fearing that Miss Bai and Dihua might have been shot to death by foreign soldiers.

He stopped at an inn for lunch and also to ask for information. It was now well past noon, and lunchtime was over, so there were very few patrons. Bohe asked the boy, who glibly replied: "Around noon today a trap did come by with two women in it, and they stopped here for lunch. They said they were in a hurry to get to Tianjin."

Bohe accepted the news at face value. "We got separated yesterday, and I need to hire a trap to take me to Tianjin," he said. "Is there anywhere I can hire one?"

"We don't have any traps in a small place like this. But even if we had a couple of stables, what with the number of people coming through these last few days, all the traps would long since have been rented out. You need to go a few miles up the road to Yang Village, where you'll find plenty of traps as well as mules."

After eating a couple of wheatcakes, Bohe set off. He walked until evening without reaching Yang Village, but found an inn in a small hamlet and stayed the night. Next morning he hurried on to Yang Village, where he arrived about noon. After a quick lunch, he hired a mule and whipping it into a canter raced off to Xigu, which he reached at sunset. In Xigu there was a livery stables to receive the mule, and he stayed there the night.

At dawn he walked across Red Bridge[5] and hired a rickshaw to rush him to the Bamboo Grove district, where he headed for the Fozhaolou to ask for information.

The Fozhaolou, which had been founded by Cantonese, was an exceptionally spacious inn. All the rich merchants and high officials stayed there when passing through Tianjin. Cantonese travelers, needless to say, would not have dreamt of staying anywhere else, which was why Bohe went directly there to ask for news. Turning in at the main gate, he inquired at the office: Had two women of such-and-such a description been in? The manager consulted his guest book. "No," he replied.

Bohe's heart sank; he was at a complete loss as to what to do. Trusting the boy at the inn, he had leapt to the conclusion that the two women must be Miss Bai and Dihua, in which case they would be in Tianjin by now, and he had been counting on seeing them as soon as he arrived. Unfortunately the boy had simply said the first thing that popped into his head, and Bohe had believed him and drawn a blank. Dejectedly he made the rounds of the smaller inns in the Bamboo Grove district without finding any trace of his companions.

The only thing to do was to go back and stay the night at the Fozhaolou. His thoughts ran along these lines: This is the place where all the Cantonese congregate. Perhaps the women will come by, and if I'm staying here we're more likely to meet. Unfortunately the manager of the Fozhaolou, noticing that Bohe had brought no luggage with him, refused to let him in. He had to relate the whole story of how he had fled the capital and been parted from his companions, and even so, it was only when he mentioned Zhang Heting, whom the manager knew, that he was allowed to stay. He took out some money and hastily bought himself some bedding, then settled in at the Fozhaolou, where he lived in hopes of seeing his companions. Whenever he heard a

5. Here and in Chapter 6 the text has Rainbow Bridge, presumably a mistake for the (Great) Red Bridge in Tianjin. ("Rainbow" and "red" are both pronounced *hong*.)

trap arriving at the gate, he would hurry out to look, and when he found that the newcomers were not Miss Bai and her daughter, he would be crushed.

But although Bohe waited anxiously for them at the Fozhaolou, Miss Bai and her daughter had never even set off for Tianjin. When the mob crashed into them, horses and traps had been sent flying in all directions, and some traps had overturned. Although their trap was not one of the latter, the extra mule hired by their driver proved to be infernally stubborn. Now, two-mule traps in the north are not like the foreign-style two-horse traps you find in Shanghai. They have only one mule between the shafts, the other being attached by a long rope to the trap itself; the two mules are not abreast but in line, one behind the other. Naturally the driver had put his own mule between the shafts and let the hired one go in front attached by a rope. When the mob crashed into them, the lead mule was knocked sideways. They had been heading south, but this animal now faced west, and its stubborn nature asserted itself. It bolted westward, and the trap wheeled and followed it. The other mule, dragged along behind, was also forced into a gallop. Jolted from his perch on top, the driver scrambled to his feet and gave chase, but it was too late. He raced frantically after the trap, shouting "Whoa! Whoa! Whoa!" over and over. Now, mules in the north do obey commands. Normally a driver has only to give one shout of "Whoa!" for a mule to come to a complete stop. But on this occasion the mule had bolted, and a thousand shouts would have made no difference.

The women were terrified when they saw such a vast crowd swarming in their direction—and even more terrified when the mule bolted and threw their driver to the ground. To make matters worse, the road was full of potholes, and the trap lurched and careened sickeningly as it raced along. Miss Bai lost her senses altogether and fainted, and Dihua seized her in her arms and began screaming for help. Finally, after bolting for miles, the mule came near a village where a man stepped into its path, grabbed its bridle, and brought it to a stop, still kicking wildly. Inside the trap Dihua was crying and screaming at her mother to wake up.

After some time the driver, puffing and panting, caught up with them and thanked the villager who had stopped the trap. Cradling her mother in one arm, Dihua pulled the curtain aside with the other.

"Hurry up and get us some boiled water!" she called out to the driver. "Someone's fainted in here, and I need it urgently to bring her around!"

"Where am I going to get any water in a place like this?" asked the driver.

"What! Someone fainted?" put in the villager. "Hurry up and pull the trap over to the village entrance. I'll see you get your boiled water." He dashed off.

The driver led his mule slowly over to the entrance. The whole village, young and old, male and female, hearing that someone riding in a trap had fainted, turned out and surrounded them to gawk and ask questions.

At this point Miss Bai's eyelids fluttered, as if she were coming to. Fortunately at that very moment the villager returned with the boiled water. Dihua thanked him, then dribbled the water slowly into her mother's mouth. Miss Bai came to her senses, opened her eyes slightly, and exclaimed: "Scared to *death,* I was!"

Outside the people began crying: "She's all right! She's all right! She's come to!"

Dihua realized that because of her mother's condition it would now be virtually impossible to travel. "What's the name of this village?" she asked. "Do you have an inn here? It's getting late and, if there is one, we'll stay the night."

"This village of ours is known as Eight Hundred," said the villager. "If you go farther west, you come to Nine Hundred, while Six Hundred is on your way south and Seven Hundred is on your way north. It's not a main road that we're on, and if you're looking for a large inn, you won't find it here. But if you don't mind a small inn, well, I happen to own one myself."

"It doesn't matter if it's small," said Dihua. The man then led the trap into the village and up to the gate of his inn. Dihua assisted her mother out, while he helped the driver take down the luggage and carry it to their room.

Miss Bai felt weak and unsteady on her feet. Her mind was confused and her breathing faint. Dihua helped her sit on the edge of

the bed, then quickly opened up the bedclothes and supported
her as she lay down.

"My dear child, do get some rest! You've done *so* much for me!
But tell me, aren't you suffering from shock yourself?"

"No, not at all. Don't worry yourself, Mother."

"What happened to Bohe?"

Dihua had suffered the initial shock of the mob's crashing into
them, then the shock of the mule's bolting, and finally the shock
of seeing her mother faint, this last being the worst of all, and in
suffering all these shocks she had forgotten about Bohe. Now, at
her mother's mention of him, she let out an involuntary *"Aiya!"*
and then, almost before the sound had escaped her lips, blushed
and choked back whatever she was about to say.

"What's the matter?" her mother asked.

"He's not here yet," murmured Dihua.

Forgetting her delicate state, Miss Bai at once sat up in bed. "I
expect he got separated from us," she said. "How dreadful! Send
someone out in search of him at once!"

"Mother, you've just had a severe shock. You must see you get
some rest and take good care of yourself. He . . ." At this point
Dihua broke off and her cheeks flushed crimson.

Miss Bai called repeatedly for Li Fu. "I've not seen Li Fu either,"
said Dihua. "I expect he got driven away, too. But he was still
there beside us when our trap was knocked sideways, and I feel
sure he saw what happened to us. Perhaps he'll find his way
here."

"If we've lost those two, we're in serious trouble. Go and find
them at once!" said Miss Bai, ordering the driver out to search.

"When that mob of people came along," said the driver, "they
were swept off to the north. It's a good ten miles from here to the
road we were traveling on, and you'd have to go still farther north
from there. What's more, I don't know exactly where they are, so
how am I ever going to find them? It's getting dark, too."

Dihua thought for a moment: "I'll give you half a tael for your
trouble. If you find them, you'll get a generous reward." She took
out some loose silver amounting to about half a tael and placed it
on the table.

The driver picked up the silver and weighed it in his hand. "All right, then, I'll go and look for them." As he left, Miss Bai sank back on the bed.

Dihua's heart was in turmoil as she wondered what had happened to Bohe. If he saw our trap, he should be able to find us, she thought. But where was he carried off to in that crush of people? He's a frail young student who's never experienced any real hardship in his life. What effect will this have on him? Someone who has just recovered from an illness mustn't be subjected to further shock. Suddenly it occurred to her that, having so recently recovered, he would have no strength left and, if he were forced to the ground in that crush of people, would surely be trampled to death. At this thought her heart broke, and tears trickled down her cheeks, but for fear her mother would notice she turned away and wept in silence. Then she began blaming Bohe for not riding on top of the trap; if he had stayed up there, he'd be with her now. Their driver fell off, it is true, but at least he had known where to come. Hadn't he eventually tracked them down?

Then it occurred to her that it was all her fault, for being so concerned about proper behavior that she had refused even to speak to Bohe. He's an extremely sensitive person, and when he saw me so concerned, naturally he didn't want to come near me. If only I'd been willing to talk to him, he'd have been happy to join me, and none of this would have occurred. Oh, Cousin Bohe, I'm the one who harmed you! If anything dreadful does happen to you, what am I going to do? If you come back to us, I won't ever try to avoid you again. At least we're properly engaged "by the command of our parents and through the good offices of a go-between!"[6]

As these chaotic thoughts were running through her head, the innkeeper appeared at their door. "Would you ladies care for any supper?" he asked.

Dihua turned and looked at her mother, who was asleep. "Yes, please bring us some when it's ready," she said.

"We don't have a set meal here," he explained. "If you want any supper, just give me the money and I'll buy you some noodles."

6. See *Stones in the Sea*, note 3.

Dihua took out seventy or eighty copper cash and handed them to him.

Then she turned and looked at her mother again. Although Miss Bai was asleep, she had a raging fever and her cheeks were a bright crimson. Dihua became nervous. She shook out a lined quilt and placed it gently over them both, then watched by her side.

It was getting dark, and the innkeeper brought in a kerosene lamp and set it down on the table. It's dark, thought Dihua. I wonder where Bohe has been carried off to in that crush of people. Where will he sleep tonight? I hope he hasn't lost the money he had on him, because without it he'll be in trouble. Then it occurred to her again that he was just a frail young student, and she hoped he wouldn't get into trouble on *account* of the money. That was the main concern in a time of such chaos, and at the very thought she felt wave after wave of sweat breaking over her.

Suddenly she heard her mother screaming: "Help, nephew! Help!" She was still screaming as she awoke.

"What is it, Mother?" said Dihua, bending over her.

Miss Bai opened her eyes. "What's the time?" she asked.

"It's only just become dark."

"Do I have a fever?"

"An awful fever. Would you like some tea?"

"Just a sip."

Dihua took out some tea and put it in the pot, then went to the door and asked the innkeeper for some boiling water.

"It's not boiling yet," said the innkeeper. "Won't be long, though. Would you like wheatcakes or soup with your supper?"

Dihua turned and asked Miss Bai. "I won't have any supper," she said. "Ask him for whatever you want."

"We won't have anything," Dihua said to the innkeeper. "Keep it for tomorrow."

The innkeeper took the teapot away with him, and Dihua went back and sat on the edge of the bed.

"Were you having a nightmare, Mother?"

"Yes. How did you know?"

"You cried out in the middle of it."

"What did I say?"

"You cried . . . you cried . . . 'Help, nephew! Help!' and woke yourself up."

"Fancy my doing that! I dreamt that that crowd we met earlier in the day came swarming in here, Bohe among them. Then a man burst in with a sword and began slashing at me. I cried out and woke up. . . ."

As she spoke, the innkeeper came in with the tea. Dihua poured out a cup and handed it to her mother, who drank it. "I have a headache and also a dizzy feeling. What am I going to do?"

"Try and get some rest, Mother. Don't upset yourself."

"Just now I saw you hiding your tears from me, and *I* felt sick at heart, too. Bohe may be my future son-in-law, but he's somebody else's son. If he's merely lost and we meet up again in a few days' time, all well and good. But if anything *has* happened to him, I shall never be able to face his parents!"

This remark stirred Dihua's own secret concerns, and tears began streaming down her cheeks despite all her efforts to control them.

"Child, stop being so miserable *this minute!* If you're going to carry on like this, you'll make me even more wretched than I am already. . . ."

As she spoke, someone burst into their room. But if you wish to know who it was, you must turn to the next chapter.

~ 4 ~

In a primitive tavern she prepares medicine
for her mother,

And along the highways she puts up notices to
find her fiancé.

Miss Bai and Dihua were just consoling each other when someone burst into the room—their driver. "Well, did you find them?"
asked Miss Bai.

The driver's face was flushed with drink, and he held a long-
stemmed pipe in one hand. His entrance made the whole room
reek of garlic. "I've looked high and low," he said, slurring his
speech. "I don't know *how* many people got lost in that ruckus
today. I asked at all the stables, and they told me they couldn't
count the number of people who'd been in looking for relatives,
so many they hadn't had time to ask their names. I've just about
run my legs off, and I haven't found a trace of them!"

"Go and get some rest," said Dihua.

"What are we to do, Mother?" asked Dihua, when the driver had
gone. "Let's not worry ourselves about what happens later on.
Right now, without a man to escort us, we'll find it next to impossible to travel. And your health—that's another concern."

"Just now I can't think what to suggest," said Miss Bai. "All I
know is that I feel faint and have a headache and palpitations as
well as a high fever. Do you think you could get them to make me
some medicinal tea?"

Dihua brought out the medicine and went to the door to call
the innkeeper, but everyone was asleep, and although she called
several times, there was no response. She took out her watch—

only nine o'clock. She would have gone and made up the medicine herself, but it was pitch dark outside. As she was dimly wondering what to do, her mother said: "Don't bother, if they're all asleep."

"They *are* asleep, but I'll see to it," said Dihua.

Her mother, who was in considerable pain, was so anxious to recover and continue their journey that she let Dihua go ahead.

Lighting a paper spill, Dihua went out to the entrance hall and looked around her. On the wall she found a kerosene lamp, which she lit. Against the wall on the west side she saw a square table piled higgledy-piggledy with chopsticks, bowls, and the like, while at the foot of the eastern wall was a ground stove, near which the floor was littered with leaves, twigs, and sorghum stalks. An iron pot stood on the stove, and beside it an earthenware jar. Dihua picked up the jar, which was empty and had no lid. She blew on the paper spill until it flared up, then went into the courtyard and looked around, but saw nothing but two mules that were tethered there. In the back court, however, she found a small crock covered with a tattered straw hat and, on picking up the hat, was delighted to see that the crock was half full of water. She went in again and fetched a bowl from the table, washed it, and used it to scoop up some water, which she tipped into the jar. There was no brazier in sight, but after a long search she found one under a pile of leaves. The jar had no lid either, so she covered it with a bowl. After scraping up a handful of twigs and leaves, she lit a fire, and before long the water came to the boil. She took off the bowl and, finding the water still perfectly clear, realized that she had forgotten to add the medicine and rushed back to the room to get it. After the mixture had simmered awhile and was more or less ready, she ladled out a bowl of it, put out the fire, turned off the lamp on the wall, and brought the medicine back to their room.

By this time her mother had fallen asleep again, but Dihua gently shook her awake: "Mother, sit up and take your medicine!"

With a great start her mother awoke from her dream. "What are you doing?"

"Don't be alarmed, Mother. It's only me."

"I fell asleep and had the craziest dream—awfully scary."

"That comes from the shock you suffered yesterday. You need complete rest now in order to get better. Your medicine's ready. Would you like to take it now?" She held out the bowl, and her mother sat up, took a few sips, and sank back again. Dihua fetched the bedclothes and covered her up, then sat beside her. After a spell of delirium her mother drifted off to sleep again.

With only the lamp for company, Dihua fell prey to a thousand cares. She wondered where Bohe was at that moment. Was he safe? If only she had someone who could take a message to him! How deeply she now regretted their mistake in leaving the capital! If they had stayed there together, they could have helped each other through this crisis, and perhaps they would not have had to part at all. She thought also of her father in Shanghai, totally unaware of the trouble she and her mother were in, and her heart began to pound. If Bohe was safe and managed to get to Shanghai, he would certainly seek out her father, and when her father learned that they had been driven apart, how anxious he would be! Oh, if only Bohe *could* reach Shanghai safely, a day or two of anxiety on her father's part would hardly matter. The essential thing was that they all get to Shanghai, for her father's anxiety would vanish as soon as they arrived. Perhaps they should send him a telegram from Tianjin to set his mind at rest. Suddenly it dawned on her that by telegraphing her father from Tianjin they could find out whether Bohe had reached Shanghai, and she was all for setting off at once in the middle of the night. Unfortunately her mother was too ill to travel, and it was unlikely they could leave the next day either. How long would it take her to get better? The sooner she did, the sooner they could learn about Bohe. But then Dihua realized that even if Bohe had set off for Shanghai, he might still be on board ship when they got to Tianjin, and so a telegram would be useless. She made a moue of disappointment. Then suddenly her thoughts became a blur, and she stopped thinking altogether and just sat beside the tiny flame of the dying lamp and stared into space.

Hearing her mother mumbling in her sleep, she bent over and felt her brow. It was covered in sweat, which she quickly wiped off with her handkerchief. Her mother awoke, mumbling over and over: "Child, I feel simply awful—so dizzy I seem to be floating on air. My body's as light as a feather, but my head's so heavy I can't seem to lift it. What am I going to do?"

"Have you perspired, Mother?"

"Yes, all over."

Dihua reached out and wiped her dry. Strangely enough, although her mother had sweated a great deal, her fever had not subsided; in fact it felt even worse, and Dihua was alarmed. Her mother asked for another dose of medicine.

"I don't think you ought to take any more," said Dihua. "After you perspired so heavily, any fever you had should have gone down. Why are you still running such a high temperature? I'm just afraid this may not be the right medicine for you."

Her mother said nothing. Dihua sat cross-legged beside her, lonelier than ever. She heard a sudden gust of wind flinging raindrops against the paper window and was overwhelmed with grief and longing. That night passed as slowly as a year. Her mother slept and awoke, awoke and slept, sweating continuously, and whenever she awoke, Dihua would wipe her down. This went on until dawn, and still Dihua had had no sleep. Her mother's illness seemed to have grown worse, and she mumbled continuously.

If Mother's illness is as bad as this, we obviously can't travel, thought Dihua. The trap is costing us fourteen taels a day, which we simply cannot afford. It's a good thing the driver was paid up through yesterday, because now we'll have to let him go. In a few days' time, when Mother's better again, we'll think about what to do next.

As soon as it was light, she told the driver of her decision. "You'd better go back now. We won't be able to travel for some time to come."

"But we had an agreement to go to Tianjin! How can you send me off when we're only halfway there?"

"We have an invalid to consider, and I don't know when she'll be well enough to travel. We can't afford your fourteen taels a day."

"If we were to set off now, it would take us only a day and a half to get to Tianjin. If you're going to send me away, you should at least pay me for that day and a half."

Revolting man, thought Dihua, just trying to cheat us. She

noticed that the innkeeper and a few other men whom she didn't recognize were standing at the entrance to the inn looking on. The extra few taels weren't of any great significance, but it wouldn't do to give wicked people any ideas by showing her money in public, so she told a lie.

"That's not the point," she said. "The trouble is that the money and bank drafts we brought are all with Master Chen. Now that he is lost, how am I going to pay you? If he were here with us, we'd have all that money he has on him and wouldn't be letting you go."

The driver digested this argument. "Even if you don't have the fare, you should at least give me a tip," he said.

Dihua took out a piece of silver weighing about a quarter of an ounce and handed it to him. He took it, harnessed up his empty trap, and drove off.

"Do you know of a good doctor around here?" Dihua asked the innkeeper.

"We don't have any doctors, but the manager of the village herbalist's shop is able to treat people. He doesn't have to take your pulse either; all he needs to know is what's wrong with you. You buy the herbs he tells you to buy, and you're right as rain."

"But is he reliable?"

"How could he cure people if he wasn't? All of us in Eight Hundred go to him when we're sick."

Dihua told the innkeeper how her mother had fallen ill from the shock, how she felt dizzy and was running a fever, and how she had taken some medicinal tea and broken into a sweat, but that her fever had not subsided, in fact it had grown worse. However, no sooner had she asked him to get her some medicine than she began worrying that he might forget the symptoms, so she fetched brush and ink and wrote them down for him. Having neglected her studies from the age of twelve, she now wrote slowly and laboriously. She couldn't be sure there weren't some mistakes in what she had written, and she was afraid people might laugh at her, but because it was crucial to get the symptoms right, she put a bold face on it and handed him the list anyway. The innkeeper, marveling at the fact that a young woman could write at all, took the sheet of paper and went off with it.

His wife, who had regarded Miss Bai and Dihua only as transient guests who would stay a single night and then move on, had paid them scant attention. But when she heard that Dihua knew how to write, she came along and praised her to the skies. "There are very few *men* in villages like ours who can read and write," she remarked, and went on to ask after Dihua's mother: "And how is madam's illness? Holy Name! What a pity it is that gentlefolk like you, who in ordinary times would hardly ever leave your houses, should run up against this sort of thing! It's no wonder she was affected by the shock!"

Dihua, who had a friendly nature, began chatting with her. Who knows, it might relieve her depression and rid her of her foolish fears. After they had been chatting a while, the innkeeper returned with the medicine. "I forgot to take any money," he said. "I got this on credit."

"How much did it come to?" asked Dihua.

"Five hundred cash."

Dihua opened the package and looked inside. The two ingredients she recognized were China root and lilyturf; the rest were unfamiliar.

"My, medicine *is* expensive here, isn't it? How did this come to five hundred?" she asked.

The innkeeper laughed. "You're from the city, miss, and don't know our country ways. In these parts a string is only a hundred and forty cash, so five hundred works out at seventy."

Satisfied, Dihua counted out seventy cash and gave them to him. She was about to go off and heat up the medicine, when the innkeeper's wife told her husband to do it for her. She wanted to go on chatting with Dihua, who now felt obliged to address her as "sister."

"Oh, no!" protested the innkeeper's wife. "My childhood name was Fivey, and that's what all my friends and neighbors call me. Please call me Fivey, too, miss!"

Dihua laughed and asked her what her surname was.

"My husband's surname is Zhang, and he's known as Fiver. My maiden name is Li, and I joined the family as a child wife, so we got into the habit of calling each other Fiver and Fivey."

This led Dihua to reflect that, villager though Fivey was, as a child wife she had never had to part from her husband. How happy they must have been! If *we* had never known each other, all well and good, she thought. Our trouble is that we lived and studied together as children, and whenever I think back on the affection we felt for each other in those days, I'm filled with longing. Moreover, while traveling with him on this journey I received countless kindnesses from him and felt ever so grateful, although I was far too embarrassed to say so. And then we had the bad luck to be driven apart, which fills me with longing even more. At this stage in her thoughts, her mind began to wander, and although Fivey launched into a long disquisition, Dihua heard none of it.

After some time Fiver brought in a bowl of medicine. With Dihua's help her mother drank it, then sank back on the bed.

Fivey asked Dihua what she would like for breakfast.

"I really couldn't eat a thing," she said. "I won't have any, thanks."

"I heard you had nothing to eat last night. If you don't eat anything today either, won't you *starve?* Let me make you a bowl of clear noodle soup. Madam's an invalid and can't take regular food, but we do have some millet in the house, and I'll make her a bowl of millet gruel." She was soon back with a bowl of noodle soup. Dihua thanked her and, after putting the bowl down, Fivey left. Dihua went over to the table and sat down, then picked up the chopsticks and began stirring the soup. She saw that the noodles were atrociously black, and took just one sip of the soup.

Fivey brought in a second bowl. "If you've lost your appetite, miss, try adding a little vinegar."

"It's very kind of you, but I really can't eat a thing." She accepted the bowl and added a little vinegar, took one more sip, forced herself to eat a couple of noodles, and stopped.

Before long Fivey was back again with the bowl of millet gruel. On seeing Dihua's mother lying there delirious, she whispered to Dihua: "It's hot. Let it cool down a bit first." Dihua nodded.

Fivey noticed that she hadn't touched the soup. "Can't you *really* eat anything, miss? Don't go starving yourself, now!"

"I can't eat, I simply can't."

Fivey took the soup and bread away and brought in a second

bowl of millet gruel. "If you can't eat that, miss, try a little gruel instead."

Dihua really *was* hungry; she was merely unable to ingest any food because of the strain she was under. However, on seeing how attentive Fivey was, she forced herself to eat something. The millet contained a good deal of grit, which grated unpleasantly between her teeth, and the only way she could get it down was to take a mouthful and swallow it in a single gulp.

Just as she was eating the last of the gruel, her mother awoke. Dihua took her the other bowl and helped her as she ate it. When she had finished, Fivey asked: "Would you like some more?"

"It's most kind of you, but no thanks," said Miss Bai. Fivey took the dishes out again.

"I've been lying down so long my joints are starting to ache," said Miss Bai. "Help me up, would you?" Dihua helped her sit up, then fetched Bohe's bedding, placed it beside her, and told her to lean back. But the mere act of moving the bedding had awakened thoughts of her own secret concerns, and she felt a sudden stab of grief and began crying again.

Her mother knew perfectly well what was troubling her daughter, but because she shared the same concerns, she could find no words to comfort her with.

Suddenly Dihua had an idea. "Mother! He . . ." she said, then abruptly stopped.

"My dear child! If there's something you want to say, say it. We're mother and daughter, and we're alone here, so there's nothing you can't tell me."

"It occurs to me that after being driven away yesterday he will certainly be looking for us. Why don't we write out a notice to say that we're waiting for him at this inn and post it up outside. When he sees it, he'll be able to find his way here."

"What a good idea! Start writing it out at once. You ought to make a few extra copies, too, and stick them up along the highway and in the entrances to livery stables and inns."

Dihua hastily got out the writing materials and, sitting at the table, began to write:

Mr. Chen Bohe—Some people at . . .

Suddenly she stopped writing and went to look for Fivey. "Does this inn have a name?" she asked.

"It was started by Fiver's grandfather and is called the Zhang Inn. It's well known in all the villages around here. But why do you want to know, miss?"

"Just asking," said Dihua. She went back to the room and continued writing:

the Zhang Inn in Eight Hundred Village are expecting you.
Hope you come soon. Anxiously awaiting you!

She read over the two dozen words. Although it wasn't neatly written, the notice was at least legible, and she copied and re-copied it until she had over twenty sheets in all. Fivey noticed them as she came in.

"What are you writing all those characters for?"

"I would like to ask your husband to do me a favor. Would he be so kind as to take these to the place where we were driven apart yesterday and post them up, so that the person who got lost will see them and know where to come?"

"Of course. But I never asked you who it was that got lost?"

Dihua blushed and could not reply. From the bed Miss Bai quickly answered for her: "Oh, a relative of ours who accompanied us out of the capital."

Fivey called Fiver in and told him to put up the notices. After Dihua had given him specific instructions to post them in prominent places along the highway as well as in the entrances to livery stables and inns, he left on his mission.

It was early afternoon when he left, and by evening he had not returned. Suddenly a party of five or six men men appeared at the door asking to stay the night, and Fivey welcomed them in.

"But what are *we* going to do?" asked Dihua. "We can't possibly be in the same room with *them!*"

"Don't worry about it! You'll move into our room," said Fivey, as she began carrying their bedding and luggage into the room opposite. Dihua helped her mother over, after which Fivey showed the men into the guest room.

Dihua steadied her mother as she sat down on the platform bed. There was a low table in the middle of it, but no other table in the room, just a couple of bamboo chairs. The walls were plastered with brightly colored pictures, each illustrating a scene from plays such as *Fourth Son Visits His Mother* and *Selling the Rouge.* . . . [7] Then suddenly beside the pictures Dihua saw a notice that gave her quite a start. But if you wish to know what it was, you will have to turn to the next chapter.

7. Two popular local operas. The first is historical adventure with a strong filial piety theme. The second is a romantic comedy set in a cosmetics shop.

~ 5 ~

An ominous dream gives rise to a lingering sorrow,

And opened bedclothes bring joy to a loving heart.

DIHUA had taken her mother into their new room and helped her sit down when suddenly she noticed a sheet of paper on the wall beside the brightly colored pictures—the very sheet that she herself had written out to describe her mother's symptoms. Privately she was rather impressed, although she could not imagine why it was there.

After her mother had rested awhile, Fivey came in with a lamp.

"While we're in your room, where are you two going to sleep?" Dihua asked.

"Don't worry about it. I'll join you in here, and we'll let Fiver sleep in the guest room."

"But won't your guests mind?"

"Miss, I can see you're not very familiar with our country ways. Our guest room often sleeps seventeen or eighteen people all squeezed in together on the platform bed. When we have more people than that, we put them in here as well, and I make up a bed for myself at the back of the inn. Fiver's in with the other guests on *those* occasions, isn't he? It happens all the time. Don't give it a second thought."

By this time Dihua's mother had grown tired and lay down again.

Fivey heated some water and invited her new guests to wash, then prepared a meal for them. Before long she brought over two bowls of millet gruel and a small dish of pickled vegetables. Dihua could not help feeling a certain embarrassment at the amount of attention they were receiving. She helped her mother eat a bowl of gruel and forced herself to eat some, too.

Then Fiver came in. "Well, I've put up all the notices," he said. "You wouldn't *believe* the excitement out there! A whole crowd of Boxers have come in, and they all say they're heading for Tianjin to kill the hairies. I've been out there watching them all this time."

Dihua grew worried again; mention of the Boxers had set her wondering about Bohe. Who knew what problems he might face if he met up with them?

After some time all was quiet at the inn.

"That medicine I took today really did me some good," said her mother. "I'm feeling a lot better. My dizziness has cleared up, and that floating feeling has gone, too. The only things still troubling me are my headache and my fever, but tomorrow I'll get some more medicine, and I expect I'll soon be well again."

Dihua was relieved. Having sat up the whole of the previous night, she now felt tired and lay down beside her mother. All her thoughts and desires, however, were still concentrated on Bohe. She wondered where he was sleeping that night, whether in all the chaos he had met with any violence, whether he had arrived safely in Tianjin—an endless list of worries that made her feel happy and sad by turns.

Then just as she was drifting off to sleep, she heard Fivey's voice saying: "Congratulations, miss! Your Master Chen is here!"

Dihua sat up at once. "Where?"

"Outside. He's just arrived. Let me take you to him."

Dihua got up and went outside with Fivey. She found a wide highway along which the horses and vehicles of the refugees were passing in an endless procession, but Bohe was nowhere to be seen. As she strained her eyes to find him, Fivey pointed up ahead. "Look over there, miss! Isn't that him?"

Dihua looked in the direction indicated and, sure enough, there was Bohe sitting astride a trap, a broad smile on his face as he came toward her. She wondered who could be inside the carriage, since Bohe was still on top. She turned and looked again: the driver was the same one they had hired as they left the capital, the same one she had dismissed that morning.

Privately she was glad. "So *he* was the one who found him for us!"

"Cousin Bohe!" she shouted, and then shouted again, but they continued to pass her by. Bohe acted as if he hadn't heard her, the driver urged on his mule, and the trap proceeded on its way south.

Dihua was crushed. He must be blaming me for avoiding his company and refusing to talk to him, she thought, and *that's* why he's upset with me. Then she felt embarrassed that she had shouted at him and was dabbing at her tears with a handkerchief when she heard a voice close beside her saying: "How cruel you were, cousin! Always ignoring me!"

She looked around. Fivey was nowhere to be seen; it was Bohe who was standing beside her. Her grief turned to joy again, and she was just about to say something, when a mule in one of the passing traps suddenly came up to her and began to bray, giving her quite a start. She turned and looked again—and this time found nothing but darkness. Bohe had vanished, but the mule was still there, braying as loudly as ever. She forced her mind to concentrate: she was still lying on the platform bed, that much was clear, and the lamp on the table had gone out. The mules of the other guests had been tied up in the courtyard and it was they who were braying. It had all been a dream.

On going over the dream in her mind, however, she began to wonder why Bohe had ignored her. It probably comes of all the anxiety I felt during the day, she thought. But suddenly she recalled seeing the driver in her dream. And she also recalled how she had told the driver, in dismissing him, that the money and bank drafts were all in Bohe's possession. I only hope he didn't remember that and then run across Bohe and murder him for the money! In a time of such chaos, law and order has completely broken down. If that happened, *I* would be the one responsible for his death! My longing for him, my dreaming of him—that's commonplace enough, but *why* did I dream of the driver? The more she thought, the more likely her fears seemed, until she felt racked by pain, wave after wave of cold sweat broke over her, and despite herself she burst out sobbing. If he loses his life over this, she thought, even if I follow him beyond the grave, I shall never be able to face him. Oh, what am I to do? The more she thought, the worse she felt, and the worse she felt, the more she cried, until the sound of her crying awoke her mother.

"Child, why are you crying?"

Dihua choked on her reply and went on sobbing.

Her mother gave a sigh. "Don't distress yourself, dear! Everything that happens to us is foreordained. I only hope Heaven does help the good man,[8] and that Bohe is safe and sound. That would be a great blessing for both our families." She stopped abruptly.

Her advice only distressed Dihua all the more, and she almost broke down and wailed. Her mother couldn't help sobbing, either, at which point Dihua at once regained her self-control. "Mother, I'm afraid your joints must be sore from all that lying down. Let me get up and give you a massage."

"I'm not sore, and I don't want a massage. Go to sleep!"

"I won't be able to sleep anyway." Dihua sat up and, groping her way over to her mother in the darkness, began gently pummeling her legs.

"What time is it?" Miss Bai asked.

"A moment ago I heard the fourth watch sounding a long way off, but I don't imagine they keep the hours too accurately in a village like this. The lamp's gone out, and I can't see my watch, so I don't know what time it is."

After she had been pummeled for a little while, her mother fell asleep again. Dihua didn't dare sob, but wept silently for fear of awakening her. Crouched over the little table, she heard the random crowing of the village roosters, and before long it was dawn.

Fivey, who was sleeping on the other side of the bed-table, awoke and, at sight of Dihua sitting up and staring into space, remarked: "You're up early, miss."

"I couldn't sleep, so at midnight I got up."

Fivey turned over on her side and looked sharply at her. "Miss, what've you been crying about? Your eyes are all red and swollen!"

"I haven't been crying about anything."

8. An ancient proverb.

Fivey sighed. "It's always hard being away from home."

She got up and went off to see to the water for washing. That day she sent Fiver out for more medicine, which Miss Bai duly took.

Only if a novelist has a lot to say will his story be a long one. To cut matters short, Miss Bai followed the same treatment for ten days, but her illness got neither better nor worse, and she continued to run a fever. We need hardly mention that Dihua found no peace of mind either, what with longing for her fiancé and worrying about her mother.

On the morning of the tenth day, however, someone came into the inn and asked: "Is this the Zhang Inn?" When Fiver said yes, it was, the newcomer continued: "Do you have a Mrs. and a Miss Zhang staying here?"

Dihua overheard the question. "Who is it?" she asked at once, starting out the door. It was Li Fu, who came forward and bowed to her. Dihua felt an inexpressible delight—as if she had been reunited with a member of her own family. Forgetting there was such a thing as decorum, she immediately asked: "The young master? Is he with you? Is he all right?"

"I couldn't find the young master, so . . ." Li Fu began.

At these words Dihua felt as if she had been deluged with icy water. The immensity of her joy shrank until it vanished altogether, to be replaced by a mere burden of grief, and she withdrew into the room. Li Fu came to the door and bowed to Miss Bai. "Ever since we were driven apart, I've been looking for the trap and the young master. I thought you'd probably gone on to Tianjin, so I hired a mule and headed there myself. I rode on and on until I came near the railroad track, where I found a number of foreign soldiers doing something or other that I couldn't quite make out. When I merely glanced in their direction, a soldier fired at me, grazing my shoulder, so I ran back and stayed at an inn to give the wound a chance to heal. I've only just recovered. According to the rumors flying about the situation is awfully tense. I don't know *how* many Boxers are supposed to be advancing on Tianjin every day. I was just going out to see, when I came upon a notice at the entrance to the inn that said someone was waiting for the young master here. I thought it had to be you, ma'am, so I made my way here to find you. It's sheer chaos at present. Many people are fleeing here from Tianjin—it's out of the question to go *there!* I'm told Shandong is the only safe place these days. Ma'am, we must set off as soon as we possibly can. We won't find any peace and quiet here, I'm afraid."

"You're right there," said Fiver, who had been standing beside Li Fu as he spoke. "Both of our neighboring villages, Seven Hundred and Nine Hundred, have invited the Brothers in and set up altars and begun doing their exercises. We've even had them here the last day or two."

Dihua was depressed and frightened by this piece of news. "Did you manage to find out where the young master went?" Miss Bai asked.

"I think he must have gone on to Tianjin, and if he made it that far, he'll be in Shanghai by now. Ma'am, it's vital that we set off as soon as possible!"

"But the mistress is sick. How can she possibly travel?" asked Dihua.

"May I ask what it is you are suffering from, ma'am?" asked Li Fu. "You won't feel any ill effects if you travel by boat. Right now it's only the waterways that are more or less safe. If we go by road again, we'll run into the same sort of trouble we had last time."

"Very well, then. Go and hire us a boat," said Miss Bai. "I couldn't stand another shock like that last one. Let's set off as soon as we can."

In tears, Dihua protested. "But he hasn't come yet. How can we leave?"

Her mother tried to reassure her. "After reaching Tianjin, he'll naturally have gone on to Shanghai. What's the point of waiting here for him? Besides, I have an idea. Fivey and her husband are good souls, both of them, and all we need do is ask them, if he should come, to tell him that we've gone on to Shandong and that he should join us there. Once we're in Shandong, we'll write out more notices of the same kind and stick them up along the highways so he'll be able to find us."

"Shandong's a very big place," said Dihua. "Just where are we going?"

"The latest refugees say Dezhou is quite safe," put in Li Fu. "I suggest we go there."

"We can easily do as you suggest," said Fivey. "If someone comes along asking for you, we'll simply give him directions."

"Mother, you'd better tell them what he looks like, so they don't go giving directions to the wrong person," said Dihua.

A nervous Miss Bai told Li Fu to go and hire a boat and at the same time gave Fivey a description of Bohe.

"There are no boats for hire around here," Fiver told Li Fu. "You'll have to go about ten miles to the southeast, to a place on the canal just east of Qinggong Village." Li Fu went out and hired a fast mule, whipped it into a canter, and raced off.

Meanwhile Miss Bai told Dihua to pack their things. Much as she missed Bohe, Dihua was afraid that her mother might not survive another shock, so she suppressed her grief and began checking their luggage. Fivey stood beside her and helped pack. Because Fivey had been so attentive, Dihua felt rather sad at the thought of parting from her. When the packing was done, she sent Fiver out to get some more medicine for her mother to take on the journey. In settling their account, she did not calculate the amount too closely, but simply handed over a five-tael piece of silver. Fiver and Fivey were delighted and thanked her profusely. Remembering Fivey's attentiveness, Dihua also took a tiny gold ring from her little finger and gave it to her. "We're ever so grateful for all you've done for us these past few days. I hope you'll accept this as a small memento."

Fivey was so astonished she began to curtsy. "How can you *say* that, miss? I'll spend my next life trying to repay you!"

"Come now, it's nothing at all, just a token of our gratitude," said Dihua.

Fivey's tongue popped out in surprise. "Miss! You say it's nothing, but no one in our village has ever *seen* this sort of jewelry, not even the older generation!"

"Is there a trap around here that we could hire?" asked Dihua. "We'll be traveling by boat, but we'll still need a trap to get us there."

"There aren't any traps for hire," said Fivey, "but old Gaffer Liu in the village has one, and I'll get Fiver to borrow it from him. It should do."

Fiver confirmed her suggestion from outside the room. "It'll be all right. I'll go over now and borrow it. I'd like to drive the ladies there myself and see them safely on board."

"Even better," said Dihua. "I'd be ever so grateful."

They had another meal, and then at about four o'clock Li Fu came riding up with a boatman. "Boats are very expensive," said Li Fu. "To take you as far as Dezhou, the larger ones are asking over two hundred taels. The one I've reserved is a small boat, with inner and outer cabins but no middle cabin, for which they want one hundred. I took the liberty of hiring it. There are only a few of us, and it should be big enough."

"So long as we have room to sit down, that's all that matters," said Miss Bai. "We can't afford to be too particular at a time like this, when we're fleeing for our lives."

After Li Fu and the boatman had loaded the luggage onto the trap, Dihua said good-bye to Fivey and helped her mother aboard, then climbed in herself. Fivey saw them to the trap and let down the curtain. The boatman hitched up the mule he had been riding, converting it into a two-mule trap. Then Li Fu, after returning his mule to its owner, joined the boatman on top, and with Fiver at the reins they set off.

The sun was already low in the sky when they arrived in Qinggong, and by the time the boatman had returned the hired mule and they had reached the shore, it was pitch dark. By the light of their lanterns, the boatmen helped Dihua and Miss Bai on board, then fetched their luggage. Dihua found a tael's worth of loose silver and offered it to Fiver with their thanks, but he was unwilling to accept it.

"You certainly won't be able to get home today," said Dihua, "and you'll need this if you're staying the night. Here, do take it." He finally accepted the money, bowed in gratitude, and left.

Dihua and her mother occupied the inner and Li Fu the outer cabin. His luggage had been in the trap when they were driven apart, and he now retrieved it. The boatmen opened the hatch and lowered the two small cases into the cabin, arranging them so that they were level and formed a berth. Dihua was afraid her mother's joints might ache from lying on such a hard surface and so, in spreading out the bedclothes, she placed her own bedding on top of her mother's, intending to sleep beside her.

"That's fine," said Miss Bai, when she noticed what Dihua was doing. "It will cushion me a little better. You can use that bedding over there." She pointed to Bohe's.

Dihua blushed. "Please let me share your bed, Mother."

"What on earth for? It's getting warmer all the time. Why do we have to squeeze in together?" She pulled Bohe's bedding over to her and opened it up.

"I understand you want to keep cool, Mother, and since you tell me to use these bedclothes, I shall," said Dihua. She opened the bedding and spread it out, then hung up her quilt as a curtain, to screen the outer cabin from view.

That night, under Bohe's bedding, Dihua's feelings overflowed into love. Her mind dwelt on the fact that, although they were still not married, she was—at her mother's express command—sleeping in her fiancé's bedding; perhaps it was a sign of a "shared quilt" in their future. These fond thoughts clung to her mind and, before she knew it, had freed her, for the time being at least, from all her sorrows and cares. Instead she contemplated how much love and respect she would show him after they were married. . . . Then she remembered how sensitive he had been to her at the inn, and how they had endured the same hardships together, and she wondered how much tender affection she would receive from him. At this joyous prospect, she experienced a desire that could not be satisfied, a desire from which she drifted into a sound sleep.

If you wish to know how long it took them to reach Dezhou, you must turn to the next chapter.

~ 6 ~

A raging inferno engulfs Tianjin city;
A traveler's illness forces a stay in Jining.

DIHUA had spent ten days at the Zhang Inn, days of fretting over her mother's illness and worrying whether Bohe was still alive. To make matters worse, the room she shared with her mother at the inn was low and cramped and held in all the stuffy air. Sometimes she would take a walk in the courtyard, but it was littered with mule and horse dung, the stench of which would drift into their room at night. For these reasons, in addition to her own anxiety, she had never enjoyed a really good night's sleep there. But now, as she boarded the boat, she found that, small though it was, it was moored beside the river, and the air inside was fresh.

On opening Bohe's quilt and pillow, she had been struck by a fond desire, her heart had brimmed with joy, and she had slipped into a sound and dreamless sleep that lasted until dawn. Awakening, she sat up and glanced at her mother, who was still asleep. The early morning air was chilly over the water. Sitting cross-legged on the bed, she drew the bedclothes up around her shoulders and let her thoughts wander, dwelling on that desire of the night before and asking herself if it could ever be realized. If only it could, she thought, I'd willingly endure even more hardships than this. But he's the one who's in trouble, and I don't even know where he's stranded. Here am I, missing him terribly, yet I expect he misses me even more! For someone who is in torment himself to have to endure the pangs of love as well—oh, I only hope his health doesn't suffer! Suddenly she remembered how as children together they used to study the *Mencius,* in which there

151

was a passage that ran: "That is why Heaven, when it is about to
place a great burden on a man, always first tests his resolution,
exhausts his frame, and makes him suffer starvation and hardship."[9] Although Bohe is only seventeen, he has already suffered
the pain of separation from his family, she thought, so perhaps he
can look forward to a brilliant future. He and I may even be hon-
ored together, I as a result of his good fortune. At this prospect
she felt a glow of contentment and stroked the quilt and pillow as
substitutes for him. Sitting on the bed as if in a trance, she stared
into space.

Her mother awoke.

"Feeling any better today, Mother?" Dihua asked.

"Only so-so," replied her mother. "Have we started yet?"

"Not yet." Dihua pulled aside the curtain and saw that Li Fu was
already up.

"Miss, could you provide a little money for breakfast, so that we
can get started?" he asked.

She took out a silver piece of about two ounces and gave it to
Li Fu, who told the boatman to weigh it and go ashore and buy
some rice, noodles, and pickled vegetables. Before long he was
back with the food, and they set off.

After traveling all day, they came upon a scene of feverish
activity, a veritable forest of masts and sails, and dropped anchor.

"What's this place called?" Dihua asked Li Fu. He didn't know
and asked one of the boatmen.

"Qinggong Village, where you came on board, is on a branch of
the river. This is the main route, known as Great West Bay. That's
Tianjin up ahead of us."

Dihua was alarmed. "But the reason we wanted to go to
Dezhou was that Tianjin was so *unsafe!* What are we doing here?"

With a laugh he reassured her. "You have to go past here and
turn south as far as Jinghai before you're on course for Dezhou.
Look at the boats moored up ahead—they're all here to avoid the
fighting. We're a fair distance from the foreign settlements, so this
isn't an important target. Just take a look at these boats. They've
been tied up for I don't know how long, but none of them wants

9. See D. C. Lau, trans., *Mencius,* p. 181.

to move. The people on board are just keeping out of harm's way and hoping that the trouble will blow over, when they'll go ashore again. They're not sailing anywhere."

They spent that night in Great West Bay and started again early the next morning, but so many boats were moored there, thousands upon thousands, one next to the other, that the river was effectively blocked, and they could not get through. The boatmen tried by every conceivable means to thread their way through the other boats, but between sunrise and sunset they had covered less than a mile and had to stop again. It was lucky their boat was so small, for it could slip through quite narrow gaps; had it been any larger, they could not have moved an inch. High tide was at midnight, and the boatmen got up and tried to thread their way through, but managed to go only a few hundred yards before finding themselves blocked once more by large boats. Again they had to anchor.

For three days they were unable to get through. Then suddenly they saw a dense pall of smoke in the distance that spread across the sky and hung there for a long time without dispersing. In great alarm the men on the other boats passed along the rumor that the Boxers had set fire to the cathedral in Tianjin.

Miss Bai was terrified, and Dihua rushed over and took her in her arms. "Don't be frightened," she said. "That's going on ashore, a long way from here. What's more, we're on the river, where nothing will happen." But even as she spoke these comforting words, she was worrying about Bohe. She wondered if he was in Tianjin, in which case he'd be in danger right now. Was there no way to find out where he was and regain her peace of mind? When night fell, the source of the smoke was transformed into a fiery glow. The boats on either side of them erupted into noisy arguments in which southern accents predominated. The disturbance went on until midnight before gradually dying away.

The fourth day was again spent in frenetic activity. "Good!" exclaimed one of the boatmen. "It looks as if there are only a hundred or so boats ahead of us now. Tomorrow we ought to be able to get through. High tide is at about two o'clock tonight, so let's wait until then before setting off."

Dihua heard this remark from the cabin and felt slightly

relieved, but she kept thinking of Bohe and couldn't help crying to herself. As they were resting after supper, a crescendo of shouts arose outside, scaring both women. Dihua opened the curtain, but another large boat blocked her view, and she could see nothing. Her mother was trembling with fear. "Don't be frightened, Mother," said Dihua. "I'll go and find out what's happening."

Pushing aside the door curtain, she called to Li Fu, but he had gone up to the bow, and although she called several times, he did not hear her.

She turned to her mother. "Don't be alarmed, it's nothing. I'm just going up to see."

"Be careful!"

"I know."

Bent low, she headed for the bow, where Li Fu saw her coming and made room for her. "Careful, miss!" he called.

She reached the bow, straightened up—and was shocked by what she saw. In the distance six or seven fires raged so fiercely that they lit up the whole sky with a ruddy glow, a glow that was reflected in the faces of the people watching from the boats. Amid the babble of voices, faint cries and screams were to be heard in the distance, and Dihua's heart began pounding violently.

"What's that on fire?" she asked Li Fu.

"We don't know for sure. The rumor is that seven or eight churches have been set on fire at the same time, all by the Boxers."

Dihua looked up again and watched as the crows and magpies roosting on the shoreline trees became startled by the fires and flew up until they covered the sky, sharply silhouetted against the glare. Even the moon turned blood-red. Dihua, who had suffered one shock after another, quickly retreated to the cabin, not daring to let her alarm show in her face.

"Well, what was it?" asked her mother.

"Oh, just another fire on shore. Those people were making a great fuss over it, but it's nothing really. No need to worry."

She sat down beside her mother, extended her wrists, and began gently pummeling her mother's legs, thinking all the while of Bohe. If he's still in Tianjin, this will be a life-and-death matter for him. Will he be able to escape? She felt overwhelmed with a grief that she could not express. In her mother's presence she didn't dare weep, but had to let the tears run down inside her.

Spasmodic cries of alarm came from the men outside. "If we can't get through tomorrow, I'll die of shock, I know I will," moaned Miss Bai. "That dizzy feeling left me after I took the medicine, but now it's coming back."

"Don't fret, mother. The boatman says we're sure to get through tomorrow!"

"If he's right, I daresay I'll survive."

Her fever grew worse, and she drifted into an uneasy sleep, leaving Dihua to face her sorrow alone. At two o'clock the boatmen got up and tried to move the boat. By dawn they had managed with great difficulty to work themselves free of the armada of ships, and everyone was overjoyed. Rowing until it got dark, they reached Jinghai, where, as bad luck would have it, the number of boats sheltering from the fighting was even larger than at Great West Bay, their masts and sails stretching as far as the eye could see. Once more the boatmen began trying to thread their way through, but at this point the river was extremely narrow, and some days they made no progress at all. Not only were Miss Bai and Dihua driven frantic, even the boatmen began to curse their luck. From Jinghai to Duli[10] ought to have been no more than a day's journey, but this time it took them over a month. All along the banks of the canal they saw groups of Boxers with red turbans and sashes, carrying swords and staffs and roaming back and forth intent on goodness knows what.

After leaving Duli, the travelers could at last sail freely. Although at each dock they came to they found numerous boats sheltering from the fighting, the boats were not jammed together as densely as before. Proceeding by regular stages, in a matter of days they had reached the outskirts of Dezhou, which they were surprised to find was virtually an armed camp. They moored at the dock but did not dare disembark; instead Li Fu and one of the boatmen ventured ashore to find out what was going on. In a

---

10. "Duli" is presumably a mistake for "Duliu," which, although a town on the Grand Canal, is actually a little north of Jinghai rather than a day's journey south. Wu Jianren was basing himself on a personal memoir that makes this mistake.

moment they were back again, and the men rushed to get started on the next stage of the journey.

"But didn't you say this was Dezhou?" exclaimed Dihua. "Why are we leaving?"

"We've just heard that the capital has been taken by foreign troops. Tianjin has fallen too," said Li Fu. "The provincial governors are raising armies to come to the aid of the royal house. Those men you saw on the bank were troops raised by Governor Yuan of Shandong. They've come this far and are now trying to commandeer boats to take them to the capital by way of the canal. That's why the boatmen were so quick to set off again. They're afraid their boat will be confiscated and they'll be set to work for practically nothing."

"But even if *they* are in danger, why do *we* have to go on? Ask them and see what they say."

Li Fu went off to the stern.

Miss Bai had a suggestion. "There's something I've been meaning to talk to you about," she said to Dihua. "Ever since we left Jinghai, we've had quite a peaceful journey, but this illness of mine has been getting steadily worse, and I finished the last of that medicine some time ago. I'm dying to get home and, rather than waste any more time here, I'd like you to talk to the boatmen about going straight through to Qingjiangpu. From Zhenjiang we could take the steamer to Shanghai."

"I've been thinking the same thing," said Dihua. "That's the best solution, I agree, but what about the arrangement we made in Eight Hundred Village to meet up in Dezhou?"

"I'm not surprised you can't forget that. It's been on my mind too. But as I see it, he's no fool and won't have wasted any time getting to Shanghai. I guarantee that when we get there we'll find him living in our house."

Dihua hung her head, absorbed in her thoughts. "But if he *should* find his way here after we've left, won't we have let him down? Wouldn't it be better if we turned back and I wrote out a few more of those notices to post at the dock and along the main road, informing him that we've gone south? Then if he does come, he'll at least know what happened."

"Good idea."

Just as they settled the matter, Li Fu returned from asking the boatmen. "They would like to go on one more stage and are hoping that you ladies will wait until the next stop before going ashore. I'm afraid I can't talk them out of it."

"We're now thinking of going straight on to Qingjiangpu," said Dihua. "Could you ask them how much more it will cost? We shall need to turn back to the dock for a moment, too. We want to go ashore and put up some more notices."

Li Fu went to the stern again, spoke with the boatmen at some length, and then reported back: "They want only another fifty taels to go on to Qingjiangpu, probably because they wouldn't mind going south themselves to get out of harm's way. I've explained to them about the notices, and they're already turning back."

Dihua took brush and paper from her covered basket and, bending over the berth, began writing out the notices. By the time the boat drew alongside the dock and the gangway was lowered, she had copied out a dozen or so, which Li Fu took ashore to post.

His thoughts were as follows: It's taken us over two months since leaving Tianjin to get this far. Even if the young master does come here, we have no idea when it will be. This is a busy place, not some country village, and the notices won't have been there more than a few days before they're covered up with others, so what's the point? Still, the young mistress wants it this way, and I can't refuse. He posted the notices and returned to the boat. The boatmen helped him aboard, then hastily pulled up the gangway and set off.

Suddenly a random volley of shots rang out on shore, scaring Miss Bai out of her wits. Dihua had never heard anything like it before, and she, too, was so frightened that her heart began to pound. At the sight of her mother's panic, however, she rallied and forced herself to offer comfort. Miss Bai suffered one fainting spell after another. A desperate Dihua clasped her mother in her arms and called to her, soothing her in every way she could think of: "That was only the army firing at the Boxer bandits. They've been driven off now, so you needn't worry. . . ." Eventually her mother did calm down a little.

"Is there a town up ahead?" Dihua asked Li Fu. "If there is, let's stop there. I want to call in a doctor to examine her."

Li Fu asked the boatmen. "Twenty miles up ahead at Four Willows there's a good-sized market town," they replied. "We'll try to make it there today."

They did get to Four Willows, but it was too late in the day to call a doctor, and they had to wait until early the next morning before Li Fu could go ashore and find one. The doctor stood in the outer cabin and felt Miss Bai's pulse through the door curtain, then pulled the curtain aside to examine her complexion and tongue. He said that her condition resulted from a sudden shock and the consequent displacement of her vital spirits by noxious summer influences. Because her illness had been neglected, it had now reached the critical stage. He wrote out a prescription to sedate her spirits and dispel the noxious influences and told her to take five doses of it over the course of the journey.

Li Fu went ashore to fetch the medicine, and while it was still being heated up, they set off again and sailed through the night. By the time they reached Majiaying, the invalid had taken her medicine for five days without any sign of improvement, and Li Fu was extremely worried. "The mistress's illness looks very serious to me," he confided to Dihua, "and a boat is no place to recover from it. That doctor's medicine doesn't seem to have done her the least bit of good. And if we're going to stop and call in a new doctor at each stage of the journey, changing doctors all the time—well, that's no way to treat an illness either. Jining is only two days from here. It's a busy place, one of the biggest ports in Shandong. In my opinion the best thing would be to go ashore at Jining and find a doctor for her there. At the same time we should write to Shanghai, perhaps suggesting that the master himself come up and advise us on what to do."

Dihua was afraid Bohe might be following them south, but her mother's illness was a more critical concern, and she accepted Li Fu's suggestion.

On reaching Jining they paid off the boatmen and went ashore to look for an inn. But they had spent only one day there before the innkeeper noticed that he had a dangerously ill guest on his hands and wanted to evict them. By now their money was all gone, and they had to get Li Fu to pawn some of their jewelry. With the proceeds they rented and furnished a house, then called in a doctor to treat Miss Bai. At the same time they sent Heting a telegram and also a letter giving a detailed account of all that had happened. From this time on Dihua and her mother remained in Jining, where we shall leave them for the present.

Meanwhile Bohe had been living at the Fozhaolou ever since he arrived in Bamboo Grove. After ten days or so, the rumors grew even more alarming, and the southerners flocked to catch steamers for the south. Only Bohe, intent on waiting for Miss Bai and Dihua, refused to leave.

Then one day the manager of the Fozhaolou himself decided to close his inn and flee to safety, and Bohe had to pack his bags and move to a one-story inn nearby. However, after only two more days the word was out that the Boxers had set a date for their attack on Bamboo Grove, and this inn wanted to close its doors, too.

It's the foreigners that the bandits hate, thought Bohe. So long as I go inland from here, I should be safe enough. But if I go inland and *they* come here, how are they going to find me? Better make for Xigu and stay at the big livery stables. If they do come this way, they'll have to pass by, and we're more likely to meet.

Once more he packed his bags. At that point the bandits were not allowing any rickshaws to go inland, so he had to hire a mule trap for the journey to Xigu, where he put up at the livery stables. Along the way he saw groups of rampaging bandits, but luckily for him they had not yet resorted to robbery. The day after his arrival in Xigu happened to be the day the churches were set on fire. By this time the bandits were growing steadily in number, and the local population rallied to their cause. Continuously, day and night, their roars were everywhere to be heard, as they paraded back and forth in an endless stream. Each day Bohe stood at the entrance to the inn watching the crowd of travelers passing by in hopes of finding Miss Bai and Dihua among them. He was watching on one particular day when a large crowd of bandits—just how many he couldn't tell—came swarming along the street shouting at bystanders to get down on their knees and welcome them. Now, Bohe was a resourceful person who would never have consented to kneel to anyone. As he considered his situation, however, with the fighting far from over and no sign of Miss Bai and Dihua, he thought it best simply to avoid the danger facing him. Returning to his room, he tore off a strip of red cloth and wound it about his head until he looked like one of the bandits, then ran out and mingled with the real bandits. From the top of Red Bridge he looked back at the stables and found them engulfed in flames. The bandits were running up and down the streets setting fires and slaughtering people, and not a single soldier came out to stop them.

As he walked along, Bohe heard a thunderous roar of gunfire from the direction of Bamboo Grove. Afraid it spelled trouble, he turned down a lane and followed its twists and turns for a few hundred yards before coming to a group of buildings that had been gutted by fire. At the very end of this scene of devastation a single building remained intact. That might be a place to hide out in, he thought, and trod through the rubble toward it, then walked all around looking for an entrance until he came to a small door. But if you are wondering what lay behind the door, you must turn to the next chapter.

～ 7 ～

A specious answer plucks safety out of danger;
Procrastination leads to a couple's murder.

BOHE went up to the little door and pushed, but it was locked. He rapped twice, and when there was no reply, feeling exhausted from the distance he had come, he leaned against the door and rested. Then after a while, hearing a faint sound of voices from inside, he put his ear to the door and listened. Suddenly it opened, and in trying to get out of the way, he stumbled inside. Four or five men were in there, all shouting at the top of their lungs, pleading with him for mercy.

Bohe suddenly realized that because of the red cloth he had around his head they had mistaken him for a Boxer bandit. Hastily removing the cloth, he bowed before them. "Gentlemen, you mustn't get the wrong impression. I'm a refugee just like yourselves. Take a look; I don't have any weapons on me. I got so tired running away that I took a breather outside your door. I never meant to give you such a shock!"

The men looked at each other in astonishment, then one of them volunteered: "It must be fate that has brought him to our door. At a time like this, with troops running amok, we ought to take him in and let him share what we have."

Much relieved, Bohe bowed in gratitude, after which someone locked the door again. Bohe saw there were five men in the room. When he asked how they came to be there, he was told that they worked in a rice store of which this building was the warehouse. The store itself, which fronted on Qianmen Avenue, had been torched and reduced to a pile of rubble that blocked the main entrance to the warehouse. The little door Bohe had fallen through was the back entrance. It opened onto a lane that was utterly deserted, which was why the men had chosen the warehouse as their place of refuge.

Bohe and the others introduced themselves, and then he offered a suggestion: "Since this is a warehouse and there are so few of us here, we'll never starve, considering the amount of rice we have on hand. But if the Boxer bandits ever find their way here, we'll be trapped. For safety's sake why don't we wait until it's dark and then go out and block up both ends of the lane with rubble?"

"That's all very well," said one of the men, "but there are only six of us, and we wouldn't have time to block up both ends of the lane in a single night. Wouldn't it be better to block up the back door with rubble, so that no one can get in? Take a look at our front door, if you don't believe me. Isn't it completely blocked?"

"But if you go out and block it up," put in Bohe, "how are you going to get back in again?"

"We'll take a ladder with us," the man replied. "Then after we've blocked up the door, we'll use the ladder to climb back over the wall."

The plan was unanimously approved, and that night they put it into effect and blocked up the door.

From this time on Bohe hid out in the warehouse. Every day he and his companions heard the sound of rifle and cannon fire, while at night a red glow lit up the sky—fortunately a long way off. The six men lived their lives in a kind of daze, oblivious to the passing of time. Numbers of people were heard going past the front door of the warehouse, but outside the back door there was never a sound.

After about a month had passed in this manner, they heard an earthshaking rumble of artillery, far more threatening than anything that had preceded it. Screams and moans were faintly audible amid the shellfire. Then for the space of ten days or more there was no sound at all save the occasional shot.

"We haven't heard a thing for a good many days now," said Bohe. "It must be safe again outside. Perhaps we ought to be thinking of how to get away."

With one voice the other men objected: "If it *was* safe, our boss would certainly have been back to check up on his warehouse. It *can't* be safe."

"Why would he be in such a hurry to check up on his warehouse the moment the fighting ends?" asked Bohe. "Anyway, you can't be sure how far people went to get out of danger. Many of them must have gone a long way off and won't have returned yet. You people have nothing else to do and can afford to wait, but there's something I need to see to, and I intend to leave."

"The doorway's all blocked up," they objected. "How will you get away? You're not going to try and tunnel your way out, are you?"

"I wouldn't dream of giving you so much trouble. No, all I'm asking is that you lend me a ladder. Once I've climbed up to the top of the wall, I'll lift the ladder over to the other side and climb down. I'll have to get one of you to pull it up again."

Realizing how determined he was to leave, the five men complied and sent him on his way.

After climbing over the warehouse wall and emerging from the lane, Bohe was confronted with devastation as far as the eye could see. All the buildings had burned down, and what remained was a sea of rubble. Numerous bodies still lay in the streets, shapeless masses of blood-caked flesh, strewn in all directions.

I've survived certain death, he thought—what an incredible piece of luck! With his head down, picking his way along the street, he was surprised by a sudden shout and turned to see who it was—a foreign soldier gripping a rifle. He took to his heels, then heard a shot and fell to the ground. As he was scrambling up again, he found the soldier at his side. The man searched him, discovered the last few taels he had left, and stalked off with them.

Bohe waited until he had gone, then got up and continued on his way. Suddenly he felt something damp against the lower part of his body. When he looked down, he found a great deal of blood oozing from his right thigh and also a bullet hole in his jacket, and realized that he had been shot. There was no hope of finding a doctor, so he hastily scraped up a handful of dirt, pressed it into the wound, and continued on his way. He had gone only a few more steps before he felt a similar dampness at the back of his thigh, and when he turned his head to look, he found blood spurting out; there was a second bullet hole at the back of his trousers. He scraped up another handful of dirt and pressed it into that wound as well. Up ahead he noticed a row of buildings with no sign of fire damage and made his way toward them. It was a street lined with shops on both sides, all of them securely locked, the most desolate scene imaginable.

His wounds now began to ache. Painfully he hobbled along, hoping to meet someone with a place where he could rest. Looking about him, he noticed one shop with a double door that, although shuttered, was still ajar, as if the bolt had not been slipped into place. He went over and gave the door a gentle push. It yielded before his hand. "Anyone at home?" he called. There was still no response after he had repeated the question several times.

By this time he was in agony. Ignoring the consequences, he struggled inside, turned and shut the door, and sank into a nearby chair. He sat there a long time without seeing a soul, then hobbled to the back of the building to investigate. He found a rear courtyard with a single large room at the opposite end of it. To one side was a kitchen, its utensils and stove covered with a thick layer of dust as if they had not been touched in ages. Plucking up his courage, he ventured into the room opposite but found no one there either, only eight large chests on the floor. Returning to the front to see what kind of shop it was, he found it was a herbalist's, completely deserted.

After bolting the shop door, he began going through the cupboards. He found some root of foxglove, sealwort, and so forth, which he gathered together, thinking to use it as food while subsisting for a few days in the shop. He also hunted out a quantity of medicinal plasters, and without caring whether they were the right kind or not, slapped two of them over his wounds. On checking himself carefully, he found that the bullet had struck the fleshy part of his thigh, fortunately missing the bone, and exited through the other side.

After he had applied the plasters, he went back to the room in which he had seen the chests and tried to lift one of them. It was very heavy. There was a bed along one side of the room with no bedding on it, but he simply brushed off the dust and flopped down. From that time onward he hid out in the shop.

Five or six days passed, and still no one came. His wounds gradually healed, but the supply of medicine suitable for food was running low, and he was wondering whether to abandon the shop and seek refuge elsewhere, when suddenly there came an urgent knocking at the door. Trouble, he thought. The owner must have come back. What am I going to tell him?

Then he heard voices outside, and they were not Chinese voices either, which only added to his fear. Not daring to open the door, he sat petrified in the back room.

The knocking grew more and more insistent. He listened. It wasn't knocking after all, but someone hammering on the door with a blunt instrument. Half scared to death, he didn't dare budge from where he was.

A crash followed, as the door burst open and a number of people surged in. He peered at them; five were foreigners and two were Chinese, and the foreigners were armed with rifles. They first looked around the shop and then came to the back. With no way of escape, Bohe lamented his fate: I'm a dead man, he told himself. One of the foreigners saw him and jabbered something that the Chinese at his side translated as "The chief wants to know who you are and what you're doing here."

Bohe realized the Chinese was an interpreter and quickly came up with an excuse. "I work here. The owner left to escape the fighting and told me to mind the shop for him while he was away."

The interpreter translated this for the foreigners' benefit, then asked: "And how long have you been minding the shop?"

"Over a month now."

The interpreter held a short discussion with the foreigners, then told Bohe: "We don't believe you. What have you been living on for the past month?"

"For a whole month I've had nothing but root of foxglove, seal-wort, and so forth, as food and black plum instead of tea." He produced some foxglove and black plum from beside his bed and showed them.

The interpreter and the foreigner held another discussion. The foreigner tasted the black plum with the tip of his tongue and laughed, then said something or other that the interpreter reported as: "The chief says it's not often one finds such an honest man among the Chinese. What valuables do you have? Where would you like to go? Tell us, and the chief will give you an official pass that will enable you to leave the area."

"There's nothing of any value here except these eight chests. The owner and I both come from Guangdong, which is where he is now. Before he left, he told me to take the chests down there for him, if I ever got the chance."

The interpreter reacted with surprise. "How is it you speak such good Mandarin if you're a Cantonese?"

"I've been living up here in the north for many years."

"In that case we're both from the same place. Can you still speak the dialect, I wonder?"

"Of course." They exchanged a few words in Cantonese, delighting the interpreter, who said something else to the foreigner. The latter took a sheet of foreign paper and a pencil from his pocket, wrote out a large number of foreign words, and handed the document to Bohe.

"This is an official pass," explained the interpreter. "Keep it on you, and if any foreigners stop you, just show it to them, and they won't give you any further trouble. Wait here while I find some men to move the chests for you. When you get to the river, hire a boat to take you to Dagu, where you'll find a freighter just in from Yantai. You can take it back to Yantai and from there get a steamer home."

Delighted at this turn of events, Bohe thanked them again and again, then saw the group to the door. Before long a dozen men arrived who declared that they had been ordered by the foreign mandarin to come and carry Bohe's luggage for him. Bohe directed them to pick up the chests and take them to the river, where he hired a small boat and had the chests loaded aboard. The men were about to leave when Bohe called to them to wait. He undid his leggings, took out a piece of gold leaf, and gave it to them as a tip. Overjoyed, they bowed low in gratitude.

The little boat then headed for Dagu. All along the way it was stopped by foreign patrol boats, but Bohe simply showed them his pass and was allowed to proceed and complete his journey without interference.

At Dagu, as the interpreter had said, dozens of grain ships lay at anchor. Bohe embarked on one of them, had the chests carried aboard, and chose a seat for himself. Taking out another piece of gold, he gave it to the boatman who had ferried him across.

He then lay back against the cabin wall and reflected on all that had happened to him since fleeing the capital—it was like a dream. His fellow passengers were all people displaced by the fighting. Some had lost sons and daughters, others parents and brothers, and now that they had been brought together in one place, it was a matter of "tear-filled eyes gazing into tear-filled eyes, broken heart facing broken heart." They sat there sighing and moaning, with tragic expressions on their faces, a sight that inevitably awakened in Bohe thoughts of his own family. He wondered what had happened to his parents and his brother, and where Dihua and her mother were stranded, and he, too, felt depressed.

He also reflected that he had told a monstrous lie and swindled someone out of eight chests, the contents of which were still a mystery to him. If they happened to be full of gold, silver, and jewels, he'd have struck it rich! At this thought his spirits began to rise.

He spent over ten days on the ship, days in which the passengers opened their hearts to one another, so he never felt unbearably lonely. When the ship had received its full complement of passengers, it weighed anchor and headed for Yantai, where Bohe took out another two pieces of gold leaf and paid his fare with them. He then hired a lighter to transport his luggage ashore and put up at an inn. On the pretext that he had lost his keys in the turmoil, he called in a locksmith to open the chests. For the most part they did contain valuables—silks and furs, gold and silver, jewelry, precious gems, and the like. In his joy at this discovery, he decided to head for Shanghai.

Occupying the room next to his at the inn was a Ningbo date merchant named Xin Shugui who made regular visits to Dongchang to buy dates. This year, with prices tumbling because of the disturbances in the north, he had seized the opportunity to buy an extra quantity at low cost. The dates had already been shipped, and he was only staying at the inn while waiting for a steamer to take him back to Shanghai. In his loneliness Bohe naturally struck up a conversation with Xin and, on learning that he, too, was going to Shanghai, arranged to travel with him.

In a few days a steamer became available, and they left for Shanghai, where they took rooms at the Hotel Dafang in the International Settlement. After depositing his luggage, Bohe went off to pay a call on his prospective father-in-law, Zhang Heting, at his imported goods shop. But at the shop he was told that Heting had become so concerned over the fate of his family that early in the fifth month he had taken passage on a ship to Tianjin, intending to go on from there to the capital and bring his family back with him. There was nothing for it but to return to the inn. From this time onward Bohe remained with Xin Shugui in Shanghai, where we shall leave him for the present.

Meanwhile Gelin, having sent his eldest son to escort Miss Bai and Dihua from the capital, had moved the rest of his family to a house on Pewter Lane outside Donghua Gate, on the assumption that, since the lane was close to the Forbidden City, it would be relatively safe there. After a few days the rumors grew even more alarming, and Gelin repeatedly told his younger son to leave, but Zhongai still refused. "It's a son's duty to stay by his parents' side. If that's true in normal times, it's even more true in times of trouble. What's the good of having a son, if he is going to abandon you in the midst of a crisis? You may say it's meaningless for all of us to die together and that I ought to escape in order to continue the family sacrifices, but my answer is that my brother has already done that. You and Mother can't possibly be left here without anyone at your side." Confronted with such arguments, Gelin had no choice but to let him stay.

On the fifteenth of that month rumors swept the capital that Dong's army had entered the city and a secretary from the Japanese embassy, Sugiyama Akira, had been killed outside Yongding Gate. The Boxers were said to be collaborating with the army in harassing foreigners, and on the streets they were the only people to be seen. In the legation quarter they were even more thickly concentrated, awaiting their chance to attack, while in the Pewter

Lane neighborhood an endless stream of them surged back and forth.

Gelin no longer dared go to his office, but locked his gate and stayed home to keep out of trouble. He kept urging Zhongai to flee.

"If you're telling me to leave on my own," replied Zhongai, "I will never agree. In my opinion the best solution would be for all of us to go together. I know you're not allowed to apply for leave, but when your life and your career are in the balance, your life is the more important. Anyway, the Ministry of Works isn't responsible for the national defense, so why do *you* need to stay behind? What's more, this upheaval is something that the nobles and high officials have actively encouraged. Why do we have to stoop to *their* level?"

"For all you say, I still have a job to do. If everybody ran away, who would see that the work of the ministry got done? Admittedly I've not been to my office the last few days, but if something comes up, they can always get a message through to me and I can go in and deal with it. There'll be time enough to leave when things get really dangerous."

Zhongai saw he could never convince his father and gave up trying.

A few days later it was rumored that the German minister had been killed by the Boxers, after which Dong's troops began a nonstop assault on the legations. Again Zhongai urged his father to flee, and again Gelin refused. Two days later the *Peking Gazette* carried an imperial decree over six hundred characters in length that condemned the foreigners and heaped praise upon the Boxers.

Gelin sighed. "It's true, as the decree says, that the foreigners have behaved atrociously, bullying us and encroaching on our territory. But why don't we work out a strategy to counter them? Why don't we summon up all our energies and try to strengthen ourselves, taking a stand where we can't be beaten and *then* confronting them? What possible advantage is to be gained from calling in an undisciplined mob to attack them with their bare hands?"

"This decree amounts to a declaration of war on the foreigners, and violence is going to break out at any moment. Father, you must leave at once!" said Zhongai.

"Let's wait another day or two," said Gelin. "If the news gets too bad, I suppose we *might* take ourselves out of harm's way for a while. . . ."

Before he had finished speaking, they heard an uproar from outside the gate, and a servant reported: "It's the Dong troops passing by, with Boxers in among them. They're on their way to the legation quarter to attack the legations."

"Father, you must leave this minute!" said Zhongai. "If you hesitate a moment longer, I'm afraid it will be too late."

Alarmed, Gelin told his wife to pack up their valuables and be ready to depart the next day.

That night they heard shouts from far and near and saw flames shooting up into the sky. Zhongai couldn't bear the suspense and went out to see what was happening. He found the streets jammed with people, all of them Boxers, yelling: "Burn the churches! Burn the legations! Kill the hairies! Kill the hangers-on!"[11]

From Qianmen Avenue Zhongai noticed a fiery glow to the west and, not daring to go any farther, turned and went back. On arriving home, however, he found the double gates wide open and was seized by a feeling of dread. He rushed in to see what had happened—only to suffer a terrible shock. But if you wish to know the reason for his shock, you must turn to the next chapter.

11. See note 4 on page 116.

~ 8 ~

In a discourse on passion an evil practice
is condemned;

As her mother departs this life, a young girl
is left alone.

AFTER leaving the house to find out what was happening in the city, Zhongai was surprised on his return to find the double gates wide open. But his surprise was nothing compared to the shock he received when he went inside and found blood everywhere and his parents lying dead on the floor. Shocked out of his senses, he fell over backwards and ended up unconscious on the ground. No one was there to revive him, but after some time he regained consciousness and began wailing with grief. Then, after grieving for some time, he called for the servants, but he received no response. He searched inside and outside the house; the rickshaw man the family employed and both their servants had vanished without a trace, while the family retainer they had brought with them from the south was lying dead in the back court. In the kitchen Zhongai found their maidservant hiding in the woodpile, cowering with fear. When he told her to get up and tell him what had happened, she was trembling too violently to speak.

"A group of Boxers got in the gate, I don't know how," she said when she had calmed down sufficiently. "They asked the master where he was from, and when he answered Guangdong, they said, 'They're hangers-on, all of them,' and killed him. Then the mistress began screaming, and they killed her, too. The servants and that rickshaw man tied red turbans around their heads and went off with them."

Zhongai forced himself to go back outside. He told the maid to
shut the gate and help him lift up the bodies, at which point he
gave way to his feelings and broke down again. When morning
came at last, he went out and bought three coffins, hired someone
to make the burial garments, and conducted a hasty laying in.
Since a funeral service was out of the question, he took the coffins
to the Guangdong Cemetery for temporary burial. That done, he
decided to flee to safety himself. However, most of the family's
valuables had been looted by the Boxers, and he knew he could
find no buyers for any of the furniture. A thorough search of all
the trunks and cases produced only a dozen or so taels that the
Boxers had overlooked.

He couldn't get very far on so little, but he had heard that Ansu
county was free of bandits and knew that the magistrate there, Li
Zhuoran, had graduated in the same year as his father and was a
close friend. His best course was to seek refuge with Magistrate Li.

Once that decision had been taken, he paid off the maidservant
and, abandoning the furniture, deposited the family paintings,
clothes, and so forth, with the Nanhai Guild on Rice Market Lane.
He then left the city through the Zhangyi Gate, where he hired a
mule and traveled by way of the Marco Polo Bridge and Chang-
xindian to Ansu county.

Li Zhuoran was deeply saddened to learn of Gelin's death and
insisted that Zhongai stay with him.

But after only two days Zhongai approached the magistrate to
ask him a favor. "Sir, I am endlessly grateful for your kindness in
taking me in and letting me stay here, but I am also deeply trou-
bled by the thought that my parents have been murdered and we
have no property to bring in an income. I can't stand idly by
when I need to see to my parents' burial, start a family of my own,
and provide for the future. I would be extremely grateful if you
could recommend me for a position in which I could make my
own way."

"I've been giving some thought to that myself," said Li. "The
trouble is that there's nothing available in the county offices at
present, and even if there were, the pay would amount to only a
few strings of cash a month. Stay here a little longer, and when an
opportunity arises, I'll see what I can do for you."

That night Wang Boshen, the county treasurer and a friend of the magistrate's, came to see Zhongai and in the course of conversation presented him with a proposal: "The magistrate is greatly impressed with your personal qualities. He has a daughter whom he wishes to honor with an alliance, and he has asked me to convey that message to you. I lack any rhetorical skills, so I can only put his offer in the plainest of words, but I wonder if you might be interested?"

"He has shown me such extraordinary kindness that I find it difficult to decline anything he might suggest. But while my father was alive, he arranged for me to marry someone else, and so I cannot do as the magistrate bids me. Let me ask you to convey that reply to him."

"That wouldn't be a pretext, now, would it?"

"*Certainly not!* He took me in when I was at my wits' end, and I am only too eager to please him. I would never dream of such a thing!"

Wang faithfully reported this reply to Li, who had a talk with Zhongai the next day. "The northern part of the country is in unbelievable turmoil. Even if there were a post to be had, I doubt that it would be any too safe. There *is* one place I'd like to recommend you to, but I wonder if you mightn't find the distance too great?"

"If you were kind enough to recommend me, sir, I would never dream of objecting to the distance. But what place did you have in mind?"

"Intendant Sun Keting of the West Qianli Circuit in Shaanxi is a sworn brother of mine. In addition to his post as intendant he is also in charge of special duties under the Shaanxi secretariat. If you joined him, you could look forward to a somewhat better position than you would get here. I've been doing a little thinking on your behalf. Seeing to your parents' funerals, setting up your own family, establishing yourself in a career, planning for the future—these are things that cannot be done on an ordinary salary, and that's what brought this place to mind. If you are at all interested, I'd be glad to write you a recommendation."

"You've been so helpful to me, I don't think I shall ever be able to repay you!"

"Come now, we're family friends after all. My one regret is that I shan't have the pleasure of your company and be able to enjoy your admirable qualities. But tell me, when your father was alive, whom did he betroth you to?"

"To a Miss Wang from Suzhou."

Magistrate Li wrote out a letter of recommendation and also provided the necessary traveling expenses, for which Zhongai duly thanked him.

The next day he set out on his long journey. Stopping only at night, he traveled for over twenty days before arriving in Shaanxi, where he went straight to the offices of the West Qianli Circuit and submitted Magistrate Li's letter of recommendation together with a request for an interview.

After reading Li's letter, Keting invited Zhongai into the parlor and greeted him. The young man's conversational abilities had always been impressive, and Keting was delighted with him and invited him to stay in his yamen and promised to find him a post. At first he was given a sinecure in the offices of the secretariat. However, within a few days of his arrival the local officials received a telegram notifying them that the allied army had seized the capital and that the Emperor and the Empress Dowager had departed on a tour of the countryside and would be taking up temporary residence in Xian. Officials at all levels scrambled to prepare for the imperial visit. The governor appointed his lieutenant-governor as director of special arrangements and the intendant as associate director. On receiving this latter position in addition to his own, Keting immediately transferred Zhongai to the office of procurement. In no time at all merchants from all over the country, hearing that Xian was engaged in procuring supplies for the imperial needs, began swarming into the city, turning it into a hive of activity.

No sooner had Zhongai taken up his post in procurement than the merchants came along to curry favor with him. Needless to say they also made cash contributions, ever so discreetly, and although Zhongai had colleagues he had to share them with, the largesse was still considerable. In addition to the money, there were all the banquets arranged by the merchants, in the course of which, needless to say, the officials got a taste of the pleasure quarter and almost inevitably became addicted to it.

Although Zhongai accompanied his colleagues to the pleasure quarter, he remained utterly indifferent. Some of his colleagues admired such maturity in a young man, while others scoffed at him as an old fogey. "I wouldn't dream of claiming to be mature," said Zhongai, "and I won't concede that I'm an old fogey. I believe myself to be a passionate man deeply enamored of women. But to be frank about it, I do find you people ridiculous—highly intelligent men who've been taken in by a novel, *The Story of the Stone*."[12]

"What do you mean?" asked his colleagues.

"Every reader of *The Story of the Stone* sees himself as Baoyu," explained Zhongai. "But with every man a Baoyu, there are not enough Daiyus and Baochais to go around, and so the Baoyus take singsong girls as their Daiyus and Baochais and apply Baoyu's passion to them. Isn't that being taken in by *The Story of the Stone?* Bear in mind that Daiyu, Baochai, and the rest were unmarried girls who in the ordinary course of events would never have set eyes on a man. When Baoyu joined them and indulged his passions, they naturally responded. But nowadays our self-appointed Baoyus rush off to prostitutes to indulge their passion, quite oblivious of the fact that one Baoyu has hardly left the prostitute before the next one arrives, so she has an endless stream of Baoyus and doesn't know which one to respond to. And as for the Baoyus, no sooner have they visited this or that Daiyu or Baochai and indulged their passion with her than they head off to another Daiyu or Baochai and indulge it again. I wonder how many Daiyus and Baochais it would take to satisfy them. Ridiculous!"

"I gather you don't feel any passion yourself?"

"Of course I do, but what *I* try to do is apply it in the right place."

12. *The Story of the Stone* (also known as *The Dream of the Red Chamber*), written in the middle of the eighteenth century, is the best-known Chinese novel. Its young hero, Baoyu, is permitted—at the request of his sister, the emperor's consort—to live in the Grand View Garden beside his girl cousins, notably Daiyu and Baochai.

"If you insist on emulating Baoyu in trying to find the right place, you'll have your work cut out for you!"

"Ah, but you see Baoyu never *did* apply his in the right place. What he did was simply immoral. The only right place for passion is with your wife or concubine. That's why I always say how lucky it is that people are so bad at emulating Baoyu. They just misapply their passion and turn into infatuated lechers. If they were any *good* at emulating Baoyu, the whole world would be awash in immorality. *The Story of the Stone* has often been condemned as a manual of lust, but lust is actually only one of the sins that that novel can be charged with!"

His companions laughed. "In that case your young lady must have enjoyed *all* of your passion."

"Hardly! We're only engaged, not married, so how can we enjoy ourselves?"

"While you're away from home, you don't want to abuse your passion," said one. "You're saving it up for later, when she'll enjoy all of it." They burst out laughing.

Zhongai continued in Shaanxi, where we shall leave him for the time being.

Meanwhile Dihua, who had been nursing her invalid mother in Jining, was by now totally dependent on pawning jewelry to pay their way. She sent two telegrams to Shanghai but received no response, and she became more and more apprehensive. Finally she sent a prepaid telegram and received the reply "HETING DEPARTED CAPITAL FIFTH MONTH FETCH FAMILY NOT RETURNED," nine words in all, which raised a whole new set of anxieties in her mind. In the midst of all these trials and tribulations, she thought, why would her father do anything so foolhardy? Only for love of her, surely. But they hadn't met along the road, so where could he be now? Oh, what a worry it all was! Her mother's illness seemed to be getting worse by the day. Doctor after doctor had been tried, all of whom said hers was a most difficult case. Dihua's heart was burdened with cares—worrying about her mother, missing her father, longing for her fiancé! And on top of that their jewelry was nearly all gone—*another* source of anxiety! As a result her own health began to suffer.

At the end of the ninth month, just when it was time to order new clothes for the winter, her mother's illness took a drastic turn for the worse. She suffered two or three fainting spells every day, scaring Dihua so badly that she didn't dare fall asleep at night. At the back of her mind she couldn't help thinking of those cases in which the ancients cured their parents with the aid of pieces of flesh cut from their own thighs. I wonder if it would work, she asked herself, because if it would, I'd never begrudge a tiny scrap of my own flesh. Obviously the doctors can do nothing for her, so there's really no hope apart from this. I know: I shan't worry about whether it works or not, I'll simply try it out and see. She waited until the middle of the night, then lit a stick of incense and said a prayer for her mother's speedy recovery. She also swore a secret vow: "Although we are taught that we inherit our bodies from our parents and must never let them come to any harm, I have no choice but to do this unfilial thing in the hope of curing my mother's illness. If it makes her better, I'll willingly atone for my sin." She bared her left arm, bit into a piece of flesh and drew it up, then with her right hand took a pair of sharp Bingzhou scissors and sheared the piece right off. Still feeling no pain, she quickly bound up the wound with a piece of cloth. The morsel of flesh, when she picked it up and examined it, was only half the size of a finger. Tiptoeing over to the medicine pot, she dropped it in, then stoked the fire and let the concoction simmer.

When her mother awoke, Dihua ladled out some medicine and offered it to her, then stayed by her mother's side until dawn, when her condition showed no sign of improvement. Dihua became even more nervous, and for the first time her wound began to ache.

Days passed, and it was the beginning of the tenth month. Her mother's mind now wandered most of the time. She knew she would not recover and was distressed to see Dihua getting thinner by the day.

"We hadn't been three days on the road before I came down with this illness," she said. "The fact that I've lingered on until now is due solely to your nursing me—a wonderful tribute to the upbringing you received! I realize there's no way I am going to get better. Child, you mustn't be too distressed when I die. And you needn't worry about your father or your fiancé, either. If we women can make it out of danger, surely the men can, too! Anyway, nothing bad is going to happen to them. If I have any ghostly powers after I die, you may be sure I shall use them to guide your fiancé out of danger and bring him safely to Shanghai so that you can be married."

As she listened to her mother, Dihua had been crying continuously, but at this point she couldn't help sobbing aloud. "Mother, we've faced all kinds of trials together and come through them safe and sound, and I was hoping to remain at your side forever. Now that you're so ill, it must be my fault for not nursing you properly. If the worst *should* happen, I'm ready and willing to go with you!"

"Child, you mustn't *say* such things! I'm not going to recover, but you have to keep in mind that you still have a father, parents-in-law, and a fiancé. You'll need to look after your own health if you're going to be a good daughter. Otherwise, I shan't have a moment's peace as a ghost."

Now more distraught than ever, Dihua gripped her mother's hands, crying as she spoke: "Mother, get better soon and be my guide forever. I'd willingly give up part of my own life for your sake. I'd exchange all the blessings in my future for the chance to stay with you."

Then she saw that her mother had fainted. In a panic, she bent down, took her mother in her arms, and cried out: "Mother, wake up!" After some time her mother half opened her eyes and muttered something in a feeble voice, "Take care, dear!" then breathed her last.

Dihua passed her hand over her mother's face and body and then broke down completely. "Mother, how could you leave me behind to suffer like this?" she cried, then suddenly she felt as light as a leaf borne by the wind, floating and whirling—sheer delight! The pain she had suffered was now entirely forgotten. If only she had been able to float as light and as free as this, riding on the wind, when they fled the capital, their journey would never have been delayed. Absorbed in these thoughts, she heard a voice calling to her over a vast distance: "Miss! Miss! Come back!" At first it was no more than a faint buzzing. Who's calling me? she wondered. The voice went on and on, getting closer and closer, until eventually it was sounding right in her ears. She listened intently; it was Wang, the maidservant they had hired. Then suddenly she remembered that her mother was dead. How could I have abandoned her to come here? she asked herself, and couldn't help crying out: "Oh, how wretched I am!" Then she opened her eyes and saw the maidservant cradling her in her arms and trying to revive her, and realized that she had fainted from grief.

Intoning Buddha's name, the maidservant cried out: "It's all right! She's come back!"

Dihua regained her senses, looked over at her mother, and began banging her head and crying bitterly again, while the maidservant tried desperately to console her and outside in the courtyard Li Fu stamped his feet. At length, after Dihua had been crying a long time, he came in and tried to calm her: "Stop crying for a moment, would you, miss? Now that the mistress has passed away and neither the master nor the young master is here, the whole responsibility rests with you. If you grieve so much that it affects your own health, who is going to take charge? The critical thing now is to see to the funeral!"

Dihua finally stopped crying long enough to tell Li Fu to call in a dressmaker to make the burial garments. She also produced a package of gold jewelry and told him to sell it and buy a coffin with the proceeds.

She then continued her piteous grieving. Perhaps her failure to cure her mother with that morsel of flesh showed that the ancients were lying, she thought. But how could their lies have been passed down over so many years without anyone seeing through them? No doubt the ancients weren't lying at all; it was her own heart that wasn't sincere enough. At this thought she began to hate herself for her insincerity, banging her head against the bed and crying herself into a state of oblivion.

Li Fu cut off a piece of material and called in a dressmaker, then went off to see that the coffin was ready. He also called in an astrologer to choose a day for the laying in.

By the time of the ceremony, the burial garments, coverlet, coffin, and coffin case were all in order. Then, just as the body was about to be placed in the coffin, a telegram arrived.

Li Fu gave it to the maid, who handed it to Dihua. She could tell from the envelope that it had been sent from Shanghai, and she feverishly pulled out the message—only to find that she couldn't understand a word of it. In her bewilderment she asked Li Fu.

"Telegrams always use foreign numbers," said Li Fu, "but I'm afraid I don't know what they mean either."

"Then hurry up and show it to someone who does, so he can tell us what it says!"

"That first telegram we got was translated for us by the telegraph office. I don't know why they didn't do the same thing this time. We'll have to take it back and get them to do it."

The messenger who had brought the telegram now broke in: "It's already been translated, and I have the message here with me, but you'll need to pay me a translation fee before I can give it to you."

Dihua told Li Fu to pay him, while she signed the receipt. The messenger then handed over the translation, which read: "HETING SETTING OFF TODAY." Dihua felt a mixture of joy and sadness—joy because her father was well and would be joining her in a few days' time, and sadness because her mother was dead, and even if her father came, he could never see her again. At this thought she broke down and cried out: "Mother, what a tragic fate you suffered!" After she had grieved once more, the laying in was at last completed.

Each morning and evening after that she offered a libation of tears to her mother's spirit. And every day she calculated her father's progress on his journey to Shandong.

She had to wait until the end of that month for his arrival. When she told him of his wife's death, father and daughter fell into each other's arms and wept bitterly, and then, after they had grieved a while, they told each other of their experiences during the crisis. Heting was concerned lest the Grand Canal freeze over, so after only a few days he took his daughter and the coffin and, accompanied by Li Fu, hired a boat and set sail with all possible speed for the south. Their maid, needless to say, was paid off.

Dihua noted that her father had nothing to say about Bohe, and she could not help feeling a certain apprehension. She longed to ask him, but was far too embarrassed to do so. His nature was very different from her mother's; all day he sat in the bow silently commiserating with himself. After several days' travel they docked at Qingjiangpu and, after crossing the Yangzi to Zhenjiang, took a steamer to Shanghai. But if you are wondering how Dihua and Bohe will meet again in Shanghai, you must turn to the next chapter.

~ 9 ~

Resigned to failure, a drifting man is caught
at the world's end;

Defying convention, a passionate girl pleads
with her wayward love.

IN THE fourth month Heting had received ominous news from the
north, news that provoked a storm of criticism in the press and
left him extremely nervous. At the end of that month he sent a
telegram to Gelin but received no reply. As soon as the Dragon
Boat Festival was over, he took the steamer to Tianjin, hoping to
get to the capital and bring his family back with him. However, on
reaching Tianjin he found the people there in a state of outright
panic. The railway from Tanggu to Tianjin was guarded by foreign
troops, and warships from the navies of the world filled Tanggu
Roads. When he visited an imported goods store on Shanghai
Avenue to look up a friend and learn the latest news—and also to
explain his reasons for going to the capital—the friend advised
him in the strongest possible terms not to go. One couldn't even
get to Bamboo Grove, let alone to the capital! "The best thing
would be to stay here in my shop for a few days before deciding,"
he said. Intent as Heting was on getting to Beijing, he could
hardly do so in the face of such warnings from the people in the
shop. So dangerous was the situation in Tianjin that refugees from
the interior who had sought safety in the foreign settlements
didn't dare move away. Within a few days heavy fighting did
indeed break out, as the Boxer bandits attacked Bamboo Grove
and the foreign troops tried to take the Dagu forts. Rumors flew
thick and fast, and since the offices of both the *National News* and

the *Tianjin Daily News* had been destroyed by the bandits, there was a complete lack of information. Within days the allied army arrived and attacked Tianjin city, and so the people who had taken refuge in the foreign settlements hid in cellars and, after their food supplies ran out, made gruel from peanuts, which gave them all diarrhea. By this time the steamers had stopped sailing between Tianjin and Shanghai, and so no one could leave the city. Even the news from Shanghai was cut off.

Not until the ninth month, when Lu Shufan organized his Relief Association[13] in Shanghai and chartered a steamship to go directly to Tianjin and bring back the refugees, did Heting manage to get a passage home, charging an officer of the association, Luo Huan-zhong, with the responsibility for finding his wife and daughter.

On his return to Shanghai Heting found the two telegrams as well as Dihua's letter waiting for him and learned that his family was now in Jining. Sending off a telegram to announce his coming, he left the city immediately. From Zhenjiang he headed for Qingjiangpu, then traveled nonstop to Jining, where he found that his wife was dead. Bringing the coffin back to Shanghai, he deposited it in Guang-Zhao Gardens.[14] Only when everything was settled did he mention to Dihua that no word had been received of Bohe since his disappearance.

In her father's presence Dihua was too embarrassed to say much, replying merely: "Now that the Relief Association has been formed, I'm sure he'll get to Shanghai. But do keep your ears open for news of him, Father."

"I have the shop, as he is well aware, and once he gets to Shanghai, he's bound to head for it. But I'm afraid that he may still be stranded up north somewhere. I'll need to send a man up to find out. And there's been no word of our in-laws either, I don't know why, which makes me very uneasy. I think I'll write them a letter and send someone to inquire."

Heting had a concubine living in Shanghai. She had given him a

13. See *Stones in the Sea,* note 46.
14. Guang-Zhao Gardens, a temporary depository for coffins before they were transported home, was one of the sights of Shanghai. It was founded for the use of Cantonese residents. ("Guang-Zhao" combines the place names Guangzhou and Zhaoqing.)

son, now two years old, who had received the childhood name of
Pup because he had been born in the year of the dog. Since
Dihua shared a house with the concubine, she was doubly careful
to abide by the rules of decorum and not express any of the
misery she felt. Only in the evenings, sitting alone beside her
lamp, did she shed any tears.

By the end of that year the situation in the north had more or
less stabilized, and once the river was open, steamship service
resumed to Tianjin.

Heting wrote a letter to Gelin in the capital and gave it to Li Fu
together with a sum to cover his travel expenses. Before long a
message arrived from Li Fu to say that Gelin and his wife had
been killed, that Zhongai had left for Shaanxi, and that Bohe's
whereabouts were still unknown, news that plunged Dihua into
an even deeper depression. In this manner more than a year
passed, during which the tears she wept in secret would easily
have filled a pitcher.

One day Heting came back from his shop in a towering rage.

"Do you know where that young swine has been all this time?"
he asked Dihua. She was so startled she didn't know what to say.

Heting pounded on the table. "He's been in Shanghai all along,
hiding out from us!"

Silently Dihua gave thanks to Buddha. So long as he still has his
health, she thought, that's what matters. Father may be angry
now, but gradually we'll get him to calm down.

"While he was in Tianjin," Heting went on, "he somehow got
off with another man's property—a lot of gold and silver jewelry,
silks, furs, and the like. Then the year before last he arrived in
Shanghai and took up with someone by the name of Xin Shugui.
With Xin leading him on, he got in with a crowd of lowlifes
and began whoremongering in a big way. In the fifth month of
last year, he married a prostitute called Jin Ruyu or something,
whom it took only a couple of months to clean him out. She went
off with everything he had, leaving him in abject poverty and
addicted to opium. Last winter he began to sink lower and lower,
living in the little opium dens of the Hongkou district. Recently
he's become so desperate that he's actually been *begging* for
money. Doesn't it make your blood boil?"

As Dihua listened to this tirade, she felt as if she had been deluged with icy water, struck on the head by a thunderbolt, pierced to the heart by a volley of arrows. All the sweetness and bitterness of life welled up in her at once, but with her father in such a rage she didn't dare utter a word.

Heting gave a furious sigh.

"This has all come about because of my ill fortune," Dihua said. "You mustn't be angry with him, Father. Don't let it affect your health."

"As a boy he always struck me as so bright. And when he grew up, he seemed decent and honorable, and I was quite pleased with him. I never imagined he'd change so drastically. I've sent someone out to look for him, and when he's been found, I'll tell him to come and live here with us. But first I'll insist that he give up opium."

Dihua hung her head. "Father, please remember that you're doing all this for love of me!" Heting heaved a sigh and left the room.

Dihua wept in silence, wondering why Bohe had so suddenly turned his life upside down. It must be the fault of those monsters he associated with, she thought. I only hope he is found and Father can bring him to his senses! Young men generally do sow a few wild oats when they leave home—that's only to be expected. He was away from his parents, without anyone to restrain him, and it's hardly to be wondered at that he should go through a silly phase. The trouble is that he has abused his health so dreadfully. As she thought and thought, she began to blame herself again for behaving so primly when they were fleeing the capital. She had discouraged him from riding in the trap with her, which had led to their being driven apart. So it was really all her fault! The longer she thought, the more remorseful she became, until to calm her nerves she had to pinch the pressure point above her lip.

Heting had a friend by the name of Bu Shuming, who owned an opium house. While Bohe still had money, he used to frequent Bu's house, spending a great deal there. The two men introduced themselves, and Bu came to learn something of Bohe's background. When one day Heting happened to mention a son-in-law who had been lost during the flight from Beijing, Bu asked the

man's name, and it turned out to be Bohe. Bu told Heting all
he knew, and Heting asked him to find his son-in-law, then
came home to give his daughter the news before returning to the
shop.

Bohe was soon brought in. He came forward and bowed to
Heting, who noticed that he was pathetically thin and had a
darker complexion than before. It was the third month, and the
weather was still raw in Shanghai, but all he had on was a thread-
bare cotton gown, and he was shivering with cold. To Heting's
eyes he looked both infuriating and ridiculous. In the presence of
Bu Shuming and his own staff he couldn't very well give Bohe a
piece of his mind, but after chatting for a while Bu took his leave,
and Heting brought Bohe home.

Seating him in the study, he asked him what had happened.

"After I was driven away from the others, I drifted to Shanghai
without a penny to my name, which is why I didn't dare call
on you."

Heting gave a snort of laughter. "We all know you picked up a
windfall in Tianjin and brought it to Shanghai, where you had a
high old time whoring around. You married a prostitute who
cleaned you out, which is why you're now so poor. But that's all
in the past, and there's no need to dwell on it. Tell me, why did
you start on opium? That stuff will haunt you the rest of your
days. It makes me furious just to see it. From now on you can live
here with us, but you'll have to swear off opium and take up your
studies seriously again in preparation for a career."

"I'm not an addict, you know. It was only a diversion for me."

"I certainly hope so. Your parents are both dead. Did you know
that?"

"When did it happen?" asked Bohe, astonished.

"You've obviously been spending your days in complete
oblivion. You never even tried to find out how they were!"

He produced Li Fu's letter and showed it to Bohe, who couldn't
help weeping.

Heting went upstairs, told his concubine to find Bohe a padded
gown, and had a maid bring it to him. Then he went over to
Dihua's room and told her that Bohe had arrived and been invited
to stay on condition that he give up opium.

Dihua flushed crimson. She was about to say something when she choked on the words.

"If you have something to say, say it," said Heting. "Why do you carry on like this?"

Dihua opened her mouth to speak but stopped again, her face flushed.

"How very odd! What can it be that you find so hard to tell me?"

Dihua finally mumbled an answer. "I've heard that when people are giving up opium, their health suffers unless they set about it the right way. If you want him to stop, Father, you should call in a doctor to monitor his health."

"Well, that's easily done. Peng Banyu[15] is an old friend of mine. I'll write him a note asking him to call in on his daily rounds." As Heting was leaving, he looked back at Dihua and smiled: "Don't worry, my dear! I shan't be too hard on him!" a remark that made Dihua's cheeks flush crimson.

As Heting went off chuckling to himself, Dihua was thinking that her father really did love her, because the anger he had so recently expressed had now completely vanished. Everything I ask him to do he does, she thought. I wonder how I had the luck to be born to such parents; I don't know how I'll ever repay them. And because Bohe had arrived and was willing to live with them and give up opium, she felt another surge of joy and looked forward to the day when he gave it up forever and regained his health, the day when all her dreams would be realized.

Let us leave Dihua with her thoughts and return to Heting, who went downstairs and gave Bohe a stern lecture on the evils of opium smoking, in the course of which Bohe merely hung his head and said nothing. After seeing him settled in the house, Heting went to his shop and told a trusted assistant to take Bohe off to the bathhouse. He also wrote a note to Dr. Peng.

From this time onward Bohe lived in his prospective father-in-law's house. Now, wouldn't it have been wonderful if he had changed his ways, given up his opium habit, and married his fiancée? Unfortunately he had so abandoned himself to license

15. Peng Banyu was the real name of a Shanghai doctor who was a close friend of the author's. A reformed opium addict himself, he invented and marketed a pill to cure addiction.

during his time in Shanghai that he never felt at ease in the Chens' house, and after three or four days there he grew restless and slipped away. If he had merely gone out for a walk and then come back, it would hardly have mattered, but he chose not to return at all. When two days had passed without a sign of him, Heting grew suspicious and looked around the study. A treasured Xuande[16] censer was missing from its place on the table. He had to go back to Bu Shuming and ask him to mount another search. After three more days Bohe was found and brought home again. The padded gown was gone, replaced by a workman's jacket and trousers. When asked about the gown, he said he had pawned it; when asked about the pawn ticket, he said he had sold it; and when asked what had happened to the Xuande censer, he said he had disposed of it at a street stall. Heting could only sigh and dismiss the matter from his mind—while delivering another stern lecture.

When Dihua saw how her father was treating Bohe, she was even more grateful than before. But Bohe was determined not to reform, and two days after his return he slipped away again. When this had happened three or four times, Heting felt so frustrated that he visited Dihua to talk the matter over with her. How could they persuade Bohe to change his ways? They both sighed in despair, and then Dihua knelt down before her father.

"Father, I have an idea, but I must ask you to forgive me for it in advance if I'm to find the courage to tell you."

"Why must you carry on like this? Get up, girl, and tell me what's on your mind!"

"I studied beside him as a child, and he and I saw a great deal of each other until the engagement, when we moved away for a few years. Then as we left the capital we found ourselves together once more, but because we weren't married, I kept my distance from him. As bad luck would have it, one of our drivers quit, leaving us with only the one trap, and I had so discouraged Bohe from riding with me that he walked beside us instead, which is how he got lost and ended up in his present state. I'm clearly the

16. The reign period 1426–1435.

one to blame in all this! Father, now that he's caught this incurable disease, he'll *never* pay any attention to your lectures."

At this point she stopped abruptly and then, after a long pause, crying once more, resumed: "It seems to me that passion between the sexes is a universal thing. When we fled from the capital, he showed me endless consideration. With your permission, Father, I would like to go downstairs and see him despite all the shame involved. I'll appeal to him face to face, and who knows, he *may* agree to reform. I only hope that you will forgive me for doing something so improper."

"Get *up,* girl!" said Heting with a sigh. "For people like you two who've known each other since childhood, it's not improper to meet once in a while. Go and see him by all means! If you can get him to change his ways, fine. But if you can't, I shall be the one who has ruined your life!"

With tears in her eyes, Dihua stood up. I might as well go off to the shop and give her a chance to persuade him, thought Heting, as he went downstairs.

Dihua was also about to go down, when a hot flush enveloped her cheeks and ears, her legs gave way beneath her, and her heart began pounding violently. She sat down to compose herself, then stood up and was about to continue, when for some reason her heart raced out of control again. She rested a moment, then forced herself to go down, gripping the banister as she went. On reaching the door she had another attack of palpitations, which she overcame with the greatest difficulty. She managed to get through the door, only to suffer another fit of blushing.

From his position on the couch, Bohe was surprised to see her come in. He felt ashamed, and the emotion showed in his face as he got up to greet her. "Cousin, won't you have a seat?"

Dihua, suffering attack after attack of palpitations, was unable to reply and simply sat herself down beside the table. A long time passed before she said anything. "It's been ages since I've seen you, cousin. You're much thinner than you were." Bohe hung his head in silence.

"I wonder how you managed to get to Shanghai after you were lost?" she went on. He still hung his head.

"You must be blaming me for all that has happened to you—I was far too concerned about the rules of behavior. But there's no need to bring up the past. Now that Father has invited you to stay, you must tell me at once if there's anything that isn't to your liking—don't keep it to yourself. Try to think of our house as if it were your own."

Bohe's face turned scarlet.

"Father had the best of intentions in trying to persuade you to give up opium, but if it doesn't agree with you to stop completely, you can always do so in stages. You don't need to be too hasty and ruin your health."

Suddenly he burst out: "I'll never be able to give up my habit as long as I live!"

After broaching the topic, Dihua was just preparing to expand upon it when interrupted by this sudden outburst. She stopped at once. He used to have such a gentle nature, she thought. Why the sudden change?

"It doesn't matter if you can't give it up," she went on. "The only trouble is that Father detests it more than anything else in the world. Even if you can't give it up permanently, perhaps you could try to stop for a few months, just to please him. Once we're married, you can smoke as much as you like. I wouldn't dream of trying to prevent you."

"Even if *my* father were alive again, I couldn't give it up—it's my life! I have nothing to my name, nothing, so how can I think of marriage? My mind is made up. If I can do as I like, fine, but if I can't, I'll become a monk!"

Dihua was taken aback. Why is he this way? she wondered. She was trying to think of how to continue the conversation when there came a knock on the door. The maid opened it to admit her father, who had brought Dr. Peng along to examine Bohe. In order to avoid the doctor Dihua let herself out through the back door and fled upstairs. There's no one in the world whose feelings can't be swayed, she thought. Why is he so indifferent to me? Perhaps my heart still isn't entirely free of insincerity, and that's the reason? Or perhaps I can't express myself well enough, and that's why I'm unable to influence him? Oh! How can I lay bare my heart and let him see me as I really am? Tears streamed down her cheeks as she tried to find an answer.

After some time Heting saw Dr. Peng out and came upstairs.

"Well, my dear, did you have any success in persuading him?" he asked.

Dihua was about to reply when a maid rushed in and announced: "Master Chen has gone again!"

If you are wondering what happened next, you must turn to the following chapter.

~ 10 ~

She enters a nunnery disillusioned with the
Heaven of Passion;

He meets his fiancée and escapes from the
Sea of Regret.

HETING heaved a deep sigh on hearing that Bohe had gone again.
"Child, this is your fate, I'm afraid. There's nothing else I can do
for you."

Dihua began to cry.

Heting did not have the heart to ask more questions and took
an awkward departure from the room. Nor did he make any
attempt to find Bohe, but left him to his debaucheries, calculating
that when he had had his fill of trouble, he might undergo a
change of heart.

As it happened, this time Bohe could not be found. Poor
Dihua's heart was in knots; words will not suffice to describe her
anguish. From time to time her stepmother would come in and try
to cheer her up, but her visits served only to remind Dihua of how
much she missed her own mother. Her health suffered, she took
little food and drink, and she began to waste away.

Heting loved his daughter dearly and would have done anything to find her fiancé and work on him—but for his fear that
Bohe would only run away again and aggravate her illness. There
seemed to be no solution.

One day, when there was little business at the shop, he
returned home to see his daughter and found her resting on her
bed. He sat down beside her and chatted a while before gradually
bringing the subject around to Bohe. "The fact is," he said with a
sigh, "I'm the one who has let you down. You and he were only
eleven or twelve when the Chens proposed the engagement, and

I should never have agreed to it so hastily. That's the root cause of all your trouble."

"Father, you mustn't *say* such things! Everything that happens in this world is foreordained. The rice was already cooked, so to speak, and I wouldn't dream of blaming either Heaven or man for it. All we can do now is let matters take their course. When I think back on those days when we lived together, Mr. and Mrs. Chen were so affectionate to me, and I was never able to do my duty to them as a daughter-in-law. Bohe had the bad luck to fall in with the wrong sort of friends, who led him into a life of self-indulgence, and I'm simply not virtuous enough to inspire him to change. So it's really all my fault. Why put the blame on yourself?"

"I have an idea. Let's find him and bring him home but not insist that he give up opium, just provide him with whatever he needs and let him smoke as much as he likes. After the wedding we'll bring him here to live with us, and it will be up to you to try and talk some sense into him. Perhaps he'll return to his studies or come and help me in the business. I do have one additional concern, though. After you're married, if he carries on the way he does now, won't your life be even harder than it is?"

"By rights a girl oughtn't to involve herself in these discussions, but things have come to such a state that I have no choice. By all means do as you suggest, Father. There's a saying of the ancients that springs to mind: 'Metal and stone will yield before a pure heart.' After we're married, I'll put my trust in a perfectly sincere heart, and perhaps, who knows, I may be able to inspire him to change. If I can't, my failure will only confirm the truth of what Mencius said: 'Whatever is done without man's doing it is from Heaven; whatever happens without man's causing it is fate.'[17] All we can do is resign ourselves to our lot, not harbor resentment against others. At the moment we don't even know where he is. But if we did know and we shilly-shallied—and in the meantime he died of his sufferings—then even you, Father, would find it hard to face his parents."

Heting nodded, then let some time pass before he spoke again. "Very well, I'll go out and look for him." He quickly left the room,

---

17. Cf. D. C. Lau, trans., *Mencius,* p. 145.

thinking: What a pity it is that a wise and virtuous daughter like mine has to be engaged to such a worthless wretch! It's all because I was so hasty in agreeing to that proposal. In the light of this experience, one should *never* accept such an arrangement!"

These thoughts running through his mind, he called in at an opium house on Third Avenue to ask Bu Shuming where Bohe was to be found.

"Lately he's been sick as well as penniless. He came by a couple of days ago and borrowed a little cash, looking terribly ill. I tried to persuade him to go home: 'Your father-in-law's been good to you,' I said. 'Why aren't you willing to stay with him? Why not go back there? They're hardly going to begrudge the cost of an extra mouth to feed!' His reply was: 'I'm not used to being at other people's beck and call.' When I heard him say that, I gave up."

Heting was neither amused nor angry. He merely sighed and asked Bu to find him again.

Bu sent out one of his assistants, who returned after a long interval. "He's terribly ill," the man reported. "He had been staying in the Guanghuachang opium den in Hongkou, but when his illness got too bad, the people there began to fear the worst and packed him off to Guang-Zhao Hospital."[18]

Alarmed, Heting said a hasty good-bye and took a rickshaw straight to the hospital.

Bohe appeared to be in a coma. Heting asked the nurse for his record and read the diagnosis: "Fever resulting from malaria. Critical." He wrung his hands and stamped his feet in agitation. Approaching Bohe's bed, he asked: "Well, how do you feel?"

Bohe opened his eyes, took one look at Heting, and closed them again. "Not so good," he said.

Heting's other questions brought no replies at all. There was nothing he could do but give the nurses repeated instructions to take good care of their patient. When Bohe recovered, he promised, they would be handsomely rewarded.

Returning home, he was in a quandary as to what to say to Dihua. It would be unwise to tell her—and equally unwise not to.

18. A hospital on Haining Road founded for Cantonese residents.

He compromised by giving her a vague report to the effect that Bohe was unwell and would be home as soon as he recovered. But Dihua peppered him with questions. What illness did he have? Where was he? Since he was ill, why not bring him home to recuperate? Unable to fend off her questions, Heting was forced to tell her the truth.

"But that won't do at all!" she cried in alarm. "Hospitals do have staff to care for the patients, but they come from the general public, after all, and he won't find it so easy to get a cup of tea whenever he wants one. Father, why didn't you bring him home to recover?"

Heting sighed. "I did ask him, but he wouldn't even give me an answer. What else could I do?"

More agitated than ever, Dihua cast all her scruples aside. "Father, would you permit me to go and see him?"

"You may if you wish, but you mustn't press him too hard to come back here. The fact that he doesn't want to come probably means he has something else in mind. In any case, he's too sick to be moved at present. It would have been simple enough to have him brought here, but he has never wanted to come, and if I had brought him against his will at a time when he couldn't resist, he'd have been bound to resent it, and when an invalid resents something, doesn't that make his condition even worse?"

He told the rickshaw man to get ready, and Dihua, taking with her a woman servant and a young maid, set off for Guang-Zhao Hospital. In the ward she found four trestle beds, three of which were empty. Bohe was lying on the fourth, fearfully emaciated, his face a greenish pallor, his lips bloodless, his eyes shut tight. Dihua couldn't suppress a surge of pity at the sight, but found herself unable to utter a word. Sitting on the edge of his bed, she gently stroked his forehead, which felt hot and dry.

When Bohe opened his eyes and looked at her, she couldn't help weeping. "Master Chen! How do you feel?" she asked.

"Exhausted," he muttered in a feeble voice.

"It's all my fault. I hope you'll take good care of yourself. When you are better, I'm fully prepared to make up for my sins by becoming your concubine instead of your wife!"

Bohe shook his head.

She bent over him. "Father meant well when he tried to persuade you to give up opium, but since you can't do it, never mind. I wonder if your sickness wasn't actually brought on by trying to stop."

"No."

"You must try to relax and get better. This place isn't at all suitable—you'd be far better off at home. I'll put aside all my shyness and concern for proper behavior and nurse you myself."

Bohe sighed. "I can't move at present. Let's see how I feel in the morning."

As he spoke, someone came in with a cup of medicine. "Time for your medicine, Mr. Chen! Shall I sit you up?"

"I don't think it's right for him to sit up," said Dihua. "Could you bring me a spoon instead?"

The nurse brought her a soup spoon, and Dihua began feeding Bohe with it. But he lacked the strength even to swallow, and each time she fed him a spoonful, the medicine would dribble out of the corners of his mouth.

Dihua felt wave after wave of anguish. "What's the matter?" she asked him.

Bohe choked once or twice before replying. "I had a fainting spell a moment ago. If you try again now, I should be able to get it down."

Dihua fed him another spoonful, but again he let half of it splash onto the floor. Quickly she wiped it up with her handkerchief, then sent the maid to the back for a cup of water, with which she rinsed out her mouth. Next she ordered both servants from the ward.

After taking a sip of the medicine, she did not swallow it, but bent over him and fed it to him mouth-to-mouth. When she saw that he had swallowed it, she took another sip, and so on until he had received more than twenty sips in all.

Bohe shook his head. "No more."

Since only a drop remained in the cup, Dihua put it aside.

"You must have a bitter taste in your mouth," said Bohe.

"It's nothing compared to the bitterness in my heart!" said Dihua. She began sobbing with great racking sobs, her tears cascading down like pearls from a broken necklace.

Bohe sighed. "Cousin! . . ." he exclaimed, and stopped.

"Husband, you mustn't call me 'cousin' anymore. I am yours now, and giving you your medicine was just part of my duty. Please try to relax and get better. Don't be upset or worry about anything."

As she spoke, Heting came in, followed by the two servants.

"Any better?" he asked.

"He's just taken his medicine," said Dihua.

Heting sat down on an empty bed.

"He's still too sick to go home," said Dihua. "The trouble is that someone who's just skin and bones can't bear to lie on a trestle bed. Father, as soon as you get back, please send over a coir rope cot. Everything in the hospital is so awfully crude. And please send us some teacups, a teapot, and so on, as well."

"That's easily done. Well, let's go home."

"I shan't be coming home today. I'm going to nurse him until he's a little better, and then we'll both come home tomorrow."

Heting hesitated. "But where will you sleep tonight?"

"I won't have any time to sleep. You needn't worry about it."

"We were in the yard at the back just now," said the servant, "and noticed that the female nurses who attend on the women patients have a separate dormitory of their own. When you get tired, you could probably arrange to sleep there."

Heting had no choice but to let his daughter have her way. He went home and sent some men over with the cot, bedding, teapot, teacups, and so forth.

Dihua told the men to dismantle the bed opposite Bohe's and replace it with the cot. Then behind her she noticed a set of opium-smoking instruments that were much the worse for wear. How could anyone *use* such things? she wondered. She told the men to borrow a set that was kept in the shop for customer use. It would do for the time being.

These were all men who did odd jobs and ran errands for Heting's shop. They knew that Bohe and Dihua were engaged but not yet married, and when they saw how she was behaving, they inevitably began whispering among themselves. Their opinions varied, some praising her as a remarkable woman, others condemning her as a shameless slut.

To return to Dihua. Having arranged the cot to her satisfaction, she asked the servant to help her lift Bohe over to it. He placed one hand on Dihua's shoulder, while she put her arm under his back and eased him onto the cot. As she did so, Bohe looked directly up at her and smiled. She started to blush, but caught herself in time. I made up my mind to come here and nurse him, she thought, and if I can get him to smile, that shows he's happy. I mustn't turn all bashful again and make him feel awkward! Provided an invalid feels relaxed and happy, his illness is easier to cure, so it's actually my *duty* to get him to relax. She flashed him a warm smile in return and helped him lie down, then sat on the edge of his bed and bent over him, her manner infinitely gentle and caring. Taking off her "double happiness" disk, she showed it to him.

"Ever since we were driven apart, this has never left my side."

Bohe could not help shedding tears.

"I only showed it to you to let you know how much I missed you," she added hastily. "You mustn't be sad."

Just then the set of opium instruments arrived. Dihua kept the young girl with her and sent the other servant home. She lit the opium pipe for Bohe but, lacking experience in such matters, had some difficulty in loading it.

Bohe did not have the strength to draw on the pipe, so she fitted a smaller bamboo pipe inside the mouthpiece. Then she held the pipe in one hand and the lamp in the other, and in that way he was able to smoke.

She nursed him all that day without eating any supper herself. At midnight he began running a high fever and became delirious. The maid was asleep, sprawled across one of the empty beds. In her anguish Dihua kept whispering "Master Chen! Master Chen!" as all that night he alternated between periods of lucidity and incoherence.

The next morning the hospital physician came in to examine him. After feeling Bohe's pulse, he shook his head and wrote out a prescription.

Dihua fed Bohe his medicine in the same way as the day before, but on this occasion the patient did not even open his eyes.

At noon Heting brought Dr. Peng in to examine him, and this time Dihua did not withdraw from the room. After the examination, Dr. Peng likewise shook his head, then picked up the prescription and read it. "It's standard hospital procedure to make out a prescription for every case. So long as the patient has a breath of life in him, they'll always prescribe *something*. There's nothing wrong with this, but it's only by way of doing everything possible. Personally I wouldn't dream of prescribing in such a case. Heting, I think you'd be well advised to start making preparations for the funeral. It's only a matter of hours away. . . ."

Suddenly they heard a crash and saw Dihua slumped on the floor in a dead faint. Heting rushed to her side, took her in his arms, and began frantically calling her name.

"That won't do any good," said Dr. Peng. "Try the pressure point above her lip."

Heting pressed hard, and Dihua suddenly uttered a great cry and burst out: "Master Chen! What suffering I've brought you!" Ignoring the doctor's presence, she rushed to Bohe's bedside, where she found him with scarlet cheeks, sallow forehead, and pallid lips. His breathing had almost stopped.

"Master Chen, do you know who I am?" she cried.

Bohe half opened his eyes. "Cousin!" he said. "I let you down!" Then his body gradually lost its warmth, the scarlet drained from his cheeks, and he died.

Dihua's grief exceeded all bounds. Indeed she cried herself into a state nearer death than life, as Heting stamped his feet and Dr. Peng merely sighed. The maid, terrified at the sight, burst into tears herself. As soon as the hospital staff heard of the death, they busied themselves carrying the corpse off to the mortuary.

Heting left to see to the funeral. Dihua, streaming with tears, personally bathed and dressed the corpse. Then, borrowing a pair of scissors from one of the female nurses, she cut her nails and a lock of her hair and, after wrapping up both items, tucked them inside one of Bohe's sleeves. "Master Chen," she said, "if you are conscious in that other world, come back soon and take me away with you!" Then she began to wail, and all those present wept with her. Someone who knew her story remarked: "And she was only his fiancée, too!" at which they were even more impressed.

But let us leave that scene and tell how, after the laying in, it was impossible to hold the funeral ceremony in the hospital, and so the coffin was left for the time being at Guang-Zhao Gardens. After a tearful farewell, Dihua returned home with her father.

Heting sat down in the living room and stared into space, while Dihua headed straight upstairs. After a time he emerged from his reverie and heaved a sigh. He was about to leave for the shop when suddenly he caught sight of his daughter descending the stairs clutching a handful of her own hair. Flinging herself into her father's arms, she sank to her knees and burst into tears. With a shock he realized that every hair of her head had been shorn off.

"Child, why did you *do* this to yourself?" he asked in horror.

Dihua cried for a while before replying: "Father, I beg you, do your unworthy daughter a great favor and let her go into a nunnery."

Heting stamped his feet in exasperation. "Child! There's no need for all this! I may be a businessman, but I'm not one of those rogues who know nothing of morality. If you want to remain a widow, *of course* I'll let you! Why did you have to go and cut off your hair without even discussing it with me?"

"Father!" cried Dihua. "My parents-in-law are dead and my brother-in-law is still unmarried—where would you have me go to preserve my widowhood? It's unthinkable to live as a widow in my parents' home! There was nothing else I could have done! All I hope is that you'll look on my leaving home as if I had married him and were now living as a widow in the Chen household. My original intention was to put an end to myself, but I was afraid that you would grieve for me too much, so I chose this as the next best solution. Show me your love and grant me my wish this one last time!"

She began wailing again, and her stepmother was unable to calm her down. Heting had no choice but to ask an intermediary to recommend her to the management of the Baode Nunnery in Hongkou, where a date was set for her induction.

When that day came, she prostrated herself before her ancestors' and her mother's tablets in the family shrine, then looked up at the sky and bade farewell to her husband. Finally she bowed to her father. "It is unfilial of me to leave you at your time of life, and I hope you'll now put me out of your mind forever! If Heaven and Earth have any compassion, I hope I can become your daughter in the next life and make up for the unfilial things I have done in this one."

Heting burst into tears. "Child! You've had such a hard fate to bear!"

Dihua then turned and knelt before her stepmother. "It's unfilial of me to leave my father at his time of life. A man approaching sixty needs someone to look after him, and I trust you will give him your loving support. In gratitude I will faithfully serve you through many lives."

She went to kowtow, but her stepmother hastily stopped her and bowed herself, crying as if her heart were breaking. After grieving for some time, Dihua hugged her four-year-old brother. "Dear brother! See you obey your father outside the home and do as your mother says inside it. When you grow up, be a good son to them both. Sister has done something terribly wrong, and you needn't think of me any more!" All of which set the four-year-old sobbing as if *his* heart was about to break. Everyone told Dihua to take good care of herself, and she departed for the Baode Nunnery and was inducted that same day.

Following the induction, Heting was left in a deep depression. Then one day someone burst into his shop and began bowing to him. He was astonished to see that his visitor was Zhongai.

"Uncle, do you happen to know where my brother is?" Zhongai abruptly asked as soon as he had finished bowing.

The sight of Zhongai made Heting feel even more depressed. He took his arm and showed him into the sitting room.

"Your brother passed away," he said.

Zhongai burst into tears. "Brother, so it *was* you after all!" he wailed, sinking to the floor. It was some time before Heting, suppressing his own feelings, managed to calm him. Zhongai then asked whether his brother had married after arriving in Shanghai, and with a sigh Heting told him the whole story, from the time the family set off from the capital and became separated along the way, to the time Bohe was admitted to the hospital in critical con-

dition and Dihua nursed him and afterwards became a nun. The
only thing he did not know was the story behind the windfall that
Bohe had picked up in Tianjin.

Zhongai wiped away his tears. "My sister-in-law is a loving wife
and a chaste widow. Brother, you let her down too cruelly!"

Heting asked Zhongai what he had been doing for the past two
years.

"I worked in procurement for over a year after arriving in
Shaanxi. In that post, with the help of the many favors that Intendant Sun did me, I managed to make a small fortune and thanks
to the good offices of Wen Tongbao got myself appointed an
inspector. After the court returned to the capital, I helped the
intendant for a few more months, then obtained leave to travel to
the capital and take my parents' coffins south for burial. I meant
to get married in Suzhou and then go on to Guangdong, but when
I arrived in Shanghai today and was depositing the coffins at
Guang-Zhao Gardens, I was surprised to find one there inscribed
'Coffin of Chen Bohe of Nanhai.' It raised a terrible suspicion
in my mind, which is why I rushed over here to ask you. But tell
me, is my sister-in-law permitted to come home now that she's a
nun? Or are men allowed to visit the nunnery? Would they let me
see her?"

"They don't allow any men visitors, I'm afraid. But today happens to be the anniversary of my wife's death, and my daughter
has come home to offer sacrifices. I expect she's still there."

"In that case I'd be greatly obliged if you'd take me to see her."

Heting took Zhongai home and showed him into the study,
then sent a maid upstairs to tell Dihua of his arrival.

In a few moments she came down wearing a nun's habit. She
looked sallow and thin, and her normal healthy glow had quite
deserted her. Zhongai burst into tears. "My brother let you down
too cruelly," he said, prostrating himself in front of her. "I couldn't
get here before, which is why all these things happened to you.
I've come to beg your forgiveness."

In tears Dihua returned his bows: "Please get up, brother-in-
law! These things came about because I wasn't destined to have a
husband. I destroyed your brother and have taken holy orders to
repent my sin. I still agonize over what I did. You mustn't say

those things you said just now. I hope you'll take good care of yourself, marry as soon as you can, have children, and name one of your sons your brother's heir. Although as a nun I can never be a mother to the boy, I care deeply for your brother."

Zhongai wept uncontrollably. After sitting with him a while, Dihua said good-bye and went upstairs again.

Zhongai was also about to leave, when Heting stopped him. "By the way, where are you staying? I don't want to impose, but why not come and stay with us?"

"As I was leaving the capital, I was given a letter of introduction to the Dechang Company, which is where my bags have been taken. Besides, I'm about to leave for Suzhou. While I'm still in mourning for my brother, it will be impossible to marry, of course, but I still need to see the girl's father and arrange a date for the wedding." He said good-bye to Heting and left.

At the Dechang Zhongai collected his bags and headed for Suzhou, where he put up at an inn and went off to call on the Wangs at the address that he had written down years before.

On arriving at the house, he was surprised to find another family in residence. From the neighbors he learned that Secretary Wang had died not long after his return to Suzhou and that, as soon as the funeral ceremony was over, his wife had taken their daughter off to Shanghai to find her a husband.

But *I'm* her husband, thought Zhongai. Who else would they be looking for? Besides, while she was still in mourning for her father, marriage would have been out of the question. But the other people he asked corroborated the story. His only recourse was to make a melancholy journey back to Shanghai, where he took up residence at the Dechang Company and lived a miserable existence. The owner, Gui Quanshu, on learning of his predicament, offered a suggestion: "Perhaps when they lost the head of the family, they moved to Shanghai to stay with relatives. Why not advertise in the paper?"

Zhongai did so, seeking information about the family of Secretary Wang Letian, but two weeks went by without a response, and he sank into an even deeper depression. I've kept myself pure all this time expecting to marry, he thought, but I got here too late, and now I don't even know where she is.

With his guest in a state of constant depression, Gui felt obliged to try and cheer him up, and so one day he invited a few friends to accompany Zhongai to a party in the pleasure quarter. Before long, amid the bright lights, sparkling wine, and loud music, they began playing guess fingers and wine forfeits with the women there, but Zhongai remained completely indifferent. Then in came a prostitute with a pretty face and a graceful figure, her long gown trailing after her. She sat down behind the friend on Zhongai's right.

Zhongai took a closer look—and froze. She bore an uncanny resemblance to Wang Juanjuan, the only difference being that she was a little taller. She kept stealing glances at him, and suddenly he recalled a joke that he and Juanjuan shared when they were children. After they became engaged, he recalled, when there was no one else present they would say: "Will we still be cousins when we grow up?" They were always saying it. She looks the image of Juanjuan, he thought, but I can't believe it's really her. Let me repeat what we used to say and see how she reacts.

He waited until the prostitute turned to look at him and said: "Will we still be cousins? . . ."

She flushed a deep red and rose abruptly to her feet. "I need to put in an appearance at another party. Wait for me," she said to her guest—and ran from the room.

Zhongai felt as if he had been deluged with icy water. The world went black before his eyes, and he keeled over in his chair and slumped unconscious to the floor. In the general alarm that followed, people assumed he had suffered an attack of colic and frantically plied him with medicine.

"I happened to faint, that's all. It's not colic, and I feel better already," protested Zhongai.

Gui Quanshu, who had no idea what lay behind Zhongai's fainting, immediately took him back to the Dechang.

Zhongai then began comparing his situation with his brother's and Dihua's with Juanjuan's, and concluded that the Creator went too far in sporting with people's destinies. No solace was to be found among the vicissitudes of fortune we encounter in this world. Arriving at this conclusion, with all his hopes in ashes, he fixed a day for his departure and took his parents' and his brother's coffins back to Guangdong for burial. There he divided up his considerable fortune among his needy relatives and friends. For himself he chose the life of a hermit, a hermit of wild and shaggy appearance, and no one knows what became of him.

> The Sea of Regret is as deep as ever;
> The Heaven of Passion[19] still needs repair.
> When marriage destinies go awry,
> Why speak of "fates that lovers share"?
> Why could not the passionless lover
> Have taken as wife the inconstant maid?
> When upheaval's joined with tribulation,
> True passion is at last displayed.

(To the tune of "Moon Over West River")

19. See *Stones in the Sea,* note 1.

About the Translator

Patrick Hanan is the Victor S. Thomas Professor of Chinese Literature at Harvard University. He is the author of *The Invention of Li Yu*, which won the Joseph R. Levenson Award of the Association for Asian Studies in 1990. He is also the author of *The Chinese Vernacular Story* and the translator of *The Carnal Prayer Mat* and *A Tower for the Summer Heat*.